PRAISE FOR
TELL ME NO LIES

_____

"This sequel delivers on the action…readers left hanging by the first volume will be intrigued to see how this story ends."

—*Booklist*

"This book will be enjoyed by mystery lovers and pop star enthusiasts alike."

—*School Library Journal*

"If you are looking for a young adult romance that isn't all hearts and flowers, that will leave you breathless and tingling with adrenaline, then this is the read for you."

—*Fangirlish*

SCARED LITTLE RABBITS

A. V. GEIGER

sourcebooks
fire

Published by Sourcebooks Fire, an imprint of Sourcebooks
P.O. Box 4410, Naperville, Illinois 60567-4410
(630) 961-3900
sourcebooks.com

Library of Congress Cataloging-in-Publication data is on file with the publisher.

Printed and bound in Canada.
MBP 10 9 8 7 6 5 4 3 2 1

To A and L, this one's for you.

Love, M

AFTER...

July 18
Winthrop Summer Maker Program—Day 18

We stand in a tight cluster, high above the lake. I couldn't say how long we've waited here. Minutes? Hours? There's no way of telling time, aside from the sun's descent toward the horizon and the growing ache in the arches of my feet. The breeze feathers my hair, but otherwise I remain completely still—as unmoving as the shelf of solid granite beneath my tennis shoes.

I shouldn't be here. Maybe I should go back down...

They warned us not to come, said not to leave our rooms. The program director's email declared the whole campus under lockdown, but we gathered anyway. One by one, we made our way up the narrow trail to this forbidden spot—this place where beauty and danger intertwine. Now, we stand shoulder to shoulder, watching and waiting. Nineteen summer students.

All but one.

No one makes a sound. Hushed words and nervous laughs have long since given way to silence. I can only hear the whisper of the wind and the crackle of the yellow caution tape fluttering against the rocks.

That tape wasn't there the last time I came to this place. Its presence feels unnatural—too bright, too glaring—slashing through my view of the white, cotton ball clouds that fill the sky and cast their shifting shadows across the landscape.

///CAUTION///CAUTION///CAUTION///

The bold, black warning seeps its way into my consciousness. It reminds me of that feeling during a dream, right before you wake— that flickering ember of doubt that catches hold and slowly spreads before the dream goes up in flame, that little voice inside your head that whispers: "Hey, Nora... Nora? Nora! Has it occurred to you that none of this is real?"

If only my brain would say that to me now. I keep waiting for it to happen, but the sick feeling in my stomach tells me I won't get out of this nightmare so easily.

I'm toward the back of the group behind the juniors and seniors. I can't tell what's going on in the water below from my vantage point, but I have a view of Maddox's profile. For once, his eyes aren't covered up by glasses. He stares straight ahead, rigidly expressionless, casting his eyes downward over the cliff's edge. A tic vibrates at the corner of his jaw. His face gives away no other hint of the emotions churning beneath the surface.

I wonder what that blank stare signifies. Hope? Fear? Guilt? I can't begin to guess. I hardly know him, after all. The thought curdles inside my throat like sour milk. Last night, I thought I might be in love with him. What a joke. It's only been a few weeks since the day we met—the day I first arrived at Winthrop Academy.

The girl beside him clasps Maddox on the arm, her fingers digging into the flesh above his wrist. I press forward and go up on my tiptoes to catch a glimpse of the water down below, as a whisper runs through the group.

"They found something… What is it?… Can you see?"

We all inch forward, craning for a better view. The surface of the lake looks calm and unbroken, except for the presence of the boat. From this distance, it reminds me of a bath toy I used to play with as a kid—a white, plastic replica of a powerboat with dark blue lettering across the hull.

POLICE

We're too far away to see the expression on the officers' faces or to hear the words exchanged. But we can see the search diver emerge from beneath the water in his black wet suit. His flippers disturb the pristine surface as he paddles his way toward the boat. He swims with one arm stretched before him, holding out the sunken treasure he's exhumed from the depths below.

"Is it…" the voices all around me murmur. "Is it…is it her?"

BEFORE...

1

INVISIBILITY

———

July 1

Winthrop Summer Maker Program—Day 1

NORA

I lean my weight against my suitcase with my back to the campus gate and its ivy-covered sign.

WINTHROP ACADEMY
FOUNDED 1813

Why did I come here again? I've been coveting a spot in this program since eighth grade, counting down the years until I was old enough to apply—then counting down the days until my parents dropped me off with hugs and kisses and orders to call home nightly.

Now here I am, waving at the red glow of their brake lights as they exit the U-shaped driveway and disappear over a rise in the twisting mountain road. My presence here is the most monumental thing I've ever accomplished. So why do I feel like a kid on my first day of kindergarten, trying desperately to hold it together before the other kids see what a crybaby I am?

I straighten my shoulders. *Get it together, Nora.* I'm not a baby. I'm sixteen years old, and I worked my butt off to earn a scholarship for this summer program. It's not like I'm moving here for life. The Winthrop Academy Summer Maker Program runs three weeks, and then my parents will be back to pick me up.

I'm here. I'm doing this…and it's going to be amazing.

With a shuddering breath, I turn my back to the road and make my way through the tall wrought-iron gates. The grandeur of this place doesn't do much to settle my nerves. I knew it would be fancy—one of the oldest and most prestigious boarding schools in New England—but I didn't expect it to be so *huge.* There must be twenty different buildings within the campus walls, interconnected by a web of gravel pathways.

I recognize the largest building straight ahead, with its brick facade and soaring clock tower. That image graced all the online application materials. It looked so welcoming on the website, pictured against a backdrop of clear blue sunny skies. But the reality before me is shadowed by a blanket of dark gray clouds.

I better figure out where I'm going before the rain starts. I grab my suitcase handle and march forward, choosing one of the angled paths at random. A pair of girls stand at the far end, and my spirits lift at the sight of them. Most of the Winthrop students have left for the summer, but the place isn't completely abandoned. I expect the girls to react to the sound of crunching gravel as I approach, but they don't turn toward me. It's weird. Can they see me? Both of them have their eyes covered by bulky sunglasses in spite of the overcast skies.

A confident person would go up to them and introduce herself. Smile. Get directions. Ask if they're part of the same program…

If only I knew someone confident like that. As for me? I turn down a different path and pull out my phone to look busy.

Maybe I can find a campus map online. I'm about to open my web browser, but something else distracts me. A new app, freshly downloaded, beckons from the bottom of my screen. At the sight of it, my whole mood shifts.

InstaLove

I got it from the app store this morning, praying my parents wouldn't notice a new download in the last-minute chaos of packing. Not that they actively forbade me to get this app—but I know if I asked permission, they'd say no. Which is why I never bothered asking.

I'll delete it before they come to pick me up, but these three weeks away from home offer my best chance to join the game. I've been dying to try InstaLove since I first read about it on TeenHack.

TEENHACK

RECOMMENDED APPS

InstaLove™: Love's a game.

Teens will fall head over heels for this location-based augmented reality game. To join, players simply download the app to their phone and upload a selfie on Instagram with hashtag #InstaLoveIsReal. Then get ready to play! The app will automatically generate a custom avatar and push an alert to other users nearby. When players encounter another InstaLover™ in real life, the app will superimpose their avatars and prompt both players with choices for how to interact. Users watch their InstaLovability™ Score increase with everyone they meet...MORE

Sounds good to me. My reality could use some "augmentation." Not that I'm obsessed with boys, but it might be nice to feel loved at some point. Or at least liked… I'm pretty sure no one has ever liked me in a non-platonic way.

I scuff the bottom of my shoe against the gravel, sending light-gray pebbles scattering. *Trevor…* Why am I still thinking about Trevor Chang?

I was so sure he liked me. That's the thing. He didn't break my heart or anything dramatic. But I spent an entire school year overanalyzing every word the boy said, and all signs pointed to "LIKE." He offered to be my lab partner in freshman biology. He asked me constantly to help him with math homework, even though we had plenty of other friends in the same class. And when I asked him to join our school's Robotics Club this spring, he said yes. He *had* to realize that was only an excuse to hang out together in the Maker Lab after school every day...

So how do you explain the look of total blankness on his face, followed by the soul-destroying thirty seconds of stammered apologies, when I finally scraped up the nerve to say something out loud?

"Gosh. I'm sorry, Nora. Damn... I—I like you a lot. For sure. You're, like, the smartest person I know. I just never... I never really... saw you... I mean, not that way..."

He never really *saw* me. Neither did those girls I passed back there. Are we sensing a theme yet? I don't know why, but people tend to overlook me. I swear if I had a superpower, I know what it would be: invisibility.

I dip my chin and return my attention to my phone. I should probably find my room and unpack before I set up my InstaLove account, but I'm in a rotten mood now. This game had better be as good as everyone says... I flick it open, and it welcomes me with a view of my own face.

> Welcome to InstaLove!
>
> Snap a selfie to begin.

I turn my head from side to side, lifting the phone higher to find a flattering angle. My face stares back, but there's something different about it. Some kind of subtle beauty filter?

I like this app already.

I take a pic and follow the prompts to post it on my Instagram, not bothering to edit the default caption.

> Love's a game. Who wants to play? #InstaLoveIsReal

I get a Like immediately, and an automatic wave of cringe-y awkwardness washes through me. Not someone from school, is it? They usually ignore everything I post. But no, to my relief, it's not from anyone I know. All part of the game.

> InstaLoveBot

It leaves a comment too.

> InstaLoveBot: Upload complete. Your avatar is ready.

That was fast! I click back to the InstaLove app, and there I am. Or, not me. My avatar. An older, prettier version of me—like a Nora 2.0, who knows how to use makeup and whose mouth isn't too wide for the rest of her face.

I smile for the first time since I got here. My fingers fly as I hit "Accept" and follow the rest of the prompts to register my account.

The camera switches angles, and the app shows a view of the path in front of me, with the back of my avatar's head visible at the bottom of the screen. I hold up the phone as I resume walking, wondering if I'll encounter other users.

Probably. InstaLove was born here, after all. I read all about that on TeenHack too. A student named Emerson Kemp created it here at Winthrop a few summers ago, and it went on to become the most commercially successful project ever to come out of the Summer Maker program.

Of course, the original concept behind InstaLove was much simpler than the game I downloaded today. The summer Emerson attended, the two most popular downloads in the App Store were Instagram and Pokémon Go—so he hacked the two together. The result was this weirdly compelling mix of social media and augmented reality. When Instagram users encountered each other in real life, his app would superimpose their profile pics over their real faces and prompt everyone to "Heart" each other's accounts. It went viral, and Emerson went on to start a software company with InstaLove as its flagship product. Now, he's this program's most famous alum. He'll be appearing here at the end of the three weeks as a guest judge for the Maker Fair, where this summer's crop of students will compete with our own projects. The thought of meeting him in person—the *real* Emerson Kemp—after all the articles I've read? My insides go all hollow and shivery every time I think about it.

At least I won't be invisible at Maker Fair. I'm not expecting to win a medal, but I have a solid plan for what I want to build. I included the proposal in my scholarship application, along with my school transcripts and programming samples.

I'll worry about work later though. Right now, InstaLove beckons, and Nora 2.0 is on the prowl. I sweep my phone from side to side, searching for any sign of other avatars as I make my way at random around the campus. *Where is everyone? Forget avatars… Where are all the humans?*

I turn the corner around a building, and I nearly crash right into one.

An avatar materializes on my screen. Brown eyes. Dark hair. A name beneath his picture that I'm too startled to read. I click the app closed and look up at the actual boy before me. He's wearing sunglasses like those girls before, but he takes them off and rubs his eyes. "That wasn't one of the choices."

"W-what?" This boy doesn't need an avatar. He looks better in real life. He runs his fingers through his hair to push it away from his face, but it flops over his forehead again, half covering his eyes. Why is it that boys look so much cuter when they're deliberately unkempt?

"You're not supposed to turn it off until you pick a choice." He nods at the phone in my hand. "It'll drop your score."

A flood of heat rushes to my face. Can he tell I'm totally new to this app? His own phone is nowhere in sight. He looks older than me, guessing by his tall frame and the breadth of his shoulders beneath his polo shirt. Probably a senior, playing this game for years.

He smiles—a burst of childlike mischief that contrasts against the squareness of his jaw—and I can't breathe.

"Where are your glasses?" he asks. "Reese will be pissed if she catches you using your phone."

Who? I stuff my phone in my pocket. Are phones not allowed? It didn't say so in the orientation packet. "I didn't know. I just got here."

He laughs. "Your secret's safe with me. I'm Maddox, by the way."

"Nora," I reply, taking his outstretched hand.

He lifts an eyebrow. "Nora… That's not short for anything, is it?"

His question takes me by surprise. I can't remember the last time someone asked me that. I usually don't mention my full name. Not that I hate it or anything, but I've never felt like it suited me. "Eleanor," I tell him. "Why?"

"Uh-oh."

He flashes that mischievous grin again, but his eyes slide past me over my shoulder, as if laughing with someone else behind me at some inside joke. Back to being invisible, I guess. For a moment there, I thought things might be different for Nora 2.0.

But no. This is the real world, and I'm still Nora.

"OK, well…" I move to step around him, rolling my suitcase

in my wake. It tumbles sideways. So much for my graceful exit. It would have yanked my arm out of its socket if he hadn't grabbed my suitcase handle to keep it upright.

"Do you need help? That thing is bigger than you are."

"I'm fine."

I'm not fine. He's staring at me now. I preferred invisibility. He lets go of the handle as I struggle to set the suitcase back on its wheels, wracking my mind for something else to say. What do you say to a boy who rescued you from a freak shoulder-dislocation accident? A beautiful boy with some weird X-ray vision super-power that allows him to see invisible girls?

Ask for directions. That's what a confident person would do. *Right.*

"Do you know where Fenmore Hall is?"

"Oh!" He points toward one of the buildings behind me. "Over there. That's one of the dorms. The rest of us are staying in Grier."

I nod in thanks and pull the suitcase toward the building he indicated. That should have been the end of the conversation, but somehow it continues. To my delight (or possibly my horror), he strolls along beside me. "I'll tell Reese you're new," he says. "She'll hook you up."

"Is Reese the director?"

"No!" He laughs. "Reese is a student. She's working on an InstaLove mod for her Maker Fair project. It lets you play hands free. Full immersion!" He waves the glasses in his hand, and I realize they aren't sunglasses after all. I know what those are. I've seen them online, but never in person. Augmented reality…AR glasses…

"Is that an InSight Visor?" I can't quite keep the awe out of my voice. "Don't those things cost, like, three thousand dollars?"

"They're pretty sweet. Reese and—"

He breaks off mid-sentence and pulls up short. Some instinct makes me look up. A girl struts down the front steps of the building we're approaching. She's the opposite of invisible, with ruby-red lipstick and dark blond hair floating in a cloud around her shoulders. Her face isn't so much beautiful, but *magnetic*. One of those people that everybody turns to look at the moment she enters any room.

Is that Reese?

"Hey, Eleanor," Maddox says beside me. His easy smile fades. His face goes still, and I'm confused. Is he talking to me? Because his eyes are on the other girl.

"What are you doing?" she demands.

"Just helping out the new kid."

The girl narrows her eyes at me and spins away from us both, striding in the opposite direction.

"Eleanor! Wait!"

Maddox jogs after her, and I'm on my own again. Guess I'll find my dorm room by myself.

2

MISSED CONNECTIONS

NORA

My narrow window looks out over the network of campus pathways down below. They're deserted. Like this room. I'm not sure what I expected in terms of accommodations, but it wasn't this—a sterile, empty dorm room, with worn-out beige carpeting and featureless white walls. The place is completely unfurnished, aside from the low sleigh bed and the wooden desk stuffed in the corner.

No bunk beds, then.

The disappointment lodges in my chest. I assumed I'd have a roommate for the duration of the program. That was one of the reasons I applied. Female bonding has never been my strong suit, but I figured this program would be full of other girls. Girls like me.

I scrunch my lips sideways. What made me so sure this

room would come furnished with an InstaBestFriend? I had all kinds of daydreams about my mythical bunkmate. Some girl my age, obsessed with TeenHack and WIRED, who would stay up half the night debating the relative merits of Java versus C++. A girl who spent her Saturday nights tinkering in the garage, figuring out how to retrofit her dad's lawn mower with a self-propelled motor and GPS navigation system. I'm not the only girl on the planet who makes robotic landscaping equipment for fun, am I?

Maybe I am. Heck, maybe that's why my "SmartMower" proposal got me accepted to this program. I bet the admissions committee read it and looked at each other all bug-eyed, like:

"Hey, should we admit this freakish freak-girl for the summer?"

"I don't know, Bob. Robotic lawn mowers? This is some next-level freakishness right here."

"Her technical skill set is impressive though."

"Clearly, this applicant has nothing more normal to do with her time."

"Perhaps we could let her in but keep her quarantined from all the non-freakish kids."

"No roommate?"

"Safer that way. This degree of freakocity might be contagious."

Ugh, the idea of people talking about me makes my skin crawl. I shudder, sinking down heavily next to my suitcase on the edge of the twin mattress. At least they didn't house me in a totally separate building. I saw a resident adviser's suite at the top of the stairs, and I can hear the echoey sound of other girls laughing somewhere down the hall.

I should probably be brave and introduce myself, but I don't budge from my perch on the bed. What if that girl is there? The one I saw outside earlier, addressed by my first name. Eleanor. The other Eleanor. The *pretty* Eleanor. The kind of Eleanor who inspires cute boys to drop conversations mid-sentence and go chasing after them.

I press my hand against my collarbone. My lungs feel like a pair of popped balloons, thoroughly deflated. I can't imagine a girl like that scrolling through a tech blog—or having *anything* in common with me other than a first name. She looked way too perfect. Perfect hair. Perfect skin. Perfect clothes. Was she even in high school? She reminded me of those ridiculous twenty-five-year-old actresses they cast to play teenagers on TV.

Maybe it's a blessing I don't have to share my room. This way I have someplace safe to hide out when I'm feeling hopelessly insecure. Which is basically anytime I'm not hunched over my laptop editing code.

I unzip my suitcase to unpack. The laughter down the hall grows louder, and I glance uncertainly toward my door. I'll meet those girls eventually. My orientation packet mentioned a welcome dinner tonight at the program director's residence. That seems like a logical place to make introductions. Official school-sponsored activities are my friend. Random socializing outside of school hours? Not so much.

I pull out the thick packet from my suitcase and look it over, although I must have reviewed it twenty times since it showed up in the mail last month. If only this program were more structured. Aside from tonight's dinner, the only other official gathering is the Maker Fair at the end of the three weeks.

The lack of routine makes my stomach hurt. I'm used to high school, with classes at set times and teachers guiding after-school activities. But this program is all about independent study and peer-based learning. In terms of faculty, there's only the program director, Dr. Carlyle, and a resident adviser living in each of the dorms. Otherwise, the students are on our own to work on self-directed projects, although we're supervised twenty-four seven from afar. It wouldn't be safe to leave a bunch of teenagers completely to our own devices. Surveillance cameras are everywhere on campus. I passed half a dozen of them earlier, including the one in the hallway outside my door. Nobody comes or goes without someone on campus security knowing about it.

At least I don't have to worry about my laptop getting stolen. My door doesn't have a lock, but I don't need one with the camera keeping watch.

I drop the orientation packet on my desk, considering what to do between now and dinnertime. My phone rests on my desk chair, and I pick it up. I'm still not sure how this InstaLove app

works. Does it keep records of all the other avatars I've encountered? There's been only one so far, but I wouldn't mind seeing
that particular avi again. The mere thought of him pops a goofy
grin onto my face.

I have to check. I can't resist.

I open InstaLove, and it shows a view of my empty room with
various options arranged in a frame around the edges. The lower
left corner shows a number:

-24

Is that my score? I tap it and an explanation fills the screen.

InstaLove (IL) Score: −24.

Show some love, Nora! There are currently 16 InstaLove
users in your area. Find them and interact to raise your
rating!

Yikes. A negative number? That should probably hurt my
feelings, but I can't help but giggle. I guess Nora 2.0 is no more
"InstaLovable" than plain old Nora. I didn't need a game to tell
me that.

I don't take it personally. I know why my score sucks so much.
Those were the first words Maddox uttered when I bumped into

him before. *"That wasn't one of the choices... It'll drop your score... You're not supposed to turn it off until you pick a choice..."*

Oops. I wonder if I dropped his score as well when I froze up. There goes any chance of talking to Maddox again. Not that there was much chance of that anyway.

I flick back to the InstaLove home screen and choose a different option from the menu. My interaction history fills the screen, organized in a three-column display.

InstaFriends	InstaCrushes	Missed Connections
		Maddox

Interesting.

Maddox's face looks different here. Am I imagining it, or did his avi change from before? No, I realize with a gasp. The avatars aren't static. They're like Animojis with different moods! My finger hovers over his lips, and his expression shifts when I touch the screen, from sad, puppy-dog eyes to a knowing smirk.

His InstaLove score appears beneath his picture.

27,048

"Oh my God," I whisper. No wonder he's smirking. My −24 looks more ridiculous by the second. How long has he been playing this game? There must be some way to see more details. Like his history… Or his age… Or his shoe size… Or whether he's straight, or gay, or otherwise inclined, or… Let's be honest. There's one thing in particular I really want to know: whether that girl who glared at me before is his girlfriend.

I lift my finger from his face, and another text bubble pops up, prompting me (or taunting me?) to do something other than stare.

InstaLove requires interaction, Nora! What did you think of Maddox? Drag his pic to put him where he belongs:

InstaFriends	InstaCrushes
People you like	People you *like* like
☺	🖤

Hint: Don't worry, no one else can see your choice! Check out our Privacy Policy.

I suck my lower lip between my teeth. Friend or crush? Obviously, I know the answer, judging from the way my pulse quickens at the thought of his easy smile and messy hair.

But I hesitate before I make my selection. Can I really trust InstaLove with all my secrets? It has to be secure, right? I mean, it has a Privacy Policy. And TeenHack recommended it. There's no way this app could get so popular if it made a habit of broadcasting everyone's secret crushes to the world…

Right. I grip my phone more firmly, annoyed by my own nervousness. I downloaded this app for the same reason I came to this program: to do something different, experience something new. To shake myself out of my comfort zone.

"InstaLove requires interaction," I mutter to myself. So what am I waiting for? What exactly am I so afraid will happen?

I press my index finger to the screen and drag his face to the second column: InstaCrushes. For a moment, his avatar smiles wide and his dark brown eyes are replaced by two red hearts.

Another text bubble emerges, but I don't have a chance to read the prompt. My head jerks up at the sound of footsteps in the corridor. They're coming toward my door. Maddox's heart eyes stare back at me, and a flush of guilty color floods my cheeks. I don't know how to exit this screen. It's too late to figure it out. Panicked, I click the phone off completely and shove it in my pocket as a knock rattles the doorframe.

Who is it?

I say the words inside my head. Not out loud. My lungs aren't functioning properly. I hold my breath as I reach for the doorknob. It's not Maddox, is it? The real Maddox? Did I summon him somehow?

I don't know why, but I have the weirdest feeling that it's him.

3

MOXIE

MADDOX

Goodbye, world. I'm screwed.

I half run, half walk in my girlfriend's wake, but she refuses to slow down. I can tell by her stride—the way her hair flounces with each step—that she's getting ready to skin me alive. What did I do this time?

Honestly, I'm not sure I care. This routine is getting old. It plays out the same way every time. Our relationship reminds me of a glitchy piece of code, stuck in an infinite loop, calling the same two functions over and over and over.

```
def relationship () :
  while boyfriend == 'Maddox':
     eleanor ('yells')
     maddox ('apologizes')
```

I only know one way to break out of a broken loop. CTRL-ALT-DELETE. Force quit.

She heads for the library, about to disappear through the glass revolving door. I don't want to have the coming conversation in there, under the scrutiny of the campus surveillance cameras. "Eleanor! Hold up!"

She spins around to face me in a swirl of whipping hair. Her icy glare is designed to freeze me in place, like I'm some well-trained puppy dog commanded by its owner to stay.

I push the thought away. Eleanor Winthrop doesn't own me—and neither does her family. Not even with their name emblazoned on this school's wrought-iron gates.

I didn't plan on having it out with her today, but I don't see any reason to delay the inevitable. I know what I need to do, and I'm prepared to live with the consequences.

"What do you want, Moxie?"

Eleanor and her nicknames… She's been calling me by that one since we were little kids, playing together in the sandbox at Riverside Park. I used to love it when she called me that, but hearing it now sets my teeth on edge.

Maybe because it's been a while since I showed an ounce of moxie in real life.

"We need to talk," I tell her.

"I'm really not in the mood."

She turns and pushes her way through the door, but I follow

her. She can't duck me that easily. I'm about to call after her again when she finally gives in with a huff and heads inside the nearest study room.

I click the glass door closed behind us. A camera hangs suspended in the corner of the room, but I ignore it. At least it records only video. No sound. That's the closest we'll come to privacy in this place.

Eleanor faces me, hands on her hips. My smart visor dangles from the cord around my neck, and she points at it. "Shouldn't you be wearing that?"

"Eleanor—"

"I mean, since your InstaLove score is the only thing you care about anymore."

"That isn't true."

She snorts. "No? So are you flirting with other girls in front of my face because you *actually* like them?"

I grit my teeth. That's why she stormed off? For real? Because I exchanged three words with that girl back there? I'm used to Eleanor's possessive streak, but she has a hell of a lot of moxie herself, giving me attitude for talking to other people.

I know what comes next in this messed up routine of ours. I'm supposed to grovel. Cajole. Wheedle my way back into her good graces until she finally breaks down and rewards me with some grudging morsel of affection.

Well, it's not going down like that. Time to break the loop. CTRL-ALT-DELETE.

"Eleanor, this isn't going to work."

Her face freezes. Her nostrils flare, but that's the only sign that she understood. I wait for her reaction. It feels like an hour ticks by before she speaks. "What are you talking about?"

But she knows what I mean. I can see the comprehension on her face, as I point toward her and back to myself again. "This. You and me. It's not working. It hasn't been working for a while."

"Wait," she answers slowly. "Are you breaking up with me?"

To her credit, she actually looks hurt. I soften my tone and take a step toward her. "I still want to be friends, but I can't—"

"No," she cuts me off, nodding toward my glasses yet again. "If you're InstaFriending me, then no. I don't accept. Request denied."

"This isn't a game, Eleanor."

"Why are you doing this? Over that little—that little nothing? That little *nobody*?" She waves her hand in the direction of Fenmore Hall.

See, this is the problem with dating a girl I've known since we were both in diapers. She knows me inside and out. She can read me too well. And the fact is, there was something interesting about that other Eleanor, or Nora as she called herself.

Nora's IL Score is 0.

Zero. Brand-new profile. I can't remember the last time I

encountered one of those. I would've looked past her under normal circumstances, but the name stopped me in my tracks. Nora… Eleanor tried that nickname on for size at some point in the distant past, before our babyish mouths had the wherewithal to pronounce the full name correctly.

But this new Nora couldn't have been more different from the Eleanor I know.

She seemed so…*real*. Nothing fake about her. Nothing calculated. No fancy clothes. No makeup. Every passing emotion written on her face. She seemed jumpy at first, but then she caught a glimpse of my InSight Visor, and she lit up like a little kid at her birthday party. Those green eyes of hers went so big and round, I thought they might swallow us both up.

The memory makes me grin, but I wipe it off my face. I am *not* breaking up with Eleanor because I want to pursue someone else.

No. I need a fresh start, that's all. I need to be my own person. I need to show some moxie for once in my life.

I swallow hard and square my shoulders. "I'm sorry. We'll still be friends. Always. We can still work together for Maker Fair. But I don't want more than that. And honestly, Eleanor, I'm pretty sure *you* don't want more than that either."

I expect her to pout. Maybe shed a tear or two. Instead, she throws back her head and laughs. Any trace of guilt evaporates at the sound of her amusement.

This is all part of the routine too.

```
def dysfunctional () :
  while 'Maddox' in doghouse :
    maddox ('begs forgiveness')
    eleanor ('laughs in his face')
```

Eleanor Winthrop has been laughing at me for as long as I can remember—from the day the Winthrops first hired my grandmother to be her nanny and let me tag along to serve as playmate for their adorable only child.

And damn if she wasn't adorable.

I used to like making her laugh. Hell, I used to *live* for it. I assumed that tinkling laughter masked some undercurrent of affection. Only recently have I realized how dysfunctional we are. I've spent my whole life as nothing more than Eleanor Winthrop's plaything.

Spring break made me see things clearly. My grandmother wasn't feeling well, so I went home to the city to take care of her. Eleanor took Reese in my place to stay at her family's five-bedroom "cabin" in Lake Tahoe. I expected to miss her during the week apart, but I barely thought of her at all. I spent the week sleeping late, blasting music, and sneaking into clubs with my fake ID. I raised my IL score to an all-time high, flirting all night with girls who laughed at my preppy clothes and utter lack of dance moves.

And Eleanor didn't miss me either. She didn't bother to text.

Our endless, private InstaLove chat stayed idle the whole time.
But I saw the way her score went through the roof while she was
in Tahoe. She was talking to someone out there, and I didn't care
enough to wonder who.

Yeah, this conversation has been brewing for a while. Eleanor's
still laughing, but I'm done.

I turn to leave the room. The glass door beckons. I'm three
steps away from my Eleanor-free future before her voice rings out.
"Where do you think you're going?"

"I said what I had to say." My hand rests on the doorknob, but
I hesitate. "It's over," I tell her softly. "And you're laughing, Eleanor.
Admit it. You're not even sad." I have my back to her, but I can see
her face reflected in the glass. I detect a tiny quiver at the corners of
her crimson lips, but she keeps her smile firmly planted.

"You *know* it's not that simple."

I drop my hand and leave the doorknob unturned. My head
comes to rest against the doorframe. *No, it's never that simple, is it?*
Not with Eleanor. Not with the Winthrops.

"You can walk away from me if you want, Moxie," she says in
that mocking tone I know so well. "But I've got some terms and
conditions."

4

LOWERCASE

NORA

I reach for my door, envisioning Maddox's visor-covered eyes on the other side. But of course it won't be him. *Welcome to reality, Nora.* No doubt Maddox forgot about me within two seconds of the end of our conversation. We exchanged only a few sentences, and he couldn't be bothered to finish his last one. He was about to tell me how those super-slick AR glasses work when…*boom.* Eleanor happened.

There's a scowl on my face, but I shake it off. At least *someone* came to my door. The knocking resumes, and I pull the door open. A girl stands in the hallway with her knuckles poised. "Good," she says, lowering her hand. "You're here."

Um. Who are you?

She pauses, eyeing me up and down, and I wait for her to say more. She's bound to introduce herself eventually. But she doesn't, and the silence of my non-reply lingers in the air a beat too long.

"Oh! Hey!" I answer finally. "Hi! Come in."

I actually sounded friendly there. Weird. I suppose that happens once in a while. In moments of high awkwardness, random words come out of my mouth—unpredictable, but occasionally friendly.

This girl does not seem overly impressed by my A-plus social skills, however. She cocks her head sideways, continuing her examination like I'm some kind of imposter. "*You're* Eleanor Weinberg?"

I nod, still confused. Could this possibly be Ms. Cleary, the resident adviser? No…I can't imagine anyone who looks like this on the faculty of a posh boarding school. This girl can't be more than a couple of years older than me, with matte magenta lipstick and sleek, shoulder-length hair dyed an unnatural shade of neon blue.

She takes a step inside the threshold. "Maddox said you're on InstaLove, right?"

I gape at her. My stomach does a somersault at the sound of that name—Maddox—and the fact that he considered me noteworthy enough to remember my existence. But the blue-haired girl brings me back down to earth. She directs her disapproval toward the area of my right hip. My hand flutters to my side, and I realize what she's glaring at: the outline of the cell phone in my pocket.

Oh. I know who this is.

I remember Maddox's warning when I first crashed into him,

eyes fixed upon my screen. *"Reese will be pissed if she catches you using your phone."*

"Sorry," I mumble, fishing in my pocket. "Are you Reese?"

She merely points over my shoulder toward the corner of my room. "The top drawer of your desk locks. That's probably the safest place to leave it."

Wait… Leave what? My phone?

She crosses her arms, and I realize it wasn't a suggestion. I get the distinct impression that she's used to being obeyed. I can't remember the last time I didn't have my cell phone on me, but…that's what people do here, apparently? I should at least *try* to fit in.

"OK, cool." I slip my phone in the drawer and don't bother to remove the metal key. Knowing me, I'd lose it. And it's not like anyone will steal my phone. There are only twenty students in the program, and a gazillion security cameras watching our every move.

When I turn back toward the doorway, it's empty, but Reese's footsteps echo down the hall. "Well, what are you waiting for?" Her voice floats back to me. "Come on!"

That didn't sound like a suggestion either.

I wipe my palms against my shorts as I step out into the hall. Reese has her hand on the doorknob of a room at the far end, waiting for me to catch up. I follow her inside.

The room is furnished identically to mine, but twice the size with double the furniture. Two desks. Two windows. Two beds. Not everyone gets assigned a single. This room is built for two, but I count four girls lounging on the beds. They must be the source of the laughter I heard earlier from my isolation chamber.

"Hi," I say softly, but I'm not sure anyone heard. The nearest two girls have their heads bent together over a laptop, blocking my view of their faces. I can see only their hair: one with a strawberry-blond pixie cut, and the other with dark springy coils pulled into a thick pouf on top of her head. A third girl in a gray beanie sits cross-legged on the other bed. She has her mouth full of bobby pins, weaving the pin-straight black hair of the fourth girl into a French braid.

None of them moves a muscle to acknowledge my presence, and my eyes dart uncertainly to Reese. She enters before me and perches herself on top of one of the desks. She clears her throat, and the rest of the girls look up.

"This is the new kid," Reese announces. "Another Eleanor."

That got their attention. The silence lengthens as all eyes turn to me. I shift my weight from side to side, raising my hand in a weak attempt to wave hello. "You can call me Nora. What are all your names?"

No one answers me. They were all laughing and chatting before I came in, but now they look grave.

"Eleanor won't like that."

"She's going to need a nickname."

I take another step into the room, approaching the bed with the two laptop girls. "Um, I have a nickname. It's Nora."

The girl with the hair pouf squints at me for a moment, before turning to the pixie-cut beside her. "What about Big Elle and Little Elle?"

"*Big* Elle?" Pixie-Cut replies. She makes a circle with her finger to indicate her own generous hips and curvy chest. "She only *wishes*."

They all erupt into a chorus of giggles. The only one who doesn't laugh is Reese. She slides off her desk and stoops in front of it, riffling through the contents of the bottom drawer. "Eleanor is Eleanor. This one"—she jerks her head in my direction—"she can be Little Elle, I suppose."

Beanie-Girl swivels her head around to look me up and down. Her eyes light up. "Lowercase L?"

The girl with the French braid smiles. "Aw, that's cute!"

"What if we just call her Lowercase?"

"Oh my gawwwd. Perfect."

I'm not sure whether I should be flattered or offended. These girls do realize that I'm still standing here, right? Not one of them has told me her own name yet, and no one seems inclined to fill me in. It reminds me of the time my family went to the animal shelter to adopt a new pet. I went around to all the cages, oohing and ahhhing and assigning each furry friend a tentative new name...but it never once occurred to me to introduce *myself*.

Clearly, these girls don't consider me a member of the same species.

I hate this feeling, hate being in this room. I have the overwhelming urge to turn and flee. In the life of an insecure teenager, there's only one situation more painful than declaring your unrequited feelings to your crush. It's called "attempting to insert yourself into a preexisting group of friends." I'd rather sew my own eyelids shut.

How do they all know each other already?

I must have said that out loud because Pixie-Cut responds. An array of photos hang on the wall across from her, and she points to the one in the center. I recognize the two girls pictured arm in arm: electric-blue hair contrasting with a cloud of dark blond curls. "Reese and Eleanor go to school here year round. The rest of us only come for the summer program."

"Don't worry," Hair-Pouf chimes in. "There are other newbies. We simply choose not to acknowledge their existence."

They all laugh again. I guess I should be flattered that they nicknamed me. "Lowercase" is a big step up from the pet names the senior girls in my high school call me, generally some variation on: "Who's-that-kid?-I-didn't-even-know-she-went-here."

But why are they talking to me if I'm some lowly newbie? Why did Reese bring me in here?

French-Braid shifts position, and my eyes light on another picture, hanging on the wall behind her head. That side of the room must belong to Eleanor. She's pictured there with her head thrown back in laughter, her back supported by the arm of a familiar-looking boy.

My face goes hot and my breath whizzes in through my teeth. *This is bad. Very, very bad.* I shouldn't react this strongly to a picture of some boy I barely know.

I look away. I didn't expect to see Maddox's face again so soon, that's all. But it occurs to me that he's the reason I'm standing here. Because Maddox—with his cute smile and his astronomical InstaLove score—vouched for me. He thought of me. Remembered me. Mentioned me.

To Reese.

She stands up from her desk and ambles toward me, holding up a pair of dark glasses before her eyes.

My tongue darts out to wet my lips. Those glasses are the same kind Maddox wore. They look like a cross between sunglasses and ski goggles. Only the thickness of the frames and the blue LED light at the bridge of the nose give away the cutting-edge technology they contain. Not glasses at all, really.

An InSight Visor.

A tingle races through me from fingertips to toes. That's why I'm in this room. That's why I'm in this *program*. To collaborate with other students on amazing projects like this. Reese sought me out because I'm an InstaLove user—and she's working on a mod.

"What's your username?" Reese asks.

"Nora241." I take a step forward and pat my front pocket, but of course it's empty. "I left my phone in my desk."

"No phone," Reese replies. Her mouth forms a grim line, not an easy feat with bubblegum-pink lipstick. The top half of her face remains hidden behind the visor as she holds it up to her eyes. "There. Found you. Password?"

I hesitate. I don't want to be rude, but...*seriously?* "Why would I—"

"I'm setting up your account," she says, pointing toward the dark lenses. "You can reset your password afterward. Is it embarrassing or something?"

I look down at my feet. Not so bad, really. Only embarrassing if you know the story behind it. "Um, it's t-r-e-v-o-r-the-number-four-e-v-e-r."

She repeats it back to me: trevor4ever. "All lowercase?" she asks.

"Yeah." Suddenly, I'm grateful that the other girls have resumed their conversation, utterly ignoring me. They don't need to know who Trevor is...or why I use some version of his name in all my pathetic passwords.

As for Reese, she couldn't care less. She takes off the glasses and holds them out. "You're good to go. Do you know how to use this?"

The answer is no, of course. *No, Reese, I've never used a $3,000 pair of smart glasses.* But I don't say that. Instead, there go those random words, falling out of my mouth again: "Um, yeah. Sure!"

"Good." She fishes for something in her pocket and pulls out a loop of black nylon cord with a silver clip in the center. She gestures for me to put it on over my head. "Best to keep your visor on a lanyard. Eleanor will kill you if you lose it."

Eleanor? What does Eleanor have to do with—

Something tells me not to ask. I slip the cord around my neck and attach the glasses to the clip, leaving them to dangle by my chest.

"You are now an official beta tester," Reese informs me. "I'll be monitoring your InstaLove usage—everything except for private messages—so only play it on your glasses. No phone for the next three weeks. Got it?"

"I have to call my parents and stuff."

"You can use the glasses for everything your cell phone does. Fully integrated text and voice communication."

"Text and voice communication," I parrot back to her. "Right. Obviously."

Satisfied, she turns her back to me and heads for the girls with the laptop. I'm the only one in the room still standing up. Am I supposed to join those girls on one of the beds, or…?

No, I realize. That was the end of the conversation. Reese turned her attention elsewhere. I'm dismissed.

"OK, see you all later." I turn to leave the room. As I exit, it occurs to me that I still don't know their names. No one except for Reese and Eleanor… The other Eleanor. The *real* Eleanor. The

Eleanor whose name serves as punctuation on the end of every conversation. The Eleanor whose specter dominates this place, demanding my renaming, even when she isn't in the room.

THE DROPBOX
(ENTRY 1)

___

ELEANOR

https://bit.ly/dropboxL

Dropbox > Personal

File Name	Created on	Visible to
Entry 1.txt	7/1/2019	Only you

I did NOT see that conversation coming. He dumped
me? One new girl smiles in his direction, and he's
gone. Wowww… Not that I'm jealous. She's probably
a lot better for him than I ever was. I'm just
surprised. I didn't think he had it in him. Honestly,
good for Moxie. Someone finally grew a spine.

But could he possibly have worse timing?

UGHHH, now what? Mox has no idea how much trouble
he's causing. And the worst part is, there's no
one I can talk to about it. No one. I shouldn't
even be writing it down. It'll come back to bite
me somehow.

But I need to get this out, even if it's only to a
library computer terminal. If I try to hold it in
any longer, I'll either scream or drown.

Not even Reese can know the truth. Not yet. I'll
have to tell her something though. There's no way I
can keep the breakup from her for long. She knows
us both too well. But she can't find out the REAL
reason I'm so annoyed about it. I'll have to play
up the "jealousy" angle for her benefit.

You got this, L. Keep it together. Get through
Maker Fair. July 21. Then you're nearly home free.
You can make it. "Fake it till you make it," right?
Isn't that what M always says?

Fake it-> Make it

Guess that's my new catchphrase for the next three
weeks.

5

OPEN DOORS

MADDOX

I pause outside Eleanor's door and flash a quick salute to the
fish-eye lens of the surveillance camera overhead. I'm not breaking any rules by being here. Students are allowed to visit each
other's rooms before eight o'clock curfew, as long as the door stays
open and we remain in full view of the camera.

What could possibly go wrong with a foolproof system like
that?

Seriously, the "remote supervision" thing is a joke. Dr. Carlyle
likes to wave his hands and say a bunch of buzzwords about
"promoting peer-based learning," but we all know it's an excuse
to cut back on faculty over the summer. Whoever came up with
this plan should be fired. As if a digital video feed can't be gamed.

Trust me, if I've learned anything from my past two summers

in the Maker Program, it's that anything can be faked. Anything can be hacked. *Anything* can be gamed.

A half smile turns up one corner of my mouth as I rap my fist against the solid oak paneling. A door can be made to look open even when it's closed. Especially when you have students like Emerson Kemp—students who know a thing or two about augmented reality. Emerson graduated a couple of years ago, but not without leaving behind his greatest legacy: some *highly* useful blocks of code for the next generation of Winthrop Academy attendees.

Looks like I won't have much use for Emerson's tricks this summer. I'll stick to the open-door policy. Eleanor and I made our deal, but strictly as a business arrangement. She wants to act like we're still a couple until the Maker Program ends? Fine. Not like I have any choice. We both know how much I have to lose. I'll go through the motions in public if she really cares that much about appearances, but there won't be anything going on between us behind closed doors.

I knock again and the door swings open. Reese stands on the other side. Eleanor's nowhere in sight.

Reese knows why I'm here. Her blue hair swings around her shoulders as she tilts her head toward the walk-in closet. A faint light emanates from the crack at the bottom of the closet door. "She's still getting dressed."

I glance at my watch. "We're late. The welcome dinner started twenty minutes ago."

"We're making a grand entrance," Reese replies. "The real party starts at eight." She offers no further explanation, but she taps the visor dangling from the cord around her neck.

InstaLove? I lift an eyebrow. Maybe this party won't be as boring as I feared. "Are you sure Dr. C will be down with that?"

But I already know the answer. Of course he's down with it. Dr. Carlyle knows where his bread is buttered. He gets his funding for the Maker Program from the Winthrops, and this InstaLove mod is their darling daughter's pet project.

I pull out my own glasses and blow on them, using the bottom of my polo shirt to wipe the lenses. I should probably tuck my shirt in, but hey, it's summer. There's no official dress code in effect. No one will look twice as long as I'm wearing a blazer over top.

I lean against the doorframe, crossing my legs at the ankles, as Reese turns away toward her laptop. I recognize the black rectangle of a text editor window. Her fingers dance across the keys, writing lines of code more fluently than most people write English sentences. She addresses me over her shoulder. "I integrated those new interaction scripts you wrote. Good stuff. I liked the one about the little rabbit…"

"You know I could've integrated them myself." I sniff, but not loudly enough for her to hear. I'm still chafing at the division of labor for this summer's project. "I'm capable of more than writing glorified text messages."

She taps the window closed and turns back toward me. "You don't have edit privileges."

"I know how to code."

"We can't have multiple people editing the same files, Maddox. That's a recipe for introducing bugs."

"I know, but…" I cast my eyes toward the ceiling and swallow the second half of my sentence. It's not worth arguing. I can't afford to get myself uninvited from Reese and Eleanor's group. We're essentially guaranteed to win first place at Maker Fair, with that tantalizing $1,500 cash prize.

But why do the two of them have to be so annoying? Eleanor I can manage, but Reese is such a control freak. I swear, she didn't used to be this bad when we were younger.

"Look," she says. "You're the one who begged to work with us. So be in our group, help where we need help, or else go do your own project. EOF."

EOF?

We're both staring each other down, but I break into a wide grin. Reese cracks me up sometimes. "Are you still saying that?" *EOF* started as a joke—using "End-of-file" for conversational purposes when any halfway normal person would say "period." Eleanor started that in seventh grade, the summer we all got serious about learning C++. That was eons ago. But I guess that's typical for Reese. Once she latches on to something, she never lets it go.

She smiles back at me, two spots of color blossoming on her cheekbones. "Never mind. I have something else you might be able to help with."

"Sure. Name it."

"How do you feel about…" She pauses, searching for the right word. "Um…human resources?"

"Excuse me?"

"You know, like personnel. Hiring. Recruitment."

I run my palm against the bottom half of my face, but I can't stop my shoulders from shaking. She's messing with me, right? *Human resources?* We're a bunch of kids at sleepaway camp!

"I'm serious, Maddox!" She whirls away and walks over to her desk. "Forget it. I'll do it myself."

I push away from the doorframe and take a step in her direction. "What do you mean, human resources?"

"Emerson wants us to recruit one of the new kids. Someone caught his eye when he was reviewing admissions applications."

Well, that's a new one, even for Emerson Kemp. Admissions applications? You have to give him credit. The kid is only twenty-one years old himself, but he's already treated like an honorary member of the faculty. "Since when did Emerson care who works in what group for Maker Fair?"

"Forget Maker Fair!" Reese glowers at me. "Didn't Eleanor tell you? Emerson might grant us a licensing deal for the visor-based module if we can show him proof of concept."

I pull up short. *That* got my attention. Eleanor didn't breathe a word about it. "Wait. What kind of deal?"

Reese rolls her eyes. She speaks slowly, enunciating her words as if talking to a toddler. "His company might license the code we develop and use it for the real app."

"So, like, pay us for it? With money?"

"Yes, Maddox. With money."

I stuff my hands in my pockets and slouch a bit to cover up my newfound interest in this conversation. Probably a good thing we aren't playing InstaLove right now. My avi would be the one with the dollar signs for eyeballs.

"Ohhh, gotcha," I say as casually as I can manage. "So how much are we talking about?"

Reese doesn't answer. Maybe she doesn't know. Or maybe she doesn't care. It's not like she needs to worry about anything so mercenary. Her biggest concern is how it will look on her college applications—as if she needs to worry about *that* either.

I clear my throat. "So what do you need me to do exactly? Recruit some phenom to our group?"

"Lowercase." Reese drops her voice and glances toward the closet.

"Excuse me?"

She whispers. "You know, the other Eleanor. We're referring to her as Lowercase."

My eyes narrow. I must be missing something. I mean, Eleanor can be petty, but I can't believe she'd throw a fit over some other girl daring to possess the same first name. "Nora" and "Eleanor" don't even sound similar…

Reese averts her eyes. "She's hurt, Maddox. Can you blame her? She saw the way you looked at that girl. Then three seconds later you broke up with her."

Oh. I wasn't sure if Eleanor told anyone about our conversation in the library. But of course she did. She and Reese tell each other everything. There are no secrets between those two.

Reese's voice drops so low, she practically mouths the words instead of speaking them. "We need to handle this *delicately.* Understood?"

"Are you saying *she*"—I nod toward the closet—"doesn't know that you're recruiting Lowercase?"

"No. That's why I need *you* to do it. Act like it was all your idea."

"Won't that make it worse?"

Reese pauses a moment before she answers. A subtle accusation dulls her tone. "You've already done your damage, Maddox. The last thing she needs is her best friend betraying her too."

I look down at the floor and scratch the back of my neck. Why do I feel like such a slime bucket? I didn't break up with Eleanor because of some love-at-first-sight InstaCrush on another girl. If that's what Reese thinks of me, she's wrong.

But I won't pretend that "Lowercase" hasn't been popping in and out of my thoughts all afternoon.

Reese's silent gaze bears down on me. I ignore it and slip on my visor, flicking and blinking through the prompts.

Nora

There she is, filed under missed connections. Her avatar greets me with those bright green eyes that first captured my attention. She hasn't finished filling out her profile yet. It consists of nothing more than her username and IL score, which has somehow dropped into negative territory. *Impressive.* I wouldn't have pegged her for some badass coder, but she must be something special if Emerson took note. That tidbit of information only adds to my curiosity about this girl.

I move her over to InstaFriends, but something makes me hesitate before I hit Confirm.

I shouldn't...

No.

Definitely a bad idea.

I shake my head, and her image sways side to side before my eyes. The next three weeks are going to be complicated enough without adding fuel to the fire.

But isn't this the reason I broke things off with Eleanor? Because she doesn't own me. She doesn't dictate who I talk to... who I look at...who I am... She doesn't get a say in my every move. Not anymore.

To hell with Reese and her guilt trips. I move Nora's avatar again.

InstaFriends	InstaCrushes	Missed Connections
	Nora	

I blink once to Confirm and slide my glasses into my back pocket as the closet door creaks open. Eleanor emerges and does a pirouette. She wears a strapless black satin cocktail dress, and the skirt swirls as she spins on sky-high heels. Anyone else would look ridiculously overdressed, but not Eleanor.

She smiles and comes toward me. I can smell her perfume: Chanel N°5, like usual. That fragrance should have been too old and stuffy for a high school student, but she makes it work. Half the girls at Winthrop started wearing it last year after Eleanor declared it her signature scent. I swear, the girl sets her own dress code everywhere she goes through sheer confidence and force of will.

She straightens the lapels of my jacket, then takes a step back to assess her handiwork. "Tuck your shirt in," she commands.

I meet her gaze, and we have a whole unspoken conversation in the long moment before I answer. "Nah. I'm good like this."

Her mouth tightens. I know that look. She isn't pleased. But she covers it with a smile and a shrug.

"Suit yourself," she says, linking her arm through mine. With her other arm, she reaches out for Reese. "Come on, you two. We're late. Let's get this party started."

6

WELCOME

NORA

There's a common nightmare, or so I've heard. The one where you show up to a party, only to realize you forgot to put on clothes. There you stand, fully naked, surrounded by the laughter and judgment of everyone in the universe you've ever wanted to impress.

I've never had that particular dream. My version is slightly less dramatic. Slightly more realistic. It involves showing up at a party, dressed in a cotton T-shirt and a pair of denim cutoff shorts, surrounded by twenty other students in skirts and dress pants and gold-buttoned blazers.

And oh yeah, there's one other key difference. My nightmare doesn't involve being asleep. It's happening to me right now, actually.

At this exact moment.

In real life.

I squeeze my eyes closed and reopen them. Everyone else in attendance must have psychic powers. I'm the only one who didn't get the memo that tonight's welcome dinner had a dress code.

I should have known when I caught sight of the program director's residence, with its pair of stone lions flanking the front entryway. The place deserves a photo spread in *Fancy People* magazine. I count a grand total of four chimneys rising from the steeply pitched roof. The sprawling house matches the stateliness of all the other buildings I've encountered here at Winthrop. Not that I've seen inside any of them besides my dormitory. I arrived ten minutes late to this party and followed the sound of chatting voices through a brick archway that led to the walled grounds out back.

I knew from my packet that the party would be held outdoors, and I dressed for a summer backyard barbecue. Instead, I walked into a fully catered garden party, set amid the program director's carefully landscaped grounds—a mix of graceful weeping willow trees, stone terraces, and well-tended flower beds.

And me? I stick out like a stray weed.

My instincts scream to turn and leave. No one here has made eye contact with me yet. I could slip out through the garden gate without drawing attention to myself. No one would notice my disappearance. If they did, I doubt they'd care.

But no. I give my head a tiny shake. This is the only officially sanctioned event for the duration of the three-week program—my only chance to introduce myself and get some face time with the faculty.

No one will look at me too closely once night has fallen. It's nearly dusk already. Paper lanterns hang from tree branches, casting the scenery in a soft, orange glow. More light emanates from lanterns at the far edge of the lawn, floating in the director's private in-ground swimming pool.

Did I mention this place was posh?

Other students stand about in clusters, with plates and glasses balanced in their hands. I avoid all of them and make a beeline for the place I feel safest: the long buffet table, bedecked with silver platters of food.

I pick up a plate and take my time filling it. As long as I keep busy, it won't look odd that I'm not talking to anyone. Unfortunately, there's a limit to how many egg rolls and mini-quiches I can fit on my plate. I reach the end of the long table and linger beside the beverages, observing the rest of the partygoers from the fringes.

Everyone is waving. Everyone is hugging. Everyone knows each other. How am I the only outsider here?

Normally, my strategy in this situation would involve staring at my phone. Nothing like some urgent fake-text-messages to hide the fact that no one wants to talk to you. Too bad I left my phone in my room. I only have my InSight Visor dangling from the cord around my neck. Several other kids here have their own glasses clipped to belt loops or poking out of bags, but nobody else has them on.

I stuff an egg roll in my mouth, searing hot inside. The filling burns my tongue. My eyes water as I abandon my plate and pour myself a glass of lemonade.

One of the girls from Reese's room stands at the other end of the drink table. She fiddles with the rubber-banded end of her French braid as her eyes rove around the party. I look toward her shyly, wondering if she'll acknowledge me.

She breaks into a bright smile and swings her arm back and forth above her head. *Really?* If anything, she seems too enthusiastic. I raise my own hand tentatively to wave back.

"Miranda!" she calls, going up on her tiptoes to see past me. "Babe! Over here!"

I turn away, using my raised hand to tuck a strand of hair behind my ear.

Smooth, Nora.

I blow out a breath and move away, scanning the other faces. There's one face in particular I'm searching for, although I'm embarrassed to admit it. *He must be here somewhere...*

Soft footsteps approach me from behind, and I spin on my heel. Too fast. The lemonade sloshes in my cup, threatening to spill. A hand reaches out to help me steady it. "Careful!"

I don't know why I expected that voice to belong to Maddox. Of course it isn't him. Instead, I find myself face-to-face with a middle-aged man with close-cropped graying hair and deep brown skin, wearing a tweed blazer and bow tie. He looks exactly like his picture on the Winthrop faculty webpage.

I swallow my mouthful of lemonade with a gulp. "Are you Dr. Carlyle?"

"I am. And you must be Miss Weinberg. Welcome to Winthrop!"

He smiles warmly, and relief floods through me. He knows my name. He didn't call security to kick me out of his backyard for trespassing, despite my raggedy cutoff shorts. Instead, he takes a step closer and holds out his hand to shake mine.

"Your application made quite a splash with our scholarship committee. We're expecting big things from you this summer!"

I take a deep breath, feeling both foolish and reassured. *Of course he knows who you are, Nora.* There's a reason I'm here in this program. For all my insecurities, I'm not actually an imposter. I have skills. I'm standing here because I earned my slot over thousands of other applicants. I need to remember that.

I smile back at him, and this time it isn't forced. It's amazing how two sentences from another human being can cast everything in a different light. He expects big things from me, and that's all I needed to hear. "Thanks," I answer, lifting my chin. "I'm really looking forward to the Maker Fair."

"Excellent! Let me know if you need any help settling in. My door is always open." He waves an arm vaguely toward the back door of his house before moving on to mingle with another group of students. I toss back a fresh mouthful of lemonade as he moves away. The liquid cools my throat, even though I can't taste the sugary tang. My poor, burned tongue feels thick and furry. Numb.

Maybe I should take the numbness as a sign. Why subject myself to another hour of cringeworthy small talk? That three-second conversation with the program director was the whole reason I came. I don't know why I allowed myself to get sidetracked by cute boys and snotty girls. None of that stuff will matter in the long run. I'm here for one reason and one reason only. Do well in the program. Impress Dr. Carlyle. Get a college recommendation at the end of it.

I set down my lemonade and eye the garden gate once more, shuffling a few steps closer to the exit. Forget making friends. I'd rather return to my laptop and get to work. Only the weight dangling around my neck makes me hesitate. My fingers rise to the visor, and I fiddle with a button on the frame.

It's not true that I only came to meet Dr. Carlyle. I was hoping for an excuse to use this thing, and I can't deny the small stab of disappointment. Tonight's gathering seemed like a natural place to give InstaLove another whirl—but I guess I'm the only one who thought so.

I turn to leave the party, but I stop dead in my tracks. A sudden hush surrounds me. The buzz of conversation turns to silence, and I sense everyone around me looking in the same direction.

The garden gate.

Three figures stand framed beneath the archway, pausing in the lantern light as they make their entrance. All three of them wear the visors that no one else dared put on. I recognize their faces instantly, even with their eyes concealed.

Reese, Eleanor, and Maddox. Arm in arm in arm.

7

MAKING A SPLASH

NORA

The three of them remain at the garden entrance, fifty feet away, but I can feel the change in the air from here. I stand transfixed, watching their graceful movements. Eleanor unlinks her elbow from Maddox and edges closer to Reese. The two girls wrap arms around each other's waists.

They make an odd pair. Reese looks edgy and dramatic, dressed in black from head to toe with a shock of bright blue hair. Eleanor, meanwhile, must have gotten lost on the way to some swank red carpet movie premiere in that semiformal cocktail dress. She smiles and waves to no one in particular as she makes her way to the middle of the stone patio.

My eyes follow her, unable to tear my gaze away. After I spent all afternoon wondering about Maddox, Eleanor is the one who keeps me planted in place. I'm not the only one watching her. The whispered questions buzz around me.

InstaLove?...here?...now? Did you bring your glasses?

My plans to leave the party evaporate, and my fingertips tingle with anticipation as I reach for the cord around my neck. For all my shyness, I won't pretend like I'm not dying to know what InstaLove looks like through these lenses.

The glasses themselves are easy enough to use. I fiddled around with them earlier in the privacy of my room. Reese set them up to auto log in to my InstaLove account, and I discovered a treasure trove of extra settings and configurations not available in the phone version of the app.

I scroll through the menu, using eye movements to make selections. I might be stuck with my own ratty clothes in real life, but Nora 2.0 can swap outfits with a few blinks. The app comes preloaded with a range of wardrobe options. I settle on a sundress, navy blue with a bright yellow sunflower print. Not as elegant as Eleanor's shimmery cocktail dress, but more appropriate than my shorts and T-shirt.

InstaMakeover complete! I'm ready. The time has come to introduce myself around.

I turn in a slow circle, scanning my lens-covered eyes around the party. I feel light-headed—not dizzy, but disconnected from solid ground—floating above the grass instead of walking through it. My movements feel weightless and frictionless, full of graceful ease. I look down at my feet and do a twirl. My lungs fill with a gasp of pleasure at the way my virtual sundress swirls around my legs.

For the first time since I arrived at Winthrop, I'm glad to be here. I've never experienced anything so magical. The InstaLove phone app might be popular, but the visor version blows it away.

I lift my head, and the hairs rise on the back of my neck. The level of detail is intense. Hard to believe that any high school student could have created all this. Everywhere I look, I see a combination of real and "augmented" scenery—not only the avatars, but the background too. I recognize the flower beds and stone terraces lined with paper lanterns, but some invisible hand has painted in a screen of palm trees at the far edge of the lawn.

Those trees weren't there before. I can't recall what they replaced though. Weeping willows, maybe? I resist the urge to lift my visor and check, not wanting to break the spell InstaLove has cast.

I glide a few paces toward the palm trees to investigate, and they no longer look fully authentic as I approach. There's something cartoonish about them. Too perfect. Too crisp. Too bright, like the background of a CGI animation film. I wonder what would happen if I tried to touch them. Could I walk right through those solid-looking tree trunks? Or would they recede farther into the distance before I got too close?

The palm fronds rustle as a cool breeze sweeps through the garden, raising goose bumps on my arms. The weather has grown colder since the sun went down. I should have brought a sweater. Maybe I should give my avatar an augmented-reality cardigan to match my dress.

The thought makes me chuckle under my breath. I'm not serious…but maybe I should be. I wonder if the mere sight of a sweater covering my arms would trick my brain into feeling a few degrees warmer.

I slow my pace and search again for the outfit customization menu, when my path is blocked by another avatar.

She looks familiar. Is that the French-braid girl who made such a point of ignoring me earlier? Her avi comes to a halt before me, with her skirt fluttering in the breeze. This time, she looks straight at me. I'm so pleased, I almost miss the fact her avatar has on an identical fake sundress to mine.

The text bubble clues me in.

> Hey, Nora, meet Samirah! Looks like you two wore the same dress (oopsies!). Do you:
>
> **A)** Compliment her good taste in clothes?
>
> **B)** Give her a dirty look and demand she change her outfit?

A nervous giggle escapes my lips. I'm not sure what the real Nora would do in this situation—probably find some deep dark hole to hide inside—but Nora 2.0 doesn't have that choice. I roll my eyes upward to highlight option "A," blinking once to confirm my selection.

Samirah's avatar breaks into a friendly smile. A text exchange pops up in the center of the screen.

> **Nora:** Hey, nice dress. You have good taste!
> **Samirah:** So do you! Maybe we should go shopping together! 😊
>
> ---
> ❤ Like ⊗ Reply

Did I just make my first InstaFriend? I eyeball the heart icon by way of response, and I practically float off the ground at the burst of newfound confidence. So much easier than real small talk! I didn't have to open my mouth once. The whole interaction played out like a pre-written script. I suddenly love this app, despite the rather limited clothing selection.

Samirah drifts away, and I follow the prompts to classify her. The InstaLove three-column display fills my field of vision.

InstaFriends…

InstaCrushes…

Missed Connections…

This is where the visor mod integrates with the basic app. The avatars look flat and lifeless by comparison. I slide Samirah's face into the empty friend column, and my new IL score flashes in the corner of the screen: 46.

A positive number!

Let's keep the momentum going, Nora 2.0. I turn and head for the thick of the party. A cluster of avatars mingle near the palm trees at the far edge of the lawn. I recognize Eleanor and Reese side by side, each talking to a different boy, but not the boy who spent all day in the back of my mind.

Maddox… Where did he go?

At the thought of him, I feel less cold. I swivel my head, searching, but I don't see his tall frame or perfectly disheveled hair. Probably for the best. I should practice a few more interactions before I run into him again. I lock eyes with a different avi—a boy who seems eager enough to talk to me. Then another girl after that.

By now I have three faces in my InstaFriend column, and my IL score keeps rising. I can't believe I'm saying this, but I'm actually having fun at a party.

It's official.

I'm in love.

With an app.

I'm never taking these AR glasses off.

My gaze flickers across Reese and Eleanor again, and I can't deny a grudging admiration. Reese must be an incredible coder to create all this. And Eleanor, with her mean-girl magnetism, inspired everyone at this party to play along. I could run over there and hug them both.

Instead, my eyes wander past them. The garden seems emptier

than before. Avatars head toward the gate in groups of two or three. There goes French Braid—I mean Samirah—holding hands with the girl she waved to earlier tonight. Beanie Girl. They must be a couple... A few other kids follow at their heels. Are they all headed back to the dorms? Maybe I should tag along.

But I can't leave yet. I stand rooted to the spot. My eyes land on another face, and he's looking in my direction.

Maddox.

My stomach drops. My hand flies to my throat, checking to make sure my head is still fully attached to my body. I expect him to ignore me—wave to someone else standing behind me. But he doesn't wave. He looks straight at me as he weaves his way past the other avatars who stand between us.

I close my eyes, gathering my nerve. *It's no big deal.* No different from all the other interactions I've had tonight. All I have to do is wait for the game to prompt me and pick the friendly choice. Then my avi will smile at him and say something non-humiliating— something halfway cute that I would never think to say in real life. And he'll have no idea about the way my thoughts are churning.

That, in a nutshell, is the brilliance behind this app. It doesn't change who you are. It merely presents the world with an enhanced version, like makeup or well-cut clothes, covering up the embarrassing blemishes in your social skills.

My main task at the moment is to stay upright. Even InstaLove can't salvage the situation if I pass out. I wipe my hands against the gauzy fabric of my sundress, caught by surprise when my fingers brush against the front pockets of my denim shorts instead.

Maddox's avatar comes up before me. A new text bubble appears, but I'm so jittery I can barely read the words.

> Hey, Nora, remember Maddox? Mutual attraction detected!
> Do you:
> **A)** Blow him a kiss?
> **B)** Run away like a scared little rabbit?

I can't breathe.

That's my choice? Really? What the heck? All the other prompts were way more chill. It must be because I lumped his avatar in the InstaCrush column. What a mistake! He can't see where I classified him, can he?

I press my lips together and gulp down against the rising panic in my chest.

I should have realized… The app's called InstaLove, after all. Not InstaGirlTalk. Not InstaShoppingBuddies. Insta*Love*. Of course it's forcing me to flirt.

How do I get out of this? There must be some way to override the script. My eyes flick up and down, highlighting each choice, but I can't find a way to exit without making a selection. Maybe I should pick choice B and run away? At least it's better than standing here like an indecisive statue.

I highlight the second option, but I can't bring myself to blink. As I hesitate, Maddox's avatar changes mood. His smile widens, and I swear those two tiny hearts flash in the pupils of his eyes.

The text message exchange opens, awaiting my response.

> **Maddox:** You look pretty tonight *blows a kiss*
> **Nora:** ...

Wait.

Wait, wait, wait.

He blew *me* a kiss?

Does that mean—

But—

But—

No.

I slam my eyes shut, pure reflex taking over. I think I just picked choice B, but I don't care. None of this feels like a game anymore. I turn and flee for real.

The fake palm trees sway before me. I stumble toward them, desperate to escape behind the leafy curtain of fronds. As I go, I turn my head to look back at Maddox over my shoulder.

He watches me with a new expression—one I haven't seen before. Eyes wide. Mouth shaped like an "O." That isn't his avatar making that face. Those are his real eyes meeting mine. He's shoved his glasses upward, propping them at his hairline.

A text bubble crashes onto my screen, highlighted on a bright red background.

> **SYSTEM**
> Nora! Eyes ahead!

How is Maddox sending me messages without his visor? That makes no sense, but I don't have time to dwell on it. I reach the augmented trees and pass through them unimpeded.

And then I realize.

I finally remember what lay at the far edge of this lawn, before we all put on our glasses. Not palm trees. Not weeping willows. Not trees at all.

Water. A glassy surface, rippling in the evening breeze, glistening in the dancing firelight of paper lanterns...

The ground beneath my feet ceases to exist. I'm falling. Sinking. I flail my arms and open my mouth, but my yelp is muffled by the splash. The icy water rushes all around me, filling my mouth and nose.

I'm fully submerged before my brain catches up with my senses, and I realize where I am: the bottom of Dr. Carlyle's in-ground swimming pool.

8

WET RABBIT

MADDOX

Ummm, did that really happen?

I stand stock-still, too stunned to move, before bounding in the direction of the pool. No one else reacts. I must have been the only one who saw Nora go under. With visors on, it would've looked like her avatar merely disappeared behind the augmented-reality palm trees. But I took my glasses off before she reached the trees, confused by the outcome of our interaction.

> **Maddox:** Hey, you look pretty tonight *blows a kiss*
> **Nora:** Eeek! Sorry, honeybunny....*hops away*

I wrote that script myself, with Nora's face in mind. I knew she was jumpy, but still… I was expecting her to pick the other option.

She was supposed to blow a kiss back, not run away so hastily that she forgot to look where she was going! And those palm trees never should have been there in the first place. Who added them to this location? Not me… Was it Reese? Or Eleanor?

Nora better not be hurt. I call out to the other students as I make my way to the water's edge. Lanterns illuminate the deck, but the water itself is dark. No sign of movement beneath the inky surface.

I whip off my blazer, preparing to go in after her, but there's no need. Nora resurfaces, thrashing and sputtering. I grasp her by the wrist, careful to keep my balance on the edge as I drag her back to safety.

A crowd has gathered at my back. I glance up, looking for Dr. Carlyle. Instead, Reese and Eleanor push their way forward.

I kneel next to Nora on the deck. My hands hover around her without making contact. I'm not sure how to help her—or if she wants my help—as she sputters and gasps for air. Reese crouches across from me at Nora's other side. Eleanor stands above us all, her face a mask of surprise. For once, something has shaken her cool composure.

Reese reaches toward Nora's face. "The visor! Is it damaged?"

I'm not sure who she's asking, but Eleanor responds. "They're supposed to be waterproof up to thirty feet deep."

Reese shakes her head. "I don't get it. How did she not get an alert—"

Seriously?

"Forget the visor!" I can't believe how crass they're being. I reach an arm around Nora's shoulders to support her as she fights to regain her breath. "Are you OK?" I ask softly, pulling her closer.

Nora coughs, too choked up to answer. Her hands move to her glasses, struggling to pull them off, but her hair tangles with the frame. Reese reaches down to tear them free. Nora lets out a yelp as Reese snatches them away and turns to Eleanor to examine them.

The crowd of other students stand around uselessly, wringing their hands. Where are all the adults? Dr. Carlyle must have left the party once the game started. There are no cameras here in the fenced-off grounds of the director's residence.

I'm about to tell Reese to go find him when I catch sight of his tweed jacket making its way through the crowd. Nora has regained her breath, but she still hasn't said a word. I can't tell if she's hurt or just embarrassed. She leans forward and buries her face in her hands.

Dr. Carlyle rests his hand on her shoulder. "Are you injured? Maddox, why don't you walk Miss Weinberg to the infirmary to get checked out."

She speaks at last, a whispered protest. "No, no." Her eyes go to the program director, big and round like the first time I met her—only now they're wide with shock, not gleaming with excitement. "I'm fine. Really."

I still have my arm around her, and she shivers in the cool evening air. I reach for my discarded blazer and wrap it around her shoulders.

Dr. C slips his wire-rim glasses down the bridge of his nose, examining her over the top of the frames. "Are you sure? If you took in any water, you should…"

Nora's chest heaves up and down again, but not for the reason Dr. Carlyle thinks. She covers her face and whispers something too soft for anyone but me to hear. "Please stop looking at me."

I glance up at the other kids around us. A few faces look concerned, but mostly I can hear their ill-suppressed laughter. "She's fine," I announce gruffly. "Show's over. Everyone put your visors back on."

I can't really blame them for laughing. This whole incident is hilarious to me too, I have to admit—but Nora is obviously not amused.

And neither are Reese and Eleanor.

Reese has Nora's visor pressed to her face, holding down the power button with her index finger, while Eleanor fidgets at her side. "Can you see anything? Did it restart?"

Reese peels the glasses off and wipes the lenses with the hem of her blouse. "They're fine." She holds them out to Nora, who still has my blazer hanging limply from her shoulders.

"Didn't you see the alert?" Eleanor snaps at her.

Nora shakes her head, her eyes pointed downward at the empty space between Reese's sneakers and Eleanor's five-inch heels. "No," she answers miserably. "I mean, it just said 'Eyes ahead.' It happened really fast."

Eleanor doesn't bother to conceal her contempt, but Reese looks more surprised than anything. She must be thinking the same thing I am. InstaLove went through some growing pains when Emerson first launched it publicly—a few scattered reports of accidents and injuries. He and his team of developers added new safety features to keep this kind of thing from happening.

"Nothing about approaching an edge?" Reese asks. "Uneven terrain? Nothing?"

"No."

I know what went wrong. I wince as I remember the few fleeting instants before Nora hit the water. InstaLove is designed to alert users to oncoming hazards, but that only works if the app can *see* the hazard. Nora had her visor pointed at the party, not the pool. "She wasn't looking forward," I explain to Reese. "She had her head turned."

She was looking over her shoulder *at me*, I add silently. But I know better than to say that out loud within Eleanor's earshot.

She's too sharp to miss the implication. Eleanor rolls her eyes, and her hands resume their usual position on her hips. "Well, then she deserved to fall in, didn't she?"

Reese matches her best friend's snippy tone. "You have to look where you're going," she tells Nora. "You're lucky these aren't broken."

Both of them need to lay off. It was an accident! I turn toward my *ex*-girlfriend, warning her with my eyes not to say another word. She glowers back at me, tilting her head a few degrees sideways.

I know that gesture. She's summoning me. Commanding me to resume my position at her side. Silently reminding me that the two of us had an agreement.

I ignore her. My hand comes to rest at the small of Nora's back. I bend closer to tell her I'll take her to the infirmary or the dorms—whichever she prefers. But before I can get a word out, Eleanor grabs my other arm and yanks me to my feet. She hauls me in the direction of the drink table, with her manicured fingernails sinking into the flesh of my inner elbow.

I open my mouth to protest, but I shut it again. *Forget it.* Everything will go more smoothly if I let her have her way. I jerk my arm free, but I keep walking at Eleanor's side. I fight the urge to glance backward over my shoulder at the soaking wet girl I abandoned.

I'm doing her a favor, I tell myself. Getting her out of Eleanor's crosshairs. We'll all be better off if I keep my eyes trained forward. Straight ahead.

9

LOWER THAN LOWERCASE

NORA

I stare up at the popcorn ceiling of my dorm room, with my blanket pulled up to my chin. My sopping clothes lay on the floor in a ball. I should wring them out before I go to sleep tonight. Otherwise, I'll awaken to a room that smells of swimming pool chlorine and mildew. But I can't summon the energy to move.

My InSight Visor sits atop my desk. My eyes dart toward it. I should put it away inside a drawer, or at least turn the lenses to face the wall instead of my bed. I can't shake the sensation that it's watching me.

Judging me, like everyone else here at Winthrop. They all stood around in a semicircle, witnessing my clumsiness. I pull the blanket over my face as if to block their view. I thought it was bad when those girls renamed me "Lowercase," but tonight, my social status plunged far lower.

Nine feet lower, to be precise: the depth of Dr. Carlyle's swimming pool.

So much for my love affair with my visor. That didn't last long. I still haven't figured out how to use it to make phone calls, and my parents are expecting me to check in with them tonight. I should retrieve my phone. Call home and tell them this program was a huge mistake. If they set out first thing tomorrow morning, they could be here by noon to pick me up.

But the thought of explaining what happened to my mom and dad only makes me feel worse. I flip over onto my stomach and bury my face in my pillow. I can't do it. I can't face talking to anyone. I'll just stay here in bed for the next three weeks until they come to fetch me as scheduled. They'll park their car in Winthrop Academy's U-shaped driveway and march proudly into the Maker Fair to see what their brilliant offspring made. They'll search and search for my name among the other students' projects, until finally, they find me. Here. In this bed. With my face buried in this pillow.

I'll tell them what I made for Maker Fair. I made a fool of myself. And the whole project took me less than a day to complete!

A muffled sound escapes my throat, somewhere between a sob and a laugh. Maybe this evening's events will seem funny to me at some point. Even in my misery, some portion of my brain knows that… But it'll take me longer than three weeks to get there.

For now, there's only one thing I can do. Tuck those smart glasses safely inside my desk and leave them there untouched. Never look at the world again through those traitorous lenses. Forget Reese. Forget Samirah. Forget my whole hard-won column full of InstaFriends.

But can I really forget Maddox?

I let out a loud sniff. Out of all those people ogling me as I pushed my way past and ran for the garden gate, Maddox was the only one *not* watching. Eleanor grabbed him by the hand and dragged him away. He went without a backward glance. He's obviously in a relationship with her—a girl light-years out of my league. What in the world made me think that he was flirting with me?

My thoughts are interrupted by a soft knock at my door.

Knock, knock, knock-knock-knock.

That must be Ms. Cleary, the resident adviser. She left the party before my graceful swan dive into loserdom, but she probably heard the story by now. No doubt Dr. Carlyle told her to check up on me, and I'd rather smother myself with this pillow than face her.

"I'm fine," I call out, lifting my head an inch. "No worries. Totally fine!"

The door clicks open a sliver. A voice penetrates through the crack, whispering my name. That's not Ms. Cleary. Is that—

"Nora? Are you awake?"

I scramble out of bed. My heart thumps loudly as my eyes fly to the door, and my thoughts shatter into a million disjointed fragments.

Him.

Maddox.

Here.

Now.

Outside my door.

Saying my name.

Maddox came to check on me.

What is life?

"Just a sec!" I thrust my fingers through my mussed-up hair, full of knots and tangles. At least it's clean. I showered to rinse off the pool water before I got in bed. I'm not still naked, am I? I look down with a strangled wheeze, but I exhale again at the sight of my striped cotton pajamas.

"Hurry up!" he whispers through the crack. "I'm not supposed to be here!"

My pajama top bunches weirdly at my waist. I missed a button when I did it up, but I don't have time to fix it...or to think about what he meant. *He's not supposed to be here.* Because he'll get in trouble with the RA at one end of the corridor? Or with his girlfriend at the other?

"Nora!" he whisper-yells, his voice growing more urgent. "Let me in!"

I swing the door open. Maddox stands before me in a short-sleeved polo shirt, rubbing his arms for warmth. I can't tear my eyes away from his shirtsleeves, clinging to his biceps, bunching and gathering as his hands run up and down.

Well, this is a first. I've never been alone before with a boy who possessed biceps. Except maybe my PE teacher, Mr. Greene. I had to stay after that one time… And he probably had some muscle definition hiding underneath that thick coat of grizzled arm hair. But Maddox's arms are… What's the word I'm looking for here?

Nice.

Nice arms.

How did I not notice those before?

"Hey," he says, seemingly unaware I had a whole conversation with myself in the time it took for him to draw breath. He slips through the door and tugs it closed behind him. A warning flares in some corner of my mind. Didn't my orientation packet say something about dormitory rules?

Students will be housed in supervised dormitories…
Students will adhere to a strict 8:00 p.m. curfew…
*Students visiting dormitory rooms to which they have not been
    assigned will keep doors open and remain in full view of
    hallway cameras at all times…*

I should probably tell him. I don't want to get in trouble. But those arms… He even has muscles in his forearms. How did I not see those at the party? Didn't his InstaLove avatar have arms?

Oh wait. No. I remember now. I close my eyes as I realize. I didn't see his arms because they were covered. Maddox, unlike some people in this room, dressed *appropriately* for the program's opening soirée. He donned that fitted polo shirt underneath a—

"Blazer," I say out loud.

He points a finger at me to confirm the reason for his presence. "Yeah. I kind of need that back."

The blood races to my cheeks. I completely stole his jacket. He draped it around my shoulders as I sat shivering at the side of the pool, and I kept it on for my frantic flight back here to Fenmore Hall. Now it sits in a ball on my floor, tangled up with my disgusting shorts and T-shirt. I lunge to pick it up before he sees.

"Sorry!" I cringe as I hold it up to the light. No stains, miraculously. "I didn't mean to—I can get this dry-cleaned."

"No, no." He takes it from me, shaking out the wrinkles. He sniffs at the lapel. "It's fine. Smells like…"

Like chlorine and humiliation?

He sniffs again, more deeply. Then he breaks into that grin of his, full of mischief. "Smells like a drowned bunny rabbit. Here, try it. It's nice."

He holds it out to me to smell for myself, but I stumble backward onto my bed. My hands rise to my face to hide my flaming cheeks, but I'm laughing through my fingers. "Sorry," I whimper.

His perfect arms disappear inside the blazer's sleeves. "No problem." He tugs at the collar and fastens the top button. "I should probably go though." He glances toward my door.

Oh right. The door. I point at it. "Are we going to get in trouble for that?"

His grin goes crooked. "Nah, I took care of it."

"What do you mean, you—"

He cocks his head sideways, and his hair flops over, covering his left eye. "This is my third summer here," he says softly. "I know my way around."

I swallow. Something about the way he said that seemed…

He's not flirting with you, Nora. I'm imagining it. Obviously. My eyes dart away from his, moving randomly until they come to rest on my desk. My glasses sit where I left them on the desktop. I move to pick them up, pretending to examine them so I don't have to meet his eyes again.

"Are they still working OK?" he asks.

The blue LED light glares at me, bright as ever. "I think so."

"Good." I can hear him smiling. "Because you picked the wrong choice last time."

My head jerks up. I suddenly remember the prompt when he approached me at the party.

> Hey, Nora, remember Maddox? Mutual attraction detected!
>
> Do you:
>
> **A)** Blow him a kiss?
>
> **B)** Run away like a scared little rabbit?

Mutual attraction? And then his avatar blew a kiss?

But that can't be. He has a girlfriend. Eleanor. There's no way he—

No.

No, no.

No, no, no.

I'm misinterpreting. Maybe Maddox didn't see the same prompt I did. He must have been prompted something different. Something where blowing a kiss would seem totally innocent and normal. Something like... Oh, I don't know...

> This awkward person is blocking your view of someone you actually find attractive. Do you:
>
> **A)** Politely ask her to move?
>
> **B)** Pretend she's invisible and blow a kiss to the person standing behind her?

Right. And it must have been the other Eleanor standing behind me. *Obviously.*

"I should go," Maddox says. He turns to leave. "See you around."

"Bye," I manage weakly.

I go to shut the door behind him, and his soft voice floats back to me over his shoulder. His parting words throw my thoughts into a whole new disarray. There's no one else in the hallway. No mistaking the way his voice drops into the back of his throat, low and seductive, his words meant only for me.

"Next time, little rabbit…don't run away."

THE DROPBOX (ENTRY 2)

ELEANOR

https://bit.ly/dropboxL

Dropbox > Personal

File Name	Created on	Visible to
Entry 1.txt	7/1/2019	Deleted
Entry 2.txt	7/2/2019	Only you

One day in, and I'm already exhausted. This is going to be harder than I thought.

I wish I could confide in Reese. It feels bizarre, keeping a secret this huge from her. She has no idea. Totally convinced by my "jealous, spurned ex-girlfriend" act.

Kind of disturbing that she considers me so petty.
Like all my fake raging about that poor girl having
the same name? Calling her "Lowercase"? So freaking
unnecessary LOL. "Nora" would be fine. No one would
ever think of me as a "Nora" anyway. Ew. We all know
"El" is the nice part of my name. "Nor" is the blah
part at the end, the part everyone i-g-N-O-R-e-s.
The name thing is a good distraction though.
Distraction, the key to illusion. Like that cheesy
magician my parents hired for my birthday party one
summer when I was little, making rabbits appear
in his hat and disappear again before our eyes.
Those tricks were always so transparent. Always a
variation of the same technique. Distract everyone's
attention with some big elaborate gesture with
one hand. Meanwhile, the other hand that nobody's
watching? That's where the real trick goes down.
And then the big reveal. Presto! Magic! A puff of
smoke!
Except with this trick, I'm not the magician. I'm
the rabbit in the hat. And when the show is over and
the smoke clears, I'll be the one who disappeared.

10

TEENHACK

NORA

My laptop perches on my knees, but my attention keeps wandering everywhere except the screen. I sit alone on a stone bench with the faint sound of footsteps crunching along the gravel path nearby. Whoever those footsteps belong to, I pray they won't turn the corner around the tall hedge that conceals my presence.

I woke this morning with a renewed sense of purpose. I didn't bother to draw my window shade last night, and I got up before my alarm, roused by the early morning light. Amazing how this campus takes on a different mood beneath a sunny sky. Last night's events—falling in the pool and Maddox's visit afterward—they never happened. It's a new dawn, and I know how to spend my morning.

I open a clean document and type words at the top of the screen.

July 2

Winthrop Academy Summer Maker Program

MAKER FAIR PROPOSAL

Nora Weinberg

That's a start. I chew my thumbnail as I contemplate the blank space beneath the heading. Maker Fair takes place in three weeks, and I don't have a clue what I'm making. My plan coming in here—the self-navigating lawn mower—seems pathetic to me now.

It's not even original. I got the idea from a post I read on TeenHack.

TEENHACK

FEATURED PROJECTS

Build a Self-Propelled SmartMower

Time Required: 3 weeks

Difficulty: Advanced

I need to come up with something better. Dr. Carlyle said it himself last night: "*We're expecting big things from you this summer.*" Big things. Not copycat things that anyone with a TeenHack account could read about and duplicate.

I tap my fingernails against the bottom edge of my laptop keyboard. If I'm going to stick it out for the full three weeks at Winthrop, then I want to do well. Make something good.

Something amazing. Something that will earn the respect of every single person who stood around and laughed at me last night. I want to leave this place with all of them calling me by my real name—Nora Weinberg, not "Lowercase"—because I made the most talked-about project to come out of this program since Emerson Kemp himself.

There's only one thing standing in my way. The empty proposal stares back at me from my computer screen, a not-so-subtle reminder of the blank feeling in my brain whenever I try to come up with an original idea.

Let's face it. Creativity has never been my strong suit. I was the kid in kindergarten who refused to do art projects and demanded extra math worksheets instead. Numbers and logic are the language I understand intuitively. But creativity? That's like some missing data set my brain keeps trying to find but can't locate the file.

"This is hopeless," I mutter. I minimize the Word doc and pull up TeenHack on my web browser instead. I know it's a bad habit—the opposite of creativity—but I always return to these user forums whenever I'm stuck for a project.

I head for the pinned section at the top.

Post your Maker Projects here

Some boy in Australia posted the SmartMower on this forum last summer, before TeenHack turned it into a "Featured Project" on their blog. I don't see the topic title anymore, pushed down behind strings and strings of other project ideas. My eyes skim through the titles, rejecting them one by one.

CRENSHAW518

Make a homemade light bulb out of a potato. It really works!

The title makes me groan. *Um, Crenshaw518? Every fifth-grade science fair participant on the planet called. They want their idea back.*

Next.

GAMERGIRL3

Help! My mom disabled in-app purchases! Anyone have a hack to get around that?

I click my tongue. Way too rudimentary. I wrote a program like that in middle school. Not that I had the guts to use it, but…

Next.

M

Turn any cell phone battery into an electroshock security device (stun gun). Detailed step-by-step instructions.

I sit up straighter. *OK, "M," you have my attention.* A stun gun?

That's surprisingly interesting, coming from someone with such a boring username. The post itself looks super-detailed. Probably legit.

But sadly not the most appropriate choice for Winthrop Academy. Granted, I would like my project to "electrify" the audience, but I can't imagine Dr. Carlyle writing me a college rec if I *tased* the judges for my Maker Fair demonstration.

Next.

WALRUS_FARTS

Make a working television out of nothing but rubber bands and popsicle sticks!

Clearly a troll post, but it makes me giggle. "Come on, TeenHack." I chuckle at the screen as I scroll down. "Don't fail me now."

Somehow, none of these posts call to me. I stifle a yawn, navigating to the next page, when the sound of crunching gravel captures my attention.

More footsteps.

Ugh. Human contact was not on my agenda for today. I should have chosen a hiding spot with an escape route. I'm cornered here, surrounded by hedges on three sides, and those footsteps keep coming closer. My AR glasses hang from my neck, tempting me with the silent promise of concealment. I scowl at them for a moment, and then I slip them on. Better to hide my face behind my avatar than remain here in plain sight.

The visor confirms the presence of another avi on the far side of the hedge.

> Nora! There are one or more InstaLove user(s) nearby.
> Interact to raise your score!

I pray it isn't Eleanor—or Reese.

Those girls are not my friends, and they made it clear last night. But more than that, the truth is, they're the reason I'm scrambling for a project. I didn't realize how advanced the other students here would be. Reese and Eleanor must have had their InstaLove mod in the works for a while. I'll never catch up with their head start. That thing played like a real, professionally designed game.

I can't help feeling jealous. Things are different here than in high school. I don't worry much about my social status back home. Everyone has their niche carved out. Some people dedicate their lives to sports. Others focus all their free time on music or art or books. And some people are computer nerds like me.

But here?

Here, the popular kids are super nerdy too. Here, I feel average at everything, and I don't know how to deal with that.

A shadow appears at the break in the hedges, followed by an avatar.

| Reese

She comes around the corner, and an InstaLove notification flashes on my screen. I expect an interaction prompt like the ones at the party last night. Instead her avi disappears before my eyes, replaced by a box of blue text.

| User Reese has signed off.
| Look for Reese now in Missed Connections. [GO]

Confused, I lift my visor. The real Reese stands before me with her glasses dangling from her hand. "There you are," she says. "I've been looking everywhere."

I feel queasy. "Why? Did you need me for something?"

"No, but I need to check that thing again. Make sure there's no residual water damage." She gestures for my visor. I pull the cord from around my neck and hand it over.

"It seems fine," I offer, but she doesn't take my word for it. I knit my fingers together, waiting as she holds my glasses to her eyes. Long moments tick by before she finally removes them.

"Well?" I stand to take the visor back, but she holds it outside my reach. I meet her eyes, expecting to see her domineering coldness. But her expression is harder to read today. There's something else in her eyes. Something almost…scared? Or maybe vaguely guilty?

"What?" I ask, inching closer. "It's not broken, is it?"

My words snap her out of whatever had been bothering her. "No, it's fine." She hands the visor back. "Listen. I had to change your username."

What?

She bites her lip. "I changed it to Lowercase."

"Are you serious?"

She shrugs, and that tinge of sheepishness crosses her face again. It's weird how much more human she seems today. Way less "mean girl" without an audience. She moves toward the stone bench and sits down, gesturing for me to sit beside her.

I hesitate for a moment, and then I take a seat. My laptop sits open where I left it. I ease it closed and hug it against my thighs. Reese stretches her legs in front of her, crossing them at the ankles. She leans back, addressing her words upward to the leafy canopy of tree limbs overhead.

"Can I give you some advice?"

I expect her to issue some warning about Eleanor. How I had the gall to steal her best friend's name, as if two girls with a common name have never attended the same school before. I look down at the silver case of my laptop, labeled in bold black lettering.

Property of Nora Weinberg

They'll probably want me to change that next. Scribble over it and write "Property of Lowercase." Or better yet, "Property of Nobody At All."

But Reese surprises me when she continues. She sits up straighter and turns to face me. "You shouldn't hide back here," she says. "Everyone's in the library or the dining hall. You should… you know…"

"Mingle?" She witnessed what happened the last time I attempted to mingle, right?

Reese must sense my skepticism. She stands and reaches out to haul me up beside her. "Trust me. Find yourself a group for the Maker Fair. Otherwise, you'll drown in the workload."

Oh.

I hadn't thought of that. I assumed I'd be flying solo. No one ever mentioned Emerson Kemp having any partners when he invented InstaLove that summer. But then again, I'm no Emerson Kemp. I'm not even an Eleanor, apparently. I'm Lowercase. Lowly Lowercase. And I'm going to need a group.

Reese heads for the gap between the hedges. She jerks her head impatiently, summoning me to follow. I stuff my laptop in my bag and hurry after her.

"Put your glasses on," she tells me when I reach her side.

I slow my pace. *No way.* It was one thing, wearing my glasses while safely seated on a bench, but I don't feel comfortable walking around with them. Not after last night. "Maybe I better not," I say, falling a few steps behind.

She stops walking and rounds on me. "You'll be fine! Just look where you're going. Eyes in front."

I dig the toe of my sneakers into the gravel. I know she's right, but still… Isn't it a slight problem with the game design if a user can never look anywhere but straight forward? I mean, was it really beyond the pale of normal human behavior for someone to turn their head?

I frown, but I hold my tongue. For all my nonexistent social skills, I know I won't endear myself to anyone by pointing out the holes in their project.

Reese folds her arms across her chest. "What is it?"

"Nothing."

"You obviously have something to say. So say it."

I scrunch my nose. Am I really that easy to read?

"Go ahead. I know what you're going to say anyway."

I'm not so sure, but I don't see any way to extricate myself from this conversation without making it worse. My voice comes out weak and fluttery, my words couched in a million qualifiers to avoid any hint of criticism. "It's just that…like…maybe there should be some functionality to detect hazards even if you're not…you know…sort of…looking directly at them?"

My eyes dart everywhere but Reese's face. I expect her to scowl at me with that icy mixture of loathing and contempt. Instead, she drops her arms and lets out a small sigh. "I know. It's a flaw. I told Emerson—"

Emerson?

"Wait, Emerson Kemp? You *talk* to him?"

"Um, yeah. Obviously." Reese gives me a funny look, but she plows on. "See, it doesn't come up when users are playing InstaLove on phones. People keep the phone pointed in the direction that they're moving." She lifts her arm in front of her, pantomiming how a user might hold up a cell phone. She walks a few steps, holding the make-believe phone in front of her while swiveling her head to glance back over her shoulder. "Like so. People don't move their phone to track with their eye gaze."

I squint at her, speaking slowly as the comprehension clicks. "Sure, but with the visor, it's attached…"

"Right, exactly!" Her expression brightens, pleased that I picked up on her train of thought. "What you did yesterday with your visor would be like a phone user doing *this*." She resumes her pantomime, this time pretzeling her arm all the way around her body to hold the nonexistent cell phone backward over her opposite shoulder. "See? This would be a highly unnatural movement."

I nod. "Not impossible though. People do weird things when they're flirting." *Especially awkward people who have no idea how to flirt.*

"I guess. Maybe interactions with InstaCrushes?" Her eyebrows draw together for a long moment, but she dismisses the thought with a flick of her hand. "Anyway, the point is, it could be a much more frequent hazard condition with the hands-free application—as you demonstrated at Dr. Carlyle's last night."

Last night… Is Reese aware that last night's fiasco took place because of my own flirtation failure with an InstaCrush?

I expect her to snicker, but her face remains totally deadpan. She's more interested in software functionality and exception testing than anything to do with the nuances of interpersonal relationships. Something about that realization makes me warm toward her. Reese isn't mocking me. Or judging me. Or icing me out. None of that high school-ish behavior. She's all business, focused on her project and making it the best it can be.

That's why Reese wants me to go on using my visor for InstaLove purposes. Nothing sinister. She needs me for her beta test, and I have no good reason to refuse. As long as I keep my eyes pointed forward, I'll be fine.

With a deep breath, I move to slip my visor on, but Reese touches my wrist to stop me. There's that indecipherable expression on her face again. Eyes narrowed. Lips tensed. Not scared, but…agitated. She leans close enough for her silky hair to tickle my shoulder as she speaks into my ear.

"Listen," she says in a near whisper. "I don't want to tell you how to run your InstaLove account, but…"

Something in her tone makes my mouth go dry. She takes my visor from me before I can protest and puts it to her own eyes once again. When she hands it back, I see she went into my history.

"You might want to move that to a different column."

Her low voice sounds its warning in my ears. My breath hitches at the sight of the avatar she highlighted.

Maddox.

In my InstaCrush column, with his eyes covered by a pair of hearts.

Hearts that are approximately the same color as my cheeks right now.

So anyhow, if any invisible swimming pools might be in the mood to materialize beneath my feet and swallow me whole, now would be a convenient moment.

"That—I didn't—I mean—" My pulse thuds in my ears, drowning out my stammered excuses. "I was curious. I was testing the...the functionality. I didn't really mean—I mean, he has a girlfriend. Right?"

Seriously, where are all the hidden bodies of water when you need them? I wonder if Reese can see the way I'm flushing from head to toe. She's covered her eyes with her own visor.

She speaks one more time before she turns to walk away. Her words hit me like a big red flashing Warning Message, impossible to ignore.

"Just watch your step," she says, drawing out each syllable to make her meaning clear. "You're heading into hazardous terrain."

11
THE GAMES WE PLAY

MADDOX

The steam wafts upward from my bowl of oatmeal as I count out the scoops of brown sugar. *One...two...three...* I've already accumulated a small mountain of light-brown crystals, but I keep going for dramatic effect. *Four scoops. Five? Would five be too extreme?*

Nah. Not when I have an audience. Eleanor stands on the opposite side of the dining hall breakfast buffet, and I can sense the waves of disapproval as she inspects my bowl.

I'm messing with her, and she knows it. I press my tongue to the roof of my mouth to keep from smiling. Eleanor's food-related edicts are another thing I'm not going to miss. My ex-girlfriend has been obsessed with my eating habits ever since my grandmother was diagnosed with diabetes. Good carbs, bad carbs, low glycemic index...

I spent the past three school years eating my morning oatmeal sweetened with nothing but fresh-cut strawberries, plus a scoop of ground flax seeds and a handful of walnuts for protein. Not very tasty, but easier than arguing with her.

Those days are over. I'm a free man. I might have agreed to play along with Eleanor's "terms and conditions" for the next three weeks, but I never said I'd pretend to be a *good* boyfriend. Nope. Not anymore. Bring on Maddox, the bad boy with his bad carbs.

I reach for the walnuts out of habit. My hand hovers above the serving spoon, but I catch myself. Good boyfriends eat walnuts. Bad boyfriends? They go for the chocolate sprinkles.

"That looks truly disgusting."

I glance up at the girl who spoke. Miranda stands at Eleanor's side, with her gray wool beanie pulled low over her forehead as usual. She nudges Eleanor with her elbow. "Are you going to let him eat that?"

Eleanor shrugs, her face a mask of innocent surprise, as if she would never dream in a million years to tell me what to eat. Instead, she picks up the container of maple syrup and holds it out to me. "Here, Moxie. You forgot this."

She smiles, and I match her cloying tone. "Thank you, my dearest darling," I reply. "Here, why don't you have some?" I apply a generous squirt of syrup to her plate of scrambled eggs before she can grab the bottle out of my hands.

Miranda looks back and forth between us, trying to get a read on the oversweetened vibe, but Eleanor changes the subject to distract her. "Hey, speaking of dearest darlings, where's your girl?"

"The hell if I know." Miranda's face darkens. *Uh-oh*. Are Samirah and Miranda having problems? I thought those two were rock solid. I put my bowl on my tray and trail after Eleanor and Miranda toward the beverage area. I can smell the drama brewing…along with a fresh pot of coffee.

"Listen," I hear Eleanor say when I catch up with them. "You're too clingy. If you really want to wrap someone around your finger, the key is to make them jealous."

I can't help but snort as I grab my own mug. Eleanor's eyes flash toward me for a split second, but she returns them to her friend.

"I don't know." Miranda looks down at her tray, tugging her woolen cap so low it covers most of her eyebrows. "That sounds like a recipe for an unhealthy relationship. No?"

Yes. I nod to myself. *Don't listen to her, M*. Apparently, there are a few things even more unhealthy than the bowl of toxic waste I concocted for my breakfast.

Eleanor lets out a tinkly laugh. "Don't be naive." She nudges the other girl with her shoulder. "Love's a game."

Her eyes lock with mine as she speaks. She's not talking about Miranda and Samirah anymore, and we both know it. She twitches her head sideways, beckoning me to follow her to our usual table in the corner. I turn away and focus my attention on stirring my black coffee. I'm not sure I have the stomach for Eleanor this morning. I was planning to eat my oatmeal in her face, relishing every diabetes-inducing bite, but that plan holds less appeal than it did a moment ago. *Love's a game, is it?* I don't know what game Eleanor's playing with her "pretend-we're-still-together" maneuver, but it won't work. I'm done.

I pour the contents of my mug into a to-go cup and abandon the rest of my tray. I've lost my appetite. I'll drink my coffee in the library instead. I pocket an apple as I make my way through the dining hall doors.

Outside, the morning sunshine warms my face. I head for the stone steps on the opposite side of Winthrop's central courtyard. There was no one in that dining hall worth talking to anyway. I looked around for any sign of a certain little rabbit the moment I walked in. Still holed up in her room, I guess.

Is that what Eleanor meant before? I can still hear her musical laughter ringing in my ears, full of mischief and bad relationship advice. *"If you really want to wrap someone around your finger, the key is to make them jealous."*

Jealous...

I wonder if she knows about the contents of my InstaCrush column. Reese has access to all the interaction data, but she has enough discretion not to share that information with her roommate.

I take a sip of coffee, but it tastes sour to me now. I chuck the half-full cup in the trash as I head through the library's revolving door.

Forget Eleanor. Forget *all* the Eleanors.

There are more important matters to attend to. The computer lab on the second floor looks empty. I take the steps two at a time and hunker down behind a computer screen, cracking my knuckles. Time for a research session. I haven't forgotten that tidbit of information Reese dropped on me in her dorm room yesterday.

"Emerson might grant us a licensing deal if we can show him proof of concept..."

Now that's a game worth playing. I might have quit Reese and Eleanor's group before I heard. Life would be much simpler if I didn't have to collaborate on a project with my ex and her best friend. And Reese's plan to throw Nora in the mix, recruited by yours truly?

Yeah. We all know how that will go.

```
ERROR
    Too many arguments.
    Incompatible types.
```

But that licensing deal...

I could use the cash. My swanky private education has been

bought and paid for by Eleanor Winthrop's parents from the day I started kindergarten. They liked to say my grandmother became part of the family the day they hired her as nanny—and they've kept their word long after she retired. But I have a feeling my bottomless tuition fund might come to an end the moment the Winthrops hear how I broke their daughter's heart.

Public school I could handle. Not exactly the senior year I envisioned, but I'd survive. A different worry made me toss and turn last night: my grandma's medical bills. I've seen the checks in the mail each month. The Winthrops have been picking up the slack since her diagnosis. They wouldn't take my misbehavior out on her, would they?

I can't risk it. Eleanor said her parents wouldn't cut me off as long as I held up my end of the bargain—which means, for all my bad-boy breakfast-cereal rebelliousness, Eleanor still owns me.

There's only one way to extricate myself. Money. A lot of it.

I didn't see that option on the table until Reese's revelation yesterday. How much would a licensing deal from InstaLove involve? I'd need thousands... Tens of thousands...

Is that anywhere within the realm of possibility? *Doubtful.*

I drum my fingertips on the edge of the keyboard. I'm getting carried away. I have no idea how much Emerson's company might have to throw around. But maybe I can find a ballpark figure.

The web browser launches, and I enter a few keystrokes, stringing together search terms that may or may not mean what I want to know: **instalove, company, funding, valuation, equity, how much money do they have?**

The search brings up a list of recent articles, all with some version of the same headline. My eyes land on a link from my favorite blog. I click it open.

TEENHACK

IN THE NEWS

Teen Phenom Turned Entrepreneur Secures $70M Series B Funding Round

San Jose, CA—
InstaLove, the augmented-reality brainchild of TeenHacker-turned-CEO Emerson Kemp, successfully raised $70 million in new financing from a range of prominent venture capital partners. In a press release, InstaLove announced that it would use the capital to invest in new forms of interactive play, including enhanced integration with next-gen wearable devices... MORE

That's a lot of words, but I stopped reading at the headline. Seventy *million*? *Dollars*?

Now we're talking.

NORA

Reese's bright blue hair sways in the breeze as she walks away. Her warning about my InstaCrush column hangs in the air.

I stand alone at a fork in the gravel pathways—at a crossroads in more ways than one. I have two choices, the way I see it. I can almost imagine the InstaLove prompt to go with this particular predicament.

> Oopsies! A frenemy has discovered your secret hopeless crush! Do you:
>
> **A)** Cry until your salty tears form a puddle deep enough to drown the cringe-y awkwardness that is your life?
>
> **B)** Block that entire conversation from your mind and pretend it never happened.

I don't know which option Nora would choose, but "Lowercase" is going with B.

An unoccupied bench rests before me, and I plunk down. My visor bounces against my chest. I chew my lower lip as I contemplate the frames, clipped to their nylon cord. When I woke this morning, I resolved not to use this visor again. *Ever.*

I didn't mean that, did I? What a monumental waste of an opportunity that would be. When am I going to get another chance to use an InSight Visor?

Don't be such a baby, Nora. I lift the glasses slowly and slip the lenses over my eyes. I'll be fine. I understand the issue with the hazard alerts now. As long as I keep my eyes pointed forward, nothing too terrible can happen.

I navigate to my history screen. Reese's avi sits at the top of my missed connections, and I file her away under InstaFriends. The column of beaming faces keeps growing—and so does my score.

> 1,023
>
> Good going, Lowercase! Your IL score has reached 1,000! You've unlocked the power to invite one of your 6 new Mutual Connections on a Private InstaQuest. Look around for the Communication Kiosk in your vicinity! [GO]

Oh! I guess that IL score actually means something. This game has more layers than I realized. I have no idea what a private InstaQuest entails, but that's not my immediate focus. There's something else. That word again. Not just connections. *Mutual* connections.

Does that mean what I think it means?

I need more information. Immediately. With a burst of energy, I rise to my feet and blink at the Go button.

The history screen disappears, replaced by a view of my

surroundings. I turn my head side to side, searching for any sign of the promised "*Communication Kiosk*." I meander backward a few steps before I catch myself.

Wow, Nora. Remember that time, three seconds ago, when you resolved to keep your eyes pointed forward? Apparently not. I forgot all about it the moment this app waved something new and shiny in front of my face.

OK, let's try that again…

I keep my head still this time, with my neck muscles clenched. My hands grope for unseen obstacles as I shuffle my feet around in a slow circle. An object materializes twenty paces down the path. I stop turning as my eyes come to rest on an old-school phone booth—like some archaeological relic from decades past. Whoever designed that thing must have watched a few too many episodes of *Dr. Who*. It would almost look real, except for the way it shimmers faintly around the edges.

That must be the kiosk. I take a few halting steps toward it. *Can I go inside?* I'll probably pass straight through like I did with those nasty palm trees last night. But something about this booth seems different. The sparkling light around the edges flares brighter, coaxing me forward until I reach the open phone booth door. I hold my breath as I step over the threshold.

Now what? None of this is real. I can't actually touch that silver telephone receiver. My brain knows that, but my hand moves anyway. My fingers close around the spot where the phone should be. In the split second before I make contact, the glimmering object gives way to a flash of pure white light. I blink hard. When my eyes reopen, the phone has disappeared. The entire booth has transformed into a larger chamber, enclosing me on all sides.

> Welcome, Lowercase! Your Communication Kiosk has been activated. Step forward to proceed.

Off-balance, I drop my head and look down at my feet. At least the ground hasn't been augmented. My sneakers remain firmly planted on the gravel walkway, and the sight of the gray pebbles banishes my sense of disorientation. *See?* I'm still at Winthrop. I haven't ventured off the walking path. If I raise up my visor and look around, I'll see nothing but stone buildings and cloudless skies.

But I resist the temptation to peek. If I do, I have a feeling this kiosk might disappear.

With a tense breath, I step forward into the center of the room. An array of buttons appears on the far wall, each with a face beside it. I recognize the avatars from my three-column display.

> Choose any one of your Mutual Connections and send a Private InstaQuest Invitation to the destination of your choice.

Interesting.

I only have enough points to choose one friend. That raises the stakes. I can feel my palms sweating from the pressure. Of course, there's one connection my mind goes to first. His avatar smirks when my eyes trace over him.

No. Wait. I should practice using this thing a few times before I venture into the deep end. I don't blink at the Invite button, but my gaze remains on his avi's face. Those dark brown eyes hold me hypnotized.

All I need to do is double blink, and the decision will be made. Huge mistake, right? I couldn't even blow this boy a kiss last night, and now I'm going to send him a private Insta-whatever? There's no way he'll see it as anything short of a confession that I like him.

That didn't go so well for me the last time.

"Gosh. I'm sorry, Nora... I just never... I never really...saw you..."

Trevor Chang gave me plenty signals of mutual attraction—a whole school year's worth of signals. At least I thought he did. Apparently, I'm not so good at discriminating between real life and my own ever-so-slightly augmented version.

"You're heading into hazardous terrain..."

No kidding. Reese didn't know the half of it. When it comes to boys, I'm doomed. There's only one thing I don't get. Why did Reese say that? First she changed my username. Then she warned me off Maddox. Why?

I gasp audibly when it hits me. There's only one good

explanation. If Reese can see my InstaCrush list, she can probably see Maddox's as well.

And lowly little Lowercase must be on it!

I press my palm to my collarbone, trying in vain to calm the wild gyrations beneath my rib cage.

I remember this sensation. I felt the same way that day in Maker Lab, right before I confessed to Trevor. I made myself ignore it at the time. I closed my eyes and took the leap…and I crash-landed.

I'm not sure I have the guts to try again.

My eyes go to Maddox one more time, searching for an answer in his avi's shifting expressions. I have to make a decision. Now or never. A new text box appears beside his face.

Hurry, Lowercase! This Communication Kiosk will deactivate in:

5…

4…

3…

2…

12

THE PROPOSAL

NORA

I hate this library.

OK, maybe not *hate*. Hate's a strong word. I can appreciate the aesthetic gorgeousness of the place, with massive skylights and soaring high ceilings. It even has a "living wall" over there, covered with enough lush vegetation to make cooped-up students feel like we're working outside.

But whatever fancy architect designed this space did not have students like me in mind—students who prefer study rooms with actual walls instead of putting us on display behind floor-to-ceiling glass. A goldfish in an aquarium would have more privacy.

With a sigh, I slide my laptop to a different section of the study table and hunker down to conceal my face behind the screen.

Who am I kidding? It's not the library stressing me out right now. It's the blank page staring back at me.

MAKER FAIR PROPOSAL

Nora Weinberg

I'm so screwed. I have no ideas that don't make me want to vomit.

I tried. I really did. After that brief vacation from reality in the communication kiosk, I came to my senses. I shut down that InstaQuest invitation unsent. Reese's other piece of advice brought me crashing back to Earth: "*Get yourself a group. Otherwise you'll drown in the workload.*"

Too bad no one in this library has any interest in working with me. No partner. No group. No interactions whatsoever, despite my app-facilitated efforts. All the other students are already holed up in their own glass-walled study chambers, clustered together in sets of three or four. Not one person looked up when I walked by, so I scurried into the nearest empty room and set up camp alone.

How do they all have groups already? Day two of the program, and somehow I missed the boat.

Am I so utterly and completely devoid of social skills? I thought things might be easier with InstaLove to grease the wheels, but no. I'm still me. Nora Weinberg. Unaugmented. No app is going to change who I am…and who I'm not.

Hot tears prick my eyes. I lean forward and bury my face in my hands.

Tap, tap, tap-tap-tap.

Tap, tap, tap-tap-tap.

Someone's knocking on the glass. Probably some other group needs the room. They came to tell me to take a hike. I mean, why would I need a whole room to myself when I'm solo?

Tap, tap, tap-tap-tap.

I swipe at my eyes and move to gather up my things.

Thunk. Thunk. Thunk.

I finally look up. Two large hands press against the clear partition, and a dark-haired head gently butts the glass.

Thunk. Thunk. Thunk.

I know that head—that shaggy mop of hair. My stomach does a half-hearted flutter. Turns out even stomach butterflies get down in the dumps. Who would've thought?

Maddox's hands must be twice the size of mine. He splays his fingers wide against the glass, and I have the strongest urge to press my own to the other side to compare.

The butterflies are making a rapid recovery. *OK, Nora. Get a grip.*

Maddox stops *thunking*. I lift a hand in a noncommittal gesture—half waving but fully prepared to convert into hair-adjustment-mode if necessary.

He breaks into a grin and waves back.

I'm never getting any work done, am I? "Go away," I mouth to him, but I don't mean it. He ignores me and pops the door open.

"What's the matter?" He hesitates in the doorway, flashing a quick glance down the long row of study rooms to make sure no one is watching. Then he comes in. "Why do you look like someone killed your puppy?"

"I'm fine."

"Homesick?"

I look away. "I'm just trying to get some work done."

He doesn't take the hint. He plops down in the chair beside me and spins it around in a circle. His feet stomp the floor when his chair faces mine. He leans in, peering at my blank computer screen.

"Interesting proposal, Miss Weinberg. I'd say it has…limitless potential."

Is he making fun of me? Is that why he came in here? I move to shut the laptop, but he stops me. The smirk leaves his face.

"Don't. I'm teasing!"

"It's fine. I was about to leave anyway."

"Wait! No. Talk to me. What's wrong?"

He looks like he actually cares. I should be flattered, but it only makes me feel worse. I place my forearms on the table and rest my head against them, hiding my face.

His hand hovers by my shoulder. He doesn't make contact, but his fingers brush against my arm when I sit back up. I can't tell whether or not his touch was accidental. Probably.

It doesn't matter. What's the point of liking a boy when I'm never going to see him again? Not after I fail to turn in a proposal tomorrow and get kicked out of this program on Day 2. "I don't belong here," I whisper.

He sticks out his lower lip, mirroring my own self-pity back at me. "That's not what I heard."

Somehow the exaggerated pout makes me forget to be forlorn for half a second. "What did you hear? That my name is Lowercase, and no one wants to be my partner because I suck at life?"

He laughs. "Nope. Actually, I heard you won first place in some huge scholastic hack-athon, and your application impressed the hell out of the admissions committee."

I blink. How does he know about my admissions application?

"Let's see it," he says, returning his attention to my laptop. "The proposal you applied with. Not the blank one."

"I deleted it."

"Permanently?"

No, not permanently. I glance down at my keyboard. I suppose I could resurrect my stupid SmartMower. That might be my only option at this point. "You don't understand. It seriously sucks!"

"Why did you propose it if it sucks?"

"I didn't know it sucked! I thought it was good!"

"And?"

"And then I saw the InstaLove mod that Reese and Eleanor are doing."

He shakes his head. "Don't try to compete with them."

"It's a competition, isn't it? Maker Fair?"

"Yeah, but they're guaranteed to win. It's not a level playing field."

What does that mean? "Because Eleanor's last name is Winthrop?"

"No," he says in a flat voice. "Because Reese's last name is *Kemp*."

I keep my eyes on the tabletop as I process this new piece of information. Of course I recognize the name. "Kemp…as in…?"

He nods in confirmation. "You've heard of Emerson Kemp, right? He's Reese's older brother."

I sit up so suddenly my chair rolls backward. I nearly fall out of my seat onto the floor. Only Maddox's quick reflexes keep me upright. He grabs me by the elbow, chuckling at my clumsiness, but not mocking me anymore. Not with the way his hand lingers a moment longer than it should. I can't help staring at his thumb, pressed against the sensitive skin of my inner arm.

Get a grip, Nora.

Literally. Get a grip. On your chair.

I latch onto the armrests and readjust.

He releases my elbow and thrusts his hand into his hair, combing it away from his forehead. I could swear his face reddens. I must be imagining that—or seeing the reflection of my own face, which has turned a subtle shade of tomato red.

"Um," I say weakly. "So does Emerson know about Reese's project?"

Maddox nods. "He's the whole reason behind it. Reese has permission to use the InstaLove corporate servers and has access to their developers to ask questions." His voice drops lower. "And she has Eleanor, of course."

Oh right. *Her.* "Don't tell me. Eleanor is some kind of supernatural coding genius?"

He shrugs. "She knows her way around a text editor. But mostly she's rich. Who do you think provided funding for all the visors?"

Something in his expression hardens when he mentions Eleanor's name. It's weird. Are the two of them in a relationship or not? "So are you and Eleanor, like—"

He interrupts before I can finish the question. "Don't worry about Reese and Eleanor. You do *you.* Tell me about your original proposal. The one you submitted when you applied."

"The one that sucks, you mean?"

He cocks his head at me. "Can I see it?"

No. Definitely not. He reaches for my laptop, but I move to close the screen. "Trust me. It's embarrassing."

"I find that hard to believe."

Somehow my hand is touching his. I pull mine away and bury it beneath my thigh.

He looks at me curiously. "Tell me about it."

Don't tell him, Nora.

Don't.

Definitely don't.

He raises one eyebrow, and the asymmetry makes his face more attractive than ever. I do my best to ignore the stomach butterflies, now fully resurrected and trying to escape. One butterfly lodges in my throat, shaking loose the words I meant to swallow.

"It's a lawn mower."

"Lawn mower..." he replies slowly. "Pretty sure those already exist."

I look away toward the glass wall of the study room, too distracted by his eyebrow to think clearly. "No, it's a...robotic... thingamajiggy. What's the word?" *How have I forgotten how to talk?* "It's like a—self—um. Self-directed..."

"Ohhh." Thankfully, he cuts me off. "Self-propelled? Like one of those robotic vacuum cleaners, but for your lawn?"

I point at him and snap my fingers. "Yes. Exactly. That's a much less confusing way to say it."

He eyes me thoughtfully, and the warmth in my cheeks spreads down my neck. I can't take the scrutiny. I reopen the laptop and pretend to hunt for the proposal, but I can see his face reflected in the screen.

He leans close, reading over my shoulder. "Don't those exist already too? I thought I read about it in TeenHack..."

I turn back to him so fast, I almost sprain my neck. "Wait. You read TeenHack?" *Oh my God. Could he get any more perfect?*

He rolls his eyes at me. "Everyone here reads TeenHack. We all saw the same post."

"Well, I didn't say it was an original invention! Just that I'm going to make one. Myself. It's a Maker Fair, right?"

He scrunches up his face. "You can do better."

His words hit me like a well-aimed dart, straight to the center of my insecurities. He's right. I'm such a copycat. I'll humiliate myself in front of everyone if I don't come up with something better. "But I don't have any other ideas."

"Sure you do. Think." He touches my arm again, feather light, an inch above my elbow—as if that's going to help me think. "There has to be some modification. Some way your version will be better than the TeenHack project."

I can only shake my head.

"Think," he whispers. His eyes go distant, and he taps his fingers against his chin. "The main limitation was the border detection, right?"

"What?"

"I'm trying to remember from that blog post," he says. He stops tapping and looks toward me. "A robot vacuum finds the edges of a room when it runs into a wall, but a lawn mower is outside, so…"

Oh! I realize where he's going with this. The lawn mower in TeenHack required an elaborate installation process. You had to bury a wire along the edge of your yard to signal the robot where to turn around. Kind of like invisible fencing for dogs.

My eyes open wide as I catch up with his train of thought. For some reason, Maddox breaks into the biggest smile ever. "Edge detection," he says slowly.

I smile back. "So I could invent one that didn't require the border wire. The user could upload a map of their property, and the lawn mower would know—"

"Not to fall into the swimming pool?"

Oh, that's why he's grinning. Back to making fun of me. "Ha," I say drily. "Funny."

"No, I'm serious." He tips forward in his chair. "Don't you get it?"

Get…what exactly?

He stands up, thrusting his hands in his pockets as he paces back and forth across the room. "I'm just thinking out loud here," he says, addressing the floor. He stops at the far end of the table and turns toward me, bouncing on the balls of his feet. "It should be doable. Why not?"

His face lights up like a light bulb. For the life of me, I can't understand this boy. "Are you really this excited about a lawn mower?"

He waves his hand back and forth to shush me. "Forget the lawn mower. We should use that idea for InstaLove!" He breaks into a little dance move, swiveling his hips and turning in a circle on his heel. "Edge detection! Remote hazard detection!"

What?

I can tell from his face that he had some brilliant idea, but I'm sadly unable to process the English language. Not with all the renewed stomach-butterfly activity. Turns out impromptu salsa moves cause stomach butterflies to spontaneously combust.

Maddox looks at me expectantly. I swallow hard. "Remote hazard detection?"

"Yes!" He claps his hands. "So scared little rabbits don't go falling in swimming pools!"

Wait...

I get it now. I just caught up. The air escapes my lungs, pushing the dead butterfly carcasses along with it. *We should use that idea for InstaLove?* That's what he said...which means...of course... "You're working on InstaLove too? With Reese and Eleanor?"

"No, no!" He comes back around the table and resumes his position at my side. "I mean, yes. But you can work with us! Partner with me."

Partner?

Partner with...

"Come on, it's perfect!" He clenches his hands and drums his fists rhythmically against his knees. "Reese and Eleanor can handle the visor implementation. You and I will focus on improving the hazard alert system."

Partner with Maddox?

He holds out his hand to shake on it, waiting for my reply. I look down at his outstretched palm. I'm not sure how long I sit there staring at it, but he loses patience after a second or two. He grabs my hand and pumps it twice. "This is awesome!"

No. Not awesome. Tempting perhaps, but definitely a bad idea. I shouldn't go along with this plan.

But for the life of me, I can't remember why.

Maddox's hand still engulfs mine, and I find myself squeezing back to signal my agreement. He grins and spins my laptop away from me, pulling up my blank proposal. His fingers flash across the keys as he picks up where I left off.

MAKER FAIR PROPOSAL

Nora Weinberg

Maddox Drake

THE DROPBOX (ENTRY 3)

ELEANOR

https://bit.ly/dropboxL

Dropbox > Personal

File Name	Created on	Visible to
Entry 1.txt	7/1/2019	Deleted
Entry 2.txt	7/2/2019	Deleted
Entry 3.txt	7/9/2019	Only you

Nine days down, twelve to go before this program ends. We're getting there…and everything would be fine if that girl didn't exist.

Nora Weinberg.

He likes her. I can tell. And it sucks.

You know what sucks about it most? The fact that under any other circumstances, I would probably like her too. There's a level of cluelessness that surpasses pathetic and just makes me want to take her under my wing. I would love a protégée. Elea-Nor and Little-Nor? How adorable would that be? My Maker Fair side project for the summer.

But no.

Somehow, "Little-Nor" is the one person here who can spoil everything if I'm not careful. Why does Mox have to like her? Why???

Forget it. I can't take over some sophomore's life. I have enough problems with my own, the way my parents insist on controlling every detail. I can't believe my mom. That informational interview she lined up? Um, OK, Mom. "Informational" my ass. Obviously, those people are going to offer me an internship. And there'll be hell to pay if I don't accept.

So transparent, I could almost laugh. My parents think they have it all mapped out. Internships-> College-> Law school-> A job offer in the state attorney's office, or maybe a judicial clerkship that *happens* to fall in my lap-> A run for office of my own someday? Why, what a delightful idea! Senator Winthrop has a nice ring to it. Although maybe the White House would make a prettier backdrop for our family Christmas cards.

And Maddox would make a fine choice for first gentleman. I know how my parents think. There's a reason they've been cultivating him all these years. They'd love nothing more than for Moxie and me to walk down the aisle someday. He fits the image, the perfect antidote to that inconvenient scent of money that follows me everywhere I go. But not Mox. He comes from nothing. An orphan, self-made, hardworking, and so verrry well-behaved.

UGH. My parents make me want to scream. Emerson and Reese don't know how lucky they are. They could fall off the edge of the earth, and it would take six months before their dad and stepmom noticed them missing. Why couldn't I be blessed with parents like the Kemps???

It doesn't matter. I'll be out from under their thumb soon enough. Once I'm 18, the whole game changes. August 1st is almost here.

But I don't need to wait around for my birthday. The two of us decided last night. After Maker Fair, we're out.

No one will see it coming. Not if we're careful. Not if my plan works.

13

LIGHT AND SHADOW

NORA

I arch my back and reach up toward my dorm room ceiling. The muscles between my shoulder blades snap like rubber bands.

How long was I hunched over my laptop? It was sometime around dusk when I first sat down to work. The eight o'clock curfew forced me to retreat from the library back to Fenmore Hall. The sky outside my window had been awash with pink and orange light, and I had to pull my window shade to block out the glare.

I stand up from my desk and peek beneath the shade. The sky looks dark—a few shades shy of pitch black—but that creeping light at the horizon isn't the last remnant of sundown. More like the first rays of dawn.

Did I stay up all night coding?

It wouldn't be the first time. Sometimes I get in the zone. The logic clicks into place, and I can visualize the whole grand plan. Every step that needs to happen. Every function. Every loop. Every if-then clause. The entire logical structure comes to me all at once, and then it's a race to get it all typed out and saved before I lose my train of thought.

I can code for hours when I get like that. Forget to eat. Forget to sleep. Forget to breathe, practically. I don't come up for air until it's done.

Done.

A warm glow of satisfaction fills me. I roll my shoulders and gather my loose hair into a ponytail, then sit back down at my desk. I just typed the final semicolon and saved my work to the InstaLove remote corporate server. Next step: debugging.

That will have to wait. My hyperfocused trance has ended, and the effects of my all-nighter hit me all at once. My head throbs. The tendons in my wrists scream for a break. I swivel in my desk chair toward my empty bed, but it's no use. Even if I lay down and closed my eyes, I wouldn't fall asleep. I'm on too much of an adrenaline rush.

I'll crash in a few hours. For now, I have only one thought. I need to show this program to my partner.

Maddox will flip when he sees it. I twirl the end of my ponytail around my finger, imagining his reaction. He's at his most adorable when he's excited, the way his eyes light up and he starts bouncing all over the room. He tends to get touchy-feely too. Lots of arm squeezes and elbow nudges.

What if he breaks out the salsa moves again? What if he takes me by the hand and pulls me close to dance with him?

The thought makes my breathing quicken. I close my eyes, savoring the warm feeling in the pit of my stomach.

The boy's a flirt. No question about it. Even when we're talking about work stuff, there's an undertone to everything he says. Like when I asked him what coding language he wanted to use for our project—C++ or Java?—and he got that sly look on his face. "I'll use any language you like…" And then he turned and whispered the next part in my ear. "But I *think* in Python."

I swear, there was something downright predatory in the look he gave me afterward. What do pythons eat for dinner? Bunny rabbits, perhaps?

Too bad, Maddox. I went with Java—easier to integrate with the real InstaLove app. Maybe he would've had a say in that decision if he hadn't left me to write the entire program myself. He was supposed to meet me at the library yesterday for a work session, but he no-showed. He was already half an hour late by the time I checked my visor and saw his message.

PRIVATE MESSAGES WITH MADDOX

Maddox: Can't make it. Start without me.

Lowercase: What happened?

Maddox: Sorry. It's Eleanor. She's being extra Eleanor-ish at the moment. 🙄

Whatever *that* meant.

Maybe it was a mistake, agreeing to work with Maddox. Sometimes I wonder why I went along with it. I mean, it made sense a week ago, sitting side-by-side with him in the library. He'd commandeered my laptop. Our whole Maker Fair proposal was his idea—using the networking capability between the visors to create a shared virtual map of potential obstacles.

"Don't you get it?" he'd insisted as he typed. "It's like crowdsourcing!"

"OK... So..."

"So if one user visits a location, it will create a virtual map of that place and share it with all the other visors in the network!"

He'd paused to correct a typo, and I finally had a chance to speed-read through his bullet points. "A shared map.... So the visor knows the terrain, even if the person wearing it has never been there?"

"Exactly!" He'd smiled at me so big and bright I almost melted. "So your visor will know to push a warning message, even if you aren't looking at the hazard."

Brilliant.

Maddox is full of good ideas, but not so helpful when it comes to the implementation. A week has come and gone since we submitted our proposal. I've been chipping away at our work plan day by day, but he has yet to contribute a single line of code. The format library he promised to build? Nowhere to be found on the server last night. You'd think he would do something, especially after all his endless whining about how Reese never gives him edit privileges!

I reach for my visor to check my private messages. I've grown accustomed to its ever-present weight around my neck—and to the absence of a cell phone in my pocket.

"Nothing," I mutter aloud.

No new texts from Maddox since our last exchange. Probably asleep. His visor will ping and wake him up if I message him. Maybe I should. Or better yet, maybe I should head over to his dorm room and pound on his door until he drags his cute/lazy butt out of bed. It would serve him right for ditching me last night.

I abandon the visor and look toward the window again. The sky has lightened to reveal an early-morning fog, cloaking the green lawns and stone buildings in misty gray. I'm not going anywhere. No way. I have a hard enough time finding my way around this campus when I can see where I'm going.

Maybe I should shower? Or at least brush my teeth and splash some water on my face? I venture out into the corridor, heading for the bathrooms a few doors down.

And that's when I see it.

I'm not the only one awake. A sliver of light escapes from the crack beneath the door at the far end of the hall. I can make out the sound of voices, whispering inside the room. Reese and Eleanor... Are they awake?

I hold my breath as I creep closer. Maddox isn't the only one I'm dying to show my program. I can't wait to see the look on Reese's face. Our group leader expressed no small amount of skepticism when Maddox called a meeting last week. The four of us gathered in one of those library study rooms, and I did my best to avoid all eye contact while Maddox ran the others through our plan. "I like the concept," Reese had agreed after reading the proposal. "But how can you possibly build that functionality in three weeks?"

"Easy," Maddox had answered. "We've got Nor—I mean, Lowercase. She's our secret weapon." He'd nudged me with his elbow. "We can do it, right, partner?"

I can't remember how I answered him. Probably blushed bright red and stared at the tabletop, desperate to ignore the death rays Eleanor was shooting at me the whole time.

Awkward!

I don't know why Eleanor hates me so much. It's weird, like some animalistic dominance ritual, marking her territory. You can practically see the smoke coming out of her ears every time Maddox speaks to me.

I can only hope she'll come around once she sees the code I wrote last night. It turns out I *am* their secret weapon, just like Maddox said. I didn't need three weeks. I got a basic version of the hazard alert system up and running in one. Reese is going to view me with a new level of respect when she sees it—and Eleanor won't be able to deny I'm an asset to the team.

Maybe she'll be willing to speak to me then. Heck, maybe I'll get my real name back. Let me be "Eleanor" for a while, and she can go by "Uppercase." See how she likes it!

A small smile curves my lips as I tiptoe down the hall. The door to Reese and Eleanor's room stands open a few inches. They must be awake. I peek inside, but the sound of voices pulls me up short.

Is that…

It sounds like…

Some instinct warns me not to make my presence known. I dart sideways, out of view of the two figures I glimpsed on the other side.

Not Eleanor and Reese after all.

Eleanor and Maddox.

I press my back to the wall beside the door. I don't think they can see my shadow from this angle. A hallway security camera looms before me, positioned directly across from the doorway at my side. If I squint, I can make out a tiny image reflected in the dark glass lens.

It's hard to tell what I'm looking at. Light and shadow, dancing behind a partially closed door. That might be Eleanor's shoulder there. Maddox has his hand on it. I can't tell if he's drawing her toward him or holding her at arm's length. She steps into the light, but she has her face lowered.

He drops his hand. "Fine. I'll see you later."

"Where do you think you're going?" I hear her whisper.

"I'm not in the mood, Eleanor."

"Are you going to *her* room?"

"No," he answers. "But so what if I did? She's my partner."

Wait a sec. Are they talking about me?

I shouldn't eavesdrop. I should tiptoe straight back to my room before they catch me lurking in the hall. But I can't. I'm rooted to the spot, paralyzed with curiosity. I still can't figure out the status between the two of them. Samirah and Miranda refused to give me the lowdown at dinner last night. The moment I brought it up, their eyes darted away, fascinated by the chalkboard displaying the evening's entrée selections. It was only Reese, behind them in the buffet line, who muttered a grudging response.

"Don't ask too many questions. It's complicated."

What does that mean though? How complicated could it be?

Maybe I'm about to find out. Their hushed words mix together with the sound of my own pulse, buzzing in my ears.

"I'm warning you, Moxie. Don't you dare embarrass me."

"Chill! You don't own me."

"Don't I? We had a deal."

"To hell with the deal. You can't expect me to—"

She cuts him off with a sudden, jerky movement. "You haven't told anyone, have you?"

Told anyone what?

"No," he whispers. "I haven't told anyone."

"And you think people won't guess, when they catch you hooking up with some sophomore?"

"I'm not hooking up with her!"

Oh my God.

Me?

Hooking up with me?

I cover my mouth with my palm to stifle the high squeaking noise threatening to come out of my throat. *What the heck?* Does Eleanor act this way toward every girl he talks to? I wonder if she knows about the push notifications that InstaLove keeps sending me.

> Lowercase! Don't leave your crush hanging!
> Resume your last interaction with Maddox now! [GO]

No wonder she hates me. She obviously doesn't realize who she's dealing with. Maybe I should clue her in with a more detailed user profile.

> **Name:** Nora
> **Age:** 16
> **Ever kissed a boy?** No
> **Ever held hands with a boy?** No
> **Ever slow danced with a boy?** No

Well, except for that one supremely awkward time with my cousin Seth at my bat mitzvah...

"Spare me," Eleanor hisses. "I have eyes, Maddox."

"There's nothing to see. There's nothing going on!"

"Why did you have to partner with *her* of all people?"

He pauses before he answers. I wait, holding my breath. I won't pretend I'm not dying to hear his answer.

"Because she'll do all the work and let me coast."

His words hit me like a slap across the face. My head flies up. I look again toward the camera-lens reflection. Eleanor is poking him in the chest, I think. But he ignores her finger and encircles her waist, drawing her toward him. His voice turns flirtatious but somehow sarcastic at the same time. "So I have more time to spend with you, my dearly beloved girlfriend, whom I most definitely did not break up with on day one of the program."

What? What does that mean?

"Don't embarrass me, Moxie," she answers him. "I will *end* you. One phone call from me, and you cease to exist."

Her hands are on his shoulders. Pushing him away...or wrapping around his neck? He touches her face. For a moment, I'm sure he's going to kiss her. Then he shakes his head and extricates himself from her arms.

Oh, no. Is he leaving?

He turns toward the door.

I have to move.

Now!

Panicked, I dart away, running on my tiptoes in the direction of my room.

14

AUGMENTED REALITY

MADDOX

Gray light filters through the skylight at the top of the dormitory stairs. I hurry onward, swearing beneath my breath. It's later than I intended. Nearly dawn. I need to get the video feeds back to their undoctored state before campus security notices anything amiss.

A tendril of unease curls its way around my abdomen. I've been messing with the security footage too often. I meant to lay off for the rest of the summer session. Keep myself out of trouble. Stick to the rules. But there was no way I could follow curfew last night.

My dorm room lies ahead—lights out, door closed—the way I left it. I make a beeline for my desk and log into my laptop. A few familiar keystrokes pull up my trusty .exe file.

```
Winthrop Secure Server [10.0.10.240]
<c> 2015 Intellisoft Solutions. All
    rights reserved.


C:\ Augmented-Reality.exe_
```

I drum my hands against my thighs. Time for some old-school "augmented reality." Little known fact, but Emerson Kemp's whole interest in AR began as nothing more than a schoolboy's efforts to circumvent curfew. I've been using his old hack for three summers now. Hard to believe no one on campus security has caught wind. They desperately need to update their cybersecurity protocols. It only takes this one script to override the password and gain full access to Winthrop security's internal server.

My fingers clench against my knees as I wait for it to work. I've gone through these motions more times than I can count, but something tonight has me unsettled. I have the weirdest feeling I'm about to be found out. What would Dr. Carlyle do if he realized that Reese, Eleanor, and I have been playing games with the camera feeds all this time?

Something tells me that Reese and Eleanor would be fine. I'm the one who would end up out on my ass with a one-way ticket back to my grandmother's apartment in New York.

I scowl. There's no reason to think that campus security will figure it out on their own. The only hitch could be if Eleanor decides to clue them in, just to screw me over. Yet another reason I have to play along with her.

How did I get myself into this mess? Everything was under control until yesterday afternoon. I was sitting right here at my desk, preparing to get started on the format libraries. Nora and I were supposed to work together after dinner, and I wanted to have something to show for myself before we met up…

But then I got that frantic text.

PRIVATE MESSAGES WITH REESE

Reese: Maddox! You need to get over here.

Maddox: Can it wait? I'm in the middle of something.

Reese: Now! Come to Fenmore. Emergency meeting!

Maddox: What happened?

Reese: Eleanor's dropping out of our group.

Maddox: Seriously? Why??

Reese: Like you don't know…

Maddox: 😖

Reese: Maddox, you need to smooth it over.

Maddox: Whatever. Are we in preschool? Let Eleanor throw her tantrum.

Reese: WE NEED HER!

Maddox: For what? Nora's a stronger coder.

Reese: Yes, but the visors are all registered to Eleanor. If she leaves, our whole project goes with her.

I'm getting really tired of Miss Winthrop and her games. I'd be perfectly content to "augment" that girl right out of my "reality." If only there was a hack for eliminating annoying exes from one's social circle.

I had no choice but to bail on Nora. By the time I got to Eleanor's room, she'd gone MIA. Reese and I spent half the night begging her to come back and talk it over before she finally deigned to grace us with her presence.

I blow out my breath with a huff. It might be best if Nora and I don't work in the library anymore. Those glass-walled rooms aren't exactly private. Someone spotted us hunched together over a laptop and sent Eleanor a pic, precipitating her latest freak-out. I guess I had my hand resting on the back of Nora's chair. Perfectly innocent. I wasn't even touching her shoulder!

At least, not that time…

A grim smile tugs at the corner of my mouth. Eleanor's not imagining things. I can lie to her and pretend my interest in Nora is all business—but the truth is, I like that girl. I like her more and more each time I'm with her.

I should have been with her last night. I hope Nora isn't pissed I ditched our work session. I haven't exactly been pulling my weight. I've had a lot on my mind lately, between the ex-girlfriend-drama and the financial fallout if the Winthrops cut me off.

But Nora doesn't know about any of that, and I can't tell her. I can't tell anyone. Not without violating the deal I made with Eleanor.

Which means I'm stuck here in this no-man's-land, tiptoeing around the truth with both of them. I walked right past Nora's room on my way out of Fenmore. Her light was on, but I didn't dare knock—not after that conversation with Eleanor.

"You haven't told anyone, have you?"

"No, I haven't told anyone."

"And you think people won't guess, when they catch you hooking up with some sophomore?"

"I'm not hooking up with her!"

That much was true. At least, not *yet…*

I bite my lip. I'm playing with fire. If I really mean to steer clear of trouble this summer, I should keep a safe ten feet of distance from my partner at all times. I gave Eleanor my word. I may be a shameless rule-breaker when it comes to stuff like curfew, but I've always been a man of my word.

Right?

I tip back my head and contemplate the ceiling. I don't know. Is a man's word binding if it's coerced?

I never would have gone along with Eleanor's nonsense if I had a choice in the matter. She's blackmailing me, essentially. So I really have no moral obligation to follow her "terms and conditions" if I can get away with it. That's why I broke up with her in the first place. So I could do my own thing. Be my own man. *Hook up with whomever I like.*

And I like Nora.

I close my eyes and groan. Life would be so much simpler if I didn't like Nora.

But I do.

I can't pretend I don't.

And I'm pretty well convinced that Nora likes me back. The girl might be a genius at Java, but she's not exactly a master of deception when it comes to hiding her feelings. She wears her emotions all over her face. Bright flaming red cheeks every time I *accidentally* brush my hand against her arm.

Honestly, Nora doesn't even need an avatar. Her face is easier to read in real life.

A flash of movement on my laptop interrupts my thoughts. My script finishes running, and the security interface logs itself in. My eyes skim over the split-screen display, and I click my mouse to maximize the windows I need. One side of my screen shows the live footage from all the cameras located on the second floor of Fenmore Hall.

All quiet. No movement. Doors closed. Lights out.

That's what the cameras appear to show, at any rate. Appearances can be deceiving.

The other half of the display shows the source code editor. There, buried halfway down the page, are the lines I added last night before my visit to Eleanor's room.

```
overlay = Image.open("CDNM.GIF")
```

A GIF…a five-second animated clip, set to the exact same frame-rate as the video input captured by the camera. This one, *CDNM*, is one of several I use on regular rotation, following the naming convention that Emerson established. CDNM stands for "closed doors no movement."

I hold down the delete key, watching the inserted commands disappear without a trace. Ready…

Now comes the risky part. I hold my breath as I hit Enter to update my changes. The footage on the other half of the screen freezes for a split-second and then jumps back to life—the fake video loop files replaced by the unaugmented live feed. To anyone watching, it would look like a momentary loss of connectivity. No obvious signs of tampering. The real footage still shows all the doors closed on Fenmore's second floor. Someone observing closely might notice the lights jump on in the crack beneath a couple of doorframes, but there's nothing so unusual about that. It merely looks like the occupants inside woke up and turned their lights on.

Done. I lean back in my chair and let out a long breath. That was a close one. It could have gotten messy if people were up and about in the hallway at the moment I reverted to the live footage. I can't take a chance like that again.

No more tampering.

At least not in the dorms.

I crack my knuckles and lean forward, adjusting the angle of

my laptop. I guess I'm not sleeping tonight. It'll be time for breakfast soon, and I still have one more thing I need to do.

I pull up a different window. My screen fills with row after
row of file folders, labeled with serial numbers and timestamps.
This server automatically stores the recorded footage from every
camera on campus for seventy-two hours—and these archives
represent the one major flaw in Emerson's hack. The inserted
GIF files only cover up the camera footage for a viewer watching
in real time. Here in the archives, the actual footage gets stored.
Only the system admin has delete privileges, which means the
truth is preserved here for three long, incriminating days.

Luckily, campus security never bothers with the archived
footage. I'm not sure they realize they have it. Still, these folders
make me nervous. I always check them before I log out, so I know
how damaging the evidence might be.

I pull up the feed from the camera outside Eleanor's room and
tap the rewind key, watching images whiz by in reverse as the time
counter races backward.

Empty hallway. All clear…

There.

I recognize my own tall form letting myself out of the room.
Hopefully that's the worst of it. I don't expect much else to crop
up as I keep rewinding. The next images race by, and it takes me
a long moment to register what I'm seeing.

"What the…"

My hand flashes to my touch pad, clicking Pause and then Play.

Was that…? I rub my palm slowly against the back of my neck. *It couldn't be…*

Nora.

I squeeze my eyes shut, hoping I'm hallucinating. But I'm not. She's there, standing in the hall outside Eleanor's room with her back pressed up against the wall. The camera angle crops half her face out of the frame, but it leaves enough visible for me to see her expression.

Her eyes are narrowed in an accusatory squint. I can practically feel them boring into me, and I slouch lower in my chair. I have the strangest sensation she can see me here, watching her, as I sit on the other side of my laptop screen.

I give my shoulders a shake to snap out of it. She's not glaring at me. This is recorded footage, not live. If it feels like we're making eye contact, that means she must've been looking straight into the security camera lens.

But her face… What exactly was she looking at? She squints harder, until her eyes are little more than two dark slits. Then her gaze shifts sideways, like she's listening—eavesdropping on the whispered conversation taking place behind that door.

Uh-oh. My mind flies backward. How much damage did I do? I can't remember half the things I said to Eleanor. All lies. Whatever I could think of to smooth her ruffled feathers.

It's not clear from Nora's face whether she can understand any of the whispered words. But then, right there at the 4:40:27 mark...

I hit pause to freeze the image, and her unmistakable expression fills my screen.

"What?" I murmur, gripping the edges of my laptop with two closed fists. "What did I say? What did you just hear?"

Her shoulders go rigid. Her mouth is slack. And those eyes—those huge green eyes I can't stop thinking about—they go all big and round.

15

DEBUGGING

NORA

I'm back in my old hiding place, the bench behind the hedge. I don't know why I bothered coming here. It's not like anyone wants to find me. My visor sits beside me on the bench, keeping me company with its steady blue light. The color hasn't changed all day. No orange flashing to signal the presence of unread messages.

I stick out my tongue at it, then tilt my face upward to bask in the afternoon sunshine. My deeply industrious "partner" has yet to explain his absence from our work session yesterday. Not that I need an explanation. He said it all last night.

"Because she'll do all the work and let me coast."

Oh really, Maddox? Will I?

I feel like throwing up. I can't get those words out of my head. No wonder Maddox keeps flirting with me. Not because he likes me. Because he's using me—and I'm so excruciatingly easy to manipulate.

This is what I get for working with a team. I should quit. Go back to solo status. I need these teammates like I need a mattress full of bedbugs creeping all over me in the dark.

That mental image makes me shudder. *Gross, Nora.* But it doesn't change the fact that I need to eradicate this so-called partnership. Time to "debug" my life.

I don't know though. Part of me doesn't want to believe Maddox meant it. Maybe Eleanor is the one he's playing—and maybe he has his reasons. I side-eye my visor with a scowl. No new messages, but the last one he sent me yesterday lingers in my mind.

> **Maddox:** Sorry. It's Eleanor. She's being extra Eleanor-ish at the moment. 🙄

She's obviously not the easiest person to get along with. I suppose I should give Maddox a chance to explain himself before I do anything rash.

At least I didn't delete the program I wrote last night. That was my first instinct at the time. I scurried back into my room before he and Eleanor could catch me lurking in the hall, and I pulled up the program file that I'd spent all night crafting.

```
RIGHT CLICK

DELETE
```

```
Warning!
This will permanently delete your program.
Are you sure?
[YES] [NO]
```

I sat there for a long time with my finger hovering over the Enter key, but I couldn't do it. In the end, I wimped out and hit No. That program was a thing of beauty. I couldn't bring myself to destroy it out of spite.

I settled for the next best thing. Why get rid of the whole program? Simply deleting a few strategic lines of code rendered it inoperable, unable to compile, and nearly impossible for anyone but me to debug.

Let Maddox coast on *that*.

As if on cue, the LED on my visor winks at me. Not orange. Flashing blue? I squint at it, wondering what that means. Did all those nonexistent messages drain down the battery?

Reluctantly, I pick it up to check, pressing the lenses to my eyes. A different notification greets me. No more texts. This came from InstaLove.

Congratulations, Lowercase!

Your crush Maddox has invited you on a True Love InstaQuest!

[CONTINUE] [DECLINE]

A *true love* InstaQuest?

OK, Maddox. Please excuse me while I gag on my laughter-vomit.

I can't let him get away with that. "Decline," I whisper to myself. *Decline it, Nora. A thousand times, Decline.* Anyone with a trace of self-respect would ignore that invitation after the things I overheard...

If I encounter any such self-respecting young ladies, I'll definitely ask them how they got that way. As for me? I stare at the Continue button.

Why am I so weak? I might not trust a word out of that boy's mouth, but I'm dying to know what a true love InstaQuest entails.

The truth is, I'm more than curious. I need Maddox. I can't blow him off. I don't have time to start from scratch on a different project. And why should I? Why should I turn my back on an opportunity, just because my partner turned out to be an untrustworthy creep? If he wants to use me for my brain, let him. I'll use *him* right back. Maddox is my ticket into Reese and Eleanor's group, guaranteed to win at the end of this program. That "first prize" trophy will look awfully nice and shiny on my college applications in a couple of years. No admissions committee will stop to wonder who I used to get it—or who used me.

I straighten my shoulders. Maybe I have some self-respect after all. I'd be a fool to drop out of the winning group. I'd only be hurting myself.

> Your crush Maddox has invited you on a True Love
> InstaQuest...

I've been eyeballing the Continue option for so long, the letters have started to blur. I can't hold my lids open any longer. With a grunt, I give in and blink.

The text flashes yellow and then disappears. My visor once again shows me a view of the green lawns and leafy foliage around me. "OK..." I say slowly. "What happened to the quest?"

That's when I see it, twenty feet from where I sit, glinting in the sunlight at a break between the hedges. *Is that really there?*

It looks like a bouquet of helium balloons, metallic pink, floating at exactly eye level. They bob and dip in the breeze as I approach, but they don't float away like real balloons would. Instead, the familiar pixilation sparkles at the edges. *Augmented reality.* Not as realistic as the palm trees painted on top of Dr. Carlyle's swimming pool, but convincing enough to trick the eye.

I ease forward and come to a halt before them. Words appear on the foil surface of the nearest balloon in the group.

> Lowercase!
> TOUCH TO BEGIN YOUR INSTAQUEST

I hesitate. Am I really going through with this? A quest? Could there be a more perfect metaphor for being led on by a boy?

But I can't turn back now. The weight of my curiosity would crush me. I reach for the balloon, poking with my index finger. The instant before my fingertip makes contact, the whole display explodes in a burst of pink confetti.

Maddox's avatar appears where the balloons hovered moments before, and words scroll through the text window beside his face. This isn't some predetermined game script. Way too specific.

> **Maddox:** Hey, Nora, this is your extremely apologetic Maker Fair partner. Sorry I skipped out on our work session last night. I suck.

His avi's expression shifts from a neutral smile to the most adorable look of contrition that has ever graced the virtual features of a boy. Gosh, he's a player—and so pathetic that I'm falling for it. That's not even his real face, and yet my mouth twitches with an involuntary smile as his words continue to scroll.

> **Maddox:** You can yell at me later. But I saw the code you wrote!!! WOW! A couple semantic errors, but I got it to compile. I think it's ready to test.

The words stop and scroll backward as I reread the last few lines. *Wait, he got it to compile?* That was no easy feat of debugging with the lines I deleted this morning. It's one thing to catch a syntax error or two, but a whole different level of skill to find a logical error lurking within a syntactically correct piece of code.

OK, so Maddox isn't as useless as he makes himself out to be. He's capable of contributing when he thinks it's worth the effort.

I skim through the rest of his message.

> **Maddox:** So that's where I could use a little help. Follow the trail I set up, and we'll see if your code works. Don't leave me hanging, Nora! Please?

"Oooh," I breathe. I get it now. This isn't what I thought. Not some pointless game designed to string me along. We're beta testing! Maddox may have been coasting up until now, but something finally lit a fire under him. He had to bust his butt to get my code running so quickly.

I might not trust him, but I can work with him…for now. And this InstaQuest might actually be fun. I bounce on the balls of my feet, awaiting my next instructions.

16

THE QUEST

NORA

A trail appears, marked by blinking red icons. They stretch before me in a direction I've never gone before. The first one sits in the center of the gravel path, twenty feet in front of me. I study it as I approach.

What is that thing, anyway? It's oddly shaped. Not a circle or a heart. More like an amoeba, or... *No, wait.* I realize what I'm looking at. Maddox must have drawn it by hand from the looks of the shaky outline. Those pointy things are ears. That bump is the cotton tail. I have to bite the inside of my lip to keep from giggling.

A little rabbit.

"Stop being so cute," I mutter to the first one as I stride past it. I crane my neck for a better view, but I can't quite tell where the rest of the trail leads.

Maddox's dorm? No… The rabbits skirt past the entrance to Grier Hall and disappear into the open field beyond. There are no more campus buildings over there. Nothing but thick trees, marking the western edge of Winthrop's grounds.

If I'd known I was going on a nature hike, I would've worn better shoes. I kneel down and slip my finger into the space where my sandal strap rubs against my heel. That better not turn into a blister. Maybe I should head back and switch to socks and sneakers before my skin is rubbed completely raw.

I turn in a slow half-circle to face the center of campus, careful to keep my eyes trained forward at all times. But a warning message flares before my eyes despite my efforts.

> **SYSTEM ALERT**
> Lowercase! Wrong way! Your InstaQuest will deactivate if you miss a checkpoint.

The sight of those words sends my heart thumping. I whip back around and let out a shaky breath as the angry red of the alert message fades.

There's no going back. Not unless I want the trail markers to disappear without a trace. I readjust my sandal strap as best I can, then resume my trek.

The path narrows as I pass the last stone building, changing from gravel to hard-packed earth. The tall grass on either side reaches to my knees. Up ahead, the trees thicken into untamed forest, rising up the side of a steep hill. The sun beats down at my back, and I quicken my pace to reach the shade. My sandals won't stop torturing me, but at least I can avoid the impending sunburn on the back of my neck.

I'm fifty yards into the trees, with the ground sloping steadily upward, when I reach my first real obstacle. A chain-link fence cuts across the path. There's a gate, locked by a heavy chain and labeled with a rusted sign.

WARNING

24-Hour Security Camera in use

NO TRESPASSING

I study it, wondering how much to trust my eyes. There's no sparkling. No pixilation around the edges. Nothing to signal that this sign is part of the game. I brush my fingertips against the embossed lettering, smooth paint, and roughened rust. This sign isn't augmented. It's real.

Now what?

As if reading my thoughts, Maddox's avatar pops into my field of vision with a text bubble.

Maddox: Problem?

Lowercase: There's a fence in the way.

> **Maddox:** So? You're a rabbit. Hop over 😉

I don't find that suggestion reassuring. I keep my feet planted on the ground as I peer through the gap in the metal fencing. The trail beyond turns sharply to the right. A few red bunnies flicker at me through breaks in the trees. It looks like they're heading skyward, up a roughly-hewn staircase made of rock.

I speak another message out loud, and the text auto-populates.

> **Lowercase:** I don't like this, Maddox.
>
> **Maddox:** It's fine! You're almost here!
>
> **Lowercase:** Are you at the end of this trail?
>
> **Maddox:** Yes! Climb the fence. It's no big deal!

Seriously? I wrinkle my nose at the "No Trespassing" sign. *Am I really going through with this?*

The fence clatters and groans beneath my weight. I reach the top and shimmy over. A metal wire snags against my shorts, and I swear under my breath as the sharp edge leaves a long scratch on the back of my thigh.

"This better be worth it." I land with a thud and glare up the stony rise. My leg is bleeding. My lungs are bursting. My heels are rubbed raw.

But that's not what bothers me most. I just had the most disturbing thought…

What if this is all a prank? Some kind of mean-spirited hazing ritual—or worse yet, what if Eleanor's behind it? What if she's with Maddox right now, safe and sound inside her room, laughing her head off at my expense?

The thought floods me with panic. *Forget this. I'm going back.* I'm about to fire off another text when I catch sight of something moving in the trees, high above my current position.

Is that him?

The avatar looks tiny from down here. I squint up at it. He emerges through a gap between the tree trunks, waving his arm back and forth over his head to attract my attention. Then he cups his hands around his mouth. The sound of his voice drifts down to me.

"Nora!"

That sounded real. Maddox's voice, not augmented in any way. He's up there.

"Nora!" he bellows again.

He wouldn't call me by my real name with Eleanor at his side.

"Come on! You have to see this!"

"Fine," I grumble, far too softly for him to hear. The word auto-populates inside another text bubble, but I don't send it. I flick my eyes sideways to clear it away, then start the long climb upward.

I'm huffing and puffing by the time I reach the final rise. The trail markers end at Maddox's feet. His avatar stands before me, holding one last pink balloon on a string. He hands it to me.

Another flurry of confetti fills the air around us as my own avi reaches out to take it.

> InstaQuest Complete!
> Congratulations, Lowercase and Maddox. Your connection
> is growing stronger. We totally ship it! 🖤

My IL score skyrockets upward. The numbers whiz past like the spinning dial on a slot machine, and Maddox's score must do the same.

"Sweet!" I hear him say beside me.

I wish I could share his enthusiasm. Hard to care about some arbitrary number when I'm bloodied, blistered, and mosquito-bitten within an inch of my life. I swear, if Maddox set up this quest just to boost our IL scores, I'm going to strangle him. We'll see if this app still "*ships it*" after that.

The game sends me a new interaction prompt, but I don't read it. With a huff, I tug my glasses upward and let them rest at the crown of my head. Hopefully, they'll block some of the disgusting sweat pouring down my temples.

Maddox lifts his own visor, and his real eyes meet mine. "Wow, you're slow," he says by way of greeting. "Turn around!"

I blink at him. *Is he for real?* He must see the irritation on my face because he takes a step closer and touches my upper arm. "Just turn," he says more softly, applying gentle pressure on my shoulder.

I roll my eyes, but I follow his instructions, turning my back to him.

"Like that. OK, stop there." He's holding both my shoulders now, angling me a few more inches with his fingertips. His breath tickles the back of my earlobe as he speaks to me from behind.

A less annoyed person might find that sensation rather enjoyable. As for me…

Well…

OK, I won't pretend I completely hate it.

"Now put your visor back on," he murmurs in my ear. He nudges the frames, and the lenses slip back down before my eyes. "You need to walk backward for the next part."

Backward? In my visor?

"Um, isn't that literally the *opposite* of what I'm supposed to do?" I turn my head to look at him, but he stops me. His fingers find the nape of my neck. A sliver of heat pierces through me as his fingertips burrow into the hair beneath my ponytail.

"Don't look back," his voice whispers, soft and smooth and warm as liquid chocolate. "You trust me, right?"

No.

I don't trust Maddox. But more worrisome than that, I don't trust *myself* when he's around. How am I supposed to judge his true intentions when his hands are on my shoulders…When I can feel his body heat inches from my back…

"You can't peek," he explains in a rushed whisper, leaning so close his visor clunks against the back of my head. "You have to back up toward a hazard without looking at it. That's the test!"

Hazard.

Hazardous terrain.

I squeeze my eyes closed. *Focus, Nora. Hazardous terrain. Beta testing.* "Wait, so we're testing the module I wrote last night? It's already running?"

"Not yet. I'm implementing it now." His hands drop from my shoulders to my elbows as I wait, but he doesn't release his hold on me. Maybe his fingertips like my arms as much as my arms like his fingertips. Or maybe he doesn't trust me not to turn around.

"There," he says at last. "Did you get an admin request?"

I open my mouth to say no when the notification flashes before my eyes.

SYSTEM

Admin.instalove-server.216.58.216.154 requests permission to install an unknown application update.

[CANCEL] [INSTALL]

I blink at the Install button, my heart skipping and fluttering inside my rib cage. Adrenaline has taken hold. The feeling is not entirely due to the way Maddox's palms felt when he ran them down my arms, warm and feathery against my skin. There's also the rush of anticipation from testing a piece of code for the first time—and the cringe-inducing, chlorine-scented memory of what happened the last time I didn't look where I was going in this visor.

"It's installing," I tell Maddox, twisting my hands together. "So what's the plan? I'm supposed to walk backward?"

"Right. I'm going to hold your arms like this so you don't trip. There's an obstacle behind us that your visor hasn't seen—"

"But your visor can see it," I murmur, following his logic.

"Exactly. I'm looking where I'm going. So if your code works, you should get an alert that you're approaching a hazard based only on the data my visor shares with yours. That's the test."

> SYSTEM
> Update completed!

I nod. The plan makes sense. It shouldn't freak me out. I mean, technically, I'm putting my life in the hands of an algorithm that I hacked between the hours of midnight and 6:00 a.m. with a boy I hardly know as my only fail-safe.

But isn't that what this Summer Program is all about? Independent study. Peer-based learning.

Right.

"There aren't any swimming pools behind me, are there?"

He only chuckles in response and draws me toward him. I

keep my eyes on the leaf-littered trail beneath my feet as I edge backward, step by step. After four or five paces, a familiar red alert message flares.

> **SYSTEM ALERT**
> Lowercase! Eyes ahead!

I freeze. "Stop."

He sounds puzzled behind me. "Did you get an alert? We're not close enough yet."

"It's the same one as before. 'Eyes ahead.'"

"Oh, you can clear that. It's just because you're not looking where you're going."

My mouth is dry. My palms are sweaty. The uncomfortable tightness in my chest has nothing to do with cute-boy-proximity anymore. I've disregarded every warning the universe has sent in my direction. The pure recklessness makes me tremble, but I don't want Maddox to see my fear. I cast my eyes sideways to flick the text box away.

I should get a different warning message if my program works. I know what it will say. I wrote the output string myself.

```
string output1 = "Warning! You are
approaching an unseen hazard. Stop
moving and proceed with extreme
caution.";
```

I need to trust, but not in the boy behind me. I need to trust myself. My program. The skills I've worked so hard to hone.

"OK," I whisper, half to myself and half to him. "Keep going."

Maddox squeezes one of my elbows. "Careful here. There's a rock. Step up." I grope behind me, nearly tripping, but his arms hold me upright as I regain my footing.

The sun's heat warms the back of my neck. We've emerged from beneath the trees into some kind of clearing, and the ground changes from soil to a shelf of solid rock. I can barely breathe with each passing step. My instincts scream to stop and go back the way I came, but I fight the feeling.

Maddox lets go of my arms. "Good," he says. "Stay still for a sec. Don't turn around!"

Is he backing away from me? "Where are you going?"

"Don't move!" he answers. "I'm recording a video of the last few feet. Wait there until I cue you."

I don't like this. Not one bit. Who made me the beta tester, anyway? Why am I the one taking all the risk?

"Good," Maddox says at last. "Now, I want you to walk backward toward my voice. Slowly. That's it."

The sun beats down from above, but a breeze flutters my hair. The cool air carries with it a faint hint of humidity. Some kind of pond or reservoir? Is that the hazard I'm approaching? I grit my teeth. "I swear, Maddox, if I end up underwater again…"

He laughs. "You're fine! Keep going. Slow and steady."

"Am I almost there?" I'm so tempted to look. My shoulders ache from tension as I keep my head pointed downward.

"I set the distance parameter to ten," Maddox answers. "You should get an alert when you're ten feet from the hazard."

Ten feet. That sounds reasonably safe. I keep inching backward. "What if it doesn't work?"

"Then I'll warn you. Don't worry!"

He sounds relaxed, but my heart is in my throat. I can barely lift my feet as I force myself to move backward another step…and another…and another…

"Almost there!" he calls to me. "Inches now. Nice and slow."

> **SYSTEM ALERT**
> Warning! You are approaching an unseen hazard. Stop moving and proceed with extreme caution.

I let out a gasp as the words appear before my eyes. Red. Flashing. Impossible to ignore. Exactly the way I planned them when I sat hunched over my laptop in the safety of my dorm room.

All my fears evaporate, replaced by a flood of triumph. "It worked! Maddox! I got the alert!"

"Awesome!" His footsteps approach. "Don't move. Stay there until I measure the distance."

"Should I clear the alert?"

"No, leave it. I want to show it on the video."

I've been holding both my fists clenched against my sides, but I force my aching fingers to unfurl. I keep my eyes trained forward so that the alert stays visible.

Maddox comes up behind me. His hand finds the small of my back. "Ten feet exactly. Can you take off your glasses without clearing the alert?"

"I think so." I remove the visor gingerly and hold it up. He cranes forward to see. I expect him to be holding a camera—or at least a cell phone—but he's only wearing his own visor, with his finger pressed to a button on the side.

"Got it!" he says.

He lets go of the button and peels his glasses off.

"The visors record video?"

"Forget the visors!" Maddox laughs. "We did it! It worked! Proof of concept!" He lets out a whoop and picks me up, swinging me around. The world spins in a whirl of color and light. Only when he sets me down do I finally take in the full 360-degree view.

All the air leaves my lungs. I thought I was backing up toward water. A pool. A pond. Maybe a lake…

But nothing prepared me for the view before me now. I stand on an outcropping of rock, surrounded on three sides by the edge of a soaring cliff with a lake far below.

I clap my hand to my chest. "Oh my God, Maddox! This is where you chose to test it?"

He grins. "Dramatic, right?" He taps his visor. "I thought about setting the distance parameter less than 10, but I figured—"

"Less than—less than—Maddox, what if it hadn't worked? What if..."

My legs go rubbery. My knees threaten to give way. Only Maddox's arm, wrapping around my waist, keeps me from sinking to the ground.

17

CLIFF'S EDGE

MADDOX

So much for keeping my distance. A safe ten feet? What a joke.

Nora leans against me with her head tucked in the crook of my shoulder. She went pale when she finally turned around and saw the scenery. Her knees looked like they might buckle, and I put my arm around her to steady her.

The color has returned to her cheeks now. I should let go. But she looks up at me, and her eyes do that thing again—so big and round, they take up half her face.

She pushes lightly against my chest, and I release her. My mouth has gone completely dry. I cover up my lack of composure by examining my visor. "Do you want to see the video?"

I hold my glasses out to her, and she puts them to her eyes. "Oh my God," I hear her breathe, a few seconds into the playback. "I can't believe you had me do that!"

"You weren't in any danger."

She hands the visor back. "I was literally walking backward toward the edge of a cliff!"

"Not within ten feet of the edge though. We can set the distance parameter higher than ten if you think—"

"That's not the point!" she interrupts. "What if the code hadn't worked? What if there was a glitch or something?"

"I would've warned you. I was standing right here."

She wraps her arms around herself and shivers, despite the heat of the sun beating down. I touch her elbow. "Come back in the shade. Do you want something to drink?"

She seems to collect herself and follows me in the direction of the trailhead. I left my backpack around here somewhere. My water bottle pokes out from a side pocket, and I hand it to her. She tips back her head and takes a long gulp. A drop of perspiration runs down the side of her neck, and I fight the urge to reach out and stop its progress before it disappears down the V of her T-shirt collar.

"Snacks. We need snacks." I snagged some extra muffins from the dining hall this morning. I rummage through my backpack and pull them out. "Blueberry or chocolate chip?"

She ignores both options and sinks down to sit on a large rock. She takes another long drag of water and then extends the bottle toward me. "I'm not really hungry," she says. She takes off her sandals and flexes her bare feet, closing her eyes with a sigh.

"You paint your toenails," I observe.

I shouldn't have said anything. Her eyes fly back open and she looks suddenly self-conscious. She draws her knees up to her chest and covers her toes with her hands.

"Don't hide them," I say, grinning. "They're cute."

I expect her to blush. I haven't missed the way her face changes color any time I look at her a certain way or accidentally brush her arm. This time though, she glowers at her feet.

Great. She's pissed. I'm not even in a relationship with this girl, but I'm already in the doghouse. Not an unfamiliar position, I'll admit. I'm going to have to smooth things over. I know how this routine goes. Same old set of functions. I'll just change out a couple of parameters for the new upgraded version.

```
def dysfunctional () :
  while 'Maddox' in doghouse :
    maddox ('begs forgiveness')
    eleanor ('laughs in his face')
    maddox ('offers muffins')
    eleanor ('glares at her feet')
```

I examine the boulder where she sits. "Move over, would you?" The rock isn't big enough for two people, but I squeeze myself beside her anyway. Nora inches sideways, perched precariously at the far corner, with a half-inch buffer zone between us. If she scooted any farther, she'd slide off the edge.

Wow, she's really not a fan of mine right now. I have a feeling I know why—and it goes beyond my choice of beta test site.

"Listen…" I take another sip of water, pausing to choose my words. "I know you overheard me talking to Eleanor this morning."

Her head snaps sideways. That took her by surprise.

"You aren't exactly super-spy material, Nora."

"No. I—I didn't mean to spy—"

"It's fine," I cut off her stammers. "I should explain."

"Whatever. I have no interest in getting in between the two of you."

"There's nothing to get between. Eleanor and I broke up." The back of my neck feels hot and prickly. I scrub my hand down the length of it, avoiding Nora's eyes. "It's just that Eleanor wants to keep that on the down-low for a while. I agreed to go along with it."

"Do you always go along with everything she says?"

Ouch. I look back up. I'm not really that pathetic, am I? "It's the price I pay to be here."

"What does that mean?"

For some reason, I can't stop thinking about what Eleanor said to me this morning—that one line in particular. "*One phone call from me, and you cease to exist.*" I know what she meant. All she has to do is tell her parents that I'm not the well-brought-up young man they thought, and *poof*: there goes life as I know it. They'll cut off my funding. I won't be able to register for fall classes. Hell, I'm not even sure I'd be able to finish out the Summer Program.

But what about my grandmother? Does Eleanor realize her parents are funding her medical bills? The thought makes me grind my teeth. I grab a muffin and take a bite to keep my mouth occupied.

"Listen." I lean closer and drop my voice. "If I tell you something, do you promise not to repeat it? Not to anyone. Promise."

Nora's eyes go all wide and innocent again.

Too wide. Too innocent.

"Maybe you better not tell me if it's such a *huge* secret."

Wait, is she being sarcastic? I can't help but smile. There are more layers to this girl than meet the eye. "What are you implying, Miss Weinberg?"

She stretches her feet before her and wiggles her fire-engine-red toes. "Nothing…" Her eyes are on her feet but I can sense them twinkling with mischief. "Just that anyone with an IL score as high as yours might be a little too good at playing games."

I clap my hand to my chest and rock backward, nearly toppling myself over with the force of my feigned indignation. She grabs my arm to steady me, but the muffin in my other hand goes flying into the underbrush, an untimely victim of my game-playing ways.

"My IL score is high because I cheat."

"You're admitting that?"

"No, no." I wave my hand back and forth as if to erase that last sentence. "Not, like, cheat at love. I mean I cheat at *InstaLove*."

She tilts her head sideways, crinkling her forehead.

"There's a hack," I explain.

"You *hacked* your score?"

"I can show you how if you want."

"Why would you bother?"

I shrug. "Why does anyone hack anything? Because I wanted to see if I could."

She nods, looking thoughtful. She studies me in silence, pinching her bottom lip between her thumb and forefinger. It's kind of cute, that gesture. I've seen her do it before when she had her attention fixed on her computer in the middle of a work session.

Finally, she speaks. "Did you hack the cameras too?"

"Huh?"

"The surveillance cameras," she says. "Is that how you're always breaking the dorm rules without getting caught?"

"Oh, yeah." I nod. "I can show you that too, if you want."

"OK…" she says slowly. "Or you could apply one-sixteenth of that much effort to working on our *actual* project."

"Hey!" Definitely sarcasm. I'm loving this sassy version of Nora. Where did she come from, anyway? "I worked on our project! I debugged your buggy-ass code!"

She rolls her eyes. "There were only bugs because I put them there on purpose."

"What? Why? I worked on that for three hours!"

She answers with a one-shouldered shrug. "I was annoyed with you."

"So you sabotaged your own program?"

She stares down at her toenails, and her voice suddenly goes dull. "I heard what you said to Eleanor. You partnered with me so you can coast…"

Oh. I suck in my breath between my teeth. Now we're getting to the heart of it. No wonder she thinks I'm a total snake. I can't say I blame her, and it bothers me way more than it should. "No, listen. I only said that because…" I scramble for some excuse to justify myself, but all I can think of is the truth. "It's complicated. Eleanor's parents are paying my way through school here."

Nora's expression changes. She pulls her eyes off her feet and looks me square in the face. "Why would they—"

I interrupt before she can finish the question. "Like I said, it's complicated. I can't just tell Eleanor to piss off. Not without serious repercussions."

"So are you in a relationship with her or not?"

Nora's hand rests on the rock between us. I cover it lightly with my own. "I broke up with her, but I agreed to act like we're still together…and not…not pursue anyone else. Romantically, that is. Not until after the Summer Program is over." This is mildly humiliating, saying it out loud. Now *I'm* the one stumbling over my words.

I can't tell if Nora believes me. Her cheeks are pink. She's staring at our hands. I rock my shoulder against hers. Then I stand and tug her hand to hoist her upright.

We stand face-to-face. There's a question in her eyes.

"Go ahead," I whisper. "Ask me anything."

"Why did you break up with her?"

That's a whole other conversation. I could give her the real answer, but it would probably take the rest of the summer to explain. Or, I could settle for the condensed version.

"Honestly," I tell her, giving her hand a squeeze. "Because I kind of started liking someone else."

NORA

I can't breathe.

I'm staring at Maddox, but I can't look away. He gazes back intently, his eyes like two magnets locking me in place.

Our fingers remain connected as he leads me back toward the exposed shelf of rock. He holds my hand lightly—an invitation to follow him, not a demand. I should probably slip free and turn away.

Instead, I clasp his hand more firmly. My sandals lie abandoned by the boulder where we sat. I follow him barefoot, tiptoeing over the rocky terrain to the open cliff. The sunbaked granite feels warm against my toes. Beyond warm. Hot, but not quite hot enough to burn.

If I could breathe, I might ask him what we're doing. Instead, his last words reverberate in the air between us.

"*Because I kind of started liking someone else.*"

There's no room for misinterpretation. He meant me. He likes *me*. And this is the part where I should say I like him back.

If only I could breathe.

We stand dead center on the clifftop now. Open space surrounds us on three sides. I'm not particularly afraid of heights, but this place unnerves me—or maybe I'm quivering like a scared rabbit because Maddox still holds my hand.

At least he stopped staring at me in that oxygen-depriving way. He turns his head and slips on his visor.

"What are you doing?" I whisper.

He releases my hand to press a button on the top edge of the frames. "Hold on. Almost done… There. Ready."

"Ready for what?"

"Put your visor on."

My lungs have resumed functioning, but several major muscle groups still aren't within my control. I stand frozen. Maddox turns his back to the cliff's edge and faces me. He reaches for the visor dangling from my neck and places it gently on the bridge of my nose.

What's happening right now?

"I had to integrate a new interaction prompt." His breath tickles my face, but I can't see how close he's standing. I can't even see his avatar. My view is blocked by the InstaLove prompt that popped onto my screen.

> Maddox would like you to consider kissing him at some
> point in the very near future. Do you:
> **A)** Say yes and pucker up.
> **B)** Tell him you're not interested and turn away.

"Wait," I whisper. "You wrote that prompt? Just now?"

"Go ahead. Pick a choice. It's totally up to you."

My feet feel disconnected from the ground. I'm off-balance, in danger of floating into space. My instincts whisper to turn and run, but I don't. Not this time. Some corner of my brain remains aware of the fact that I'm surrounded by a ledge with a two hundred foot drop-off. I reach forward, groping for some handhold to anchor me. My fingers land on his wrist. I grip tightly, and I can feel his pulse. Fast, like my own, but firm and steady.

The tip of my tongue darts out to wet my lips. "Reese will see. She can see all our interactions."

"I know."

"Eleanor will see it too."

"Good."

I've never kissed a boy before. Never in my life. I've dreamed about it a time or two. Not going to pretend I haven't. In fact, I may have dreamed about it with this boy who stands before me.

He shuffles a half-inch closer. His wrist slips loose from my grip, and the dizzy feeling returns the moment I lose contact. I draw in a sharp breath, and his hands rise to my shoulders to steady me.

"Nora," he whispers. "I've got nothing to hide. I'm not cheating. Eleanor and I are broken up."

"But—"

"Don't overthink it. Just pick a choice. I highly recommend the first one."

Say yes and pucker up.

My eyes track over the words. All I need to do is blink. I want to, more than anything. So why am I still hesitating? Has the electrical charge between us caused my eyelids to malfunction?

His hands run up and down my arms, and his fingertips feel cool against my heated skin. Somehow, his touch calms me.

It feels good. It feels right. It feels like a boy who wants to kiss me in real life.

I focus on the sensation, and blink twice.

THE DROPBOX (ENTRY 4)

ELEANOR

https://bit.ly/dropboxL

Dropbox > Personal

File Name	Created on	Visible to
Entry 1.txt	7/1/2019	Deleted
Entry 2.txt	7/2/2019	Deleted
Entry 3.txt	7/9/2019	Deleted
Entry 4.txt	7/10/2019	Only you

So, it turns out Maddox is a liar and a cheat.
He's getting up to something behind my back, although
Reese is doing her best to cover for him. Whatever,
Reese. Whose side is she on? I don't even feel

guilty anymore about the surprise "announcement" I
have planned. No, I'm done. I'm telling her tomorrow
at breakfast. I was going to break it to her gently,
but why bother? She obviously has no consideration
for my feelings. She won't shut up about Lowercase
and that program.

I saw the program too. It's good. I'm big enough
to admit that. The girl has talent. Very logically
structured. So logical, in fact, that it would only
take one keystroke to throw the whole thing off.
That distance parameter… All I can think is how
unfortunate it would be for their Maker Fair demo
if someone made a little typo.

Too bad I don't have edit privileges, or I could
really have some fun :)

18
NORA 2.0

NORA

"Because I kind of started liking someone else."

That's what Maddox said yesterday at the summit of our InstaQuest—which also marked the high point of my summer and possibly the high point of my life. I haven't been able to stop thinking about it. He had a certain look on his face when he uttered those words, a look I now have filed away in a previously undiscovered corner of my brain called: HAPPINESS.

```
Nora's Internal File Server
Awkwardness—35,786,542 files
Anxiety—68,532,797 files
Happiness—1 file
```

"Because I kind of started liking someone else."

An insecure person would record that under ANXIETY and come up with a long list of other people he must have been talking about. I mean, there are seventeen other people in this program *not* named Eleanor, not to mention seven billion other people on this planet.

Good thing I don't know any insecure people like that. If I did, I would tell them to stop selling themselves short. As for me, I know with one hundred percent certainty who Maddox meant. I could see it from the way he kept looking at me, alternately staring at my painted toenails, and then my eyes, and then my lips.

Like he might, at some point in the future, find it not altogether unpleasant to do something more than stare.

And then that kiss between our avatars…

Does it count as a first kiss if only your virtual lips make contact?

It didn't feel real. And I don't just mean the InstaKiss. That whole conversation, sitting beside him on the rock, felt like some out-of-body experience. Not the real me interacting with him. More like watching some augmented rendering of myself, acting all the ways I wish the real live Nora could act.

I don't know if it was the adrenaline from finding myself ten feet from the edge of a cliff, or my irritation with Maddox for putting me in that position, but somehow I forgot to feel self-conscious around him. I forgot the endless stream of self-criticism that usually runs through my head. I was just *me*. Nora Weinberg. Unfiltered and unaugmented.

And he liked me.

I've been floating on air since that moment. I'm still floating now, a day later, although deflating a bit, like a helium balloon that's slowly leaking out its insides. If he likes me (and he's as single as he claims), then why hasn't he laid a finger on me since? If anything, Maddox was *less* handsy than usual on the hike back down to campus. No more accidental brushes of his fingertips, leaving trails of gooseflesh on my skin. It's been twenty-four hours, and he hasn't touched me once.

He still stares at me though. I caught him at dinner last night with one of those long-simmering looks, when he thought my eyes were on my tray. I know I'm not imagining it. What does it mean if a boy says he likes you with his words and his eyes, but not with his lips or fingertips?

I wish I had someone I could turn to for advice. Girl talk. That's what I need. I'm so sick of being stuck inside my own head. If there's ever been a time for an InstaBFF to walk into my life, this is it.

Too bad I'm a social pariah, with my single dorm room and social status of a flea. The other students interact with me through InstaLove prompts, but no one seems interested in spending more than three seconds in my presence without the benefit of visors.

No one except Maddox.

What does he want? Does he like me or not? Maybe he's waiting for me to make the next move?

I frown, fighting back the questions that swirl round and round. I need to stop thinking so much. Be that girl from The Overlook. Confident Nora. Comfortable-in-her-own-skin Nora. If I could be that Nora on a regular basis, life would be golden.

The library building looms ahead. I push my way through the revolving door, mentally rehearsing all the clever things I'll say when I see him. I refuse to think about the fact I'm here for a group meeting with the other members of our foursome. Reese and Eleanor have some new side project they're working on for their half of the presentation, although they haven't told us what.

Do they know about the "kiss"? Probably.

Wow, this is going to be awkward.

The prospect should fill me with dread, but I won't let it. Why am I so intimidated by Eleanor Winthrop? She's just a girl—a girl Maddox no longer wants to be his girlfriend. *Because why, Maddox? Oh, that's right...*

"Because I kind of started liking someone else."

A smile steals across my lips as I make my way up the library's central staircase—a modern minimalist affair, suspended by nothing but wire cables that hang from the sky-high ceiling.

Guess who's back to floating on air again? Nora 2.0.

This good mood of mine is dangerous. Last time I felt this giddy, I was using my visor for the first time at Dr. Carlyle's garden party, and we all know how that ended: face first in a swimming pool.

I need to keep my wits about me. I haven't forgotten Reese's warning, when she caught me with Maddox's face at the top of my InstaCrush column. At the time, I was too embarrassed to think about what she meant, but I get it now. This breakup between Maddox and Eleanor is a messy situation. Complicated. *Hazardous terrain.* The last thing I want is to get caught in the cross fire between the two of them—or worse, used as a pawn in some chess match I don't understand.

Is Maddox manipulative like that? Is it possible that our whole clifftop flirtationship was fake?

I mean, technically, it *was* fake. His avatar kissed mine. Our actual lips did not come anywhere close to meeting. So, maybe it meant nothing. Maybe he's playing games.

The old insecure Nora would jump to that conclusion. Maddox was flirting, but not *really* flirting. Old Nora would then proceed to dissect and rehash every word that Maddox had ever said to her.

But the old Nora is retired. Rendered obsolete. Nora 2.0 is here to take her place. So Reese can take her ambiguous warning message and stuff it. I'll put Maddox in my InstaCrush column if I want. I'll InstaKiss him, and I'll kiss him for real if the opportunity arises. A boy I like actually likes me back, for the first time in the history of my life.

I refuse to let anything—or anyone—destroy that.

I pause at the top of the staircase and make a quick scan of the second floor. A lone figure sits in the study room at the far corner. I can't see his face with the bright blaze of sunlight streaming through the skylights overhead, but I'm sure that's Maddox. I recognize him by his posture. He has a certain way of slouching anytime he sits in a chair.

Why are boys with bad posture so much cuter than boys who sit up straight? Especially when they do that thing where they tip their chair backward and put their feet up on the desk. I've seen Maddox do that only once, when he was hanging out in the dining hall after lunch the other day. He tipped too far and almost toppled backward. I thought the rolled-up cuffs of his shirt might burst wide open, the way his forearms flexed when he reached to catch himself.

The mental image sends a wave of heat rolling through me. "Oh my God," I whisper as I make my way toward the room. I like a boy with muscles in his *forearms*, and I think he likes me back. *How is this real life?*

I slow my roll. He hasn't seen me yet. If he had, he would've waved. The girl's bathroom beckons, and I dash inside. Not that my newfound confidence has abandoned me or anything. Just because I caught sight of a cute boy sitting in a slouched configuration? Why would that send me into a tailspin?

No, no. I'm fine. I ignore the stalls and head for the wall of bathroom mirrors. Even the uber-confident Nora 2.0 needs to check her hair before she sees her InstaCrush.

Ugh. Who am I kidding? I'm blushing so severely, my entire face is the same color as the inside of my mouth. *Cute.*

Before I can do anything other than gawk at myself, the bathroom door swings open. A pair of girls walk in. I recognize Miranda in her ever-present beanie, followed by Celeste, the girl who made that crack on day one about us clueless "newbies" whose existence she preferred to ignore.

Hopefully they'll both ignore me now. They better not go all Mean Girls on me again. They speak in hushed voices, hiding their mouths with their hands, but they stop talking the moment they see me.

"Sorry," I say, not sure why I'm apologizing. I turn on the water tap and look as busy as possible scrubbing my hands.

"Are you OK?" Celeste peers over my shoulder. "Your face…"

Is it that noticeable? My cheeks flame even hotter, and I bend forward to splash some water on them. Miranda scoots herself onto the sink beside me, leaning her back against the mirror. She pulls off her knit cap and fluffs her hair—a cloud of wild, brown frizz that matches the freckles on her pale cheeks. "You're not crying too, are you?"

Crying? I look at Miranda, confused. "Why would I be—"

"Never mind." She reaches for the paper towels and hands me one to dry my face.

Celeste pulls out a makeup bag and leans over the sink on my other side. She sweeps some powder across her cheekbones, highlighting the dark copper glow of her skin. "I don't think she was crying," Celeste says to the mirror. She puckers at herself, then adds a coat of gloss to her russet lips. "I think she got all red like that from yelling."

I turn toward her. "Why would I be yelling?"

"Not you! Reese and Eleanor." Her voice drops lower, and she glances toward the bathroom door before she continues. "Did you miss breakfast? The two of them had world war three in the dining hall this morning."

Wait a sec…

This isn't Mean Girls. We're actually having…girl talk…in a girl's bathroom. A bunch of female friends, gossiping while we reapply our makeup! Or, well…OK, while Celeste reapplies her makeup, and I wait for my face to return to a semi-human-looking color. But same general idea.

Friendship goal achieved!

I pat my face with a towel and try to look way more chill than I feel. "What were they fighting about?" I ask. *And did it have anything to do with a recent InstaLove interaction between two avatars?*

There's no way Reese didn't notice that. Two avatars sharing an augmented reality kiss? And there's no way Reese wouldn't tell Eleanor what she saw. But why would that trigger a fight between the two of them? I could see Eleanor taking it out on Maddox, but on Reese? Talk about shooting the messenger.

"—early admission. She's starting in the fall."

I glance at Miranda in the mirror. I missed the first half of that sentence. Early admission? "You mean to college?"

Miranda nods. "I thought Reese was going to have a stroke."

"I don't understand. Why *wouldn't* Reese apply to college?"

"No!" Celeste shakes her head at me. "Not Reese! Eleanor!"

"OK…so?" I meet my own eyes in the mirror and frown. Apparently this fight had nothing to do with InstaLove—or with me. *Way to be self-centered, Nora 2.0.*

Miranda sees my puzzlement. "She doesn't know about the plan," she says over her shoulder to Celeste.

Am I in this conversation or not? I can't quite tell. "What plan?"

"The college plan," Celeste answers. As if that explains anything.

Miranda turns back toward me, speaking rapid-fire to catch me up. "Reese had this plan since forever that she and Eleanor would go to MIT and Harvard—"

"And share an apartment in Central Square," Celeste finishes with a giggle.

"That's specific…" I say slowly. "Where's that? Boston?"

Miranda side-eyes me impatiently. "Cambridge. Halfway between Harvard Square and Kendall!"

Gee, sorry I haven't memorized the exact topography of Cambridge, Massachusetts.

I leave that retort unsaid. My footing in this conversation feels far too precarious to attempt sarcasm. "Oh," I reply instead. "Right. Duh."

"Anyway, that's not important. The point is Eleanor bailed on the entire eastern seaboard. She got accepted early to Stanford. She's skipping her senior year. EOF."

Both girls laugh in unison. "EOF…"

End-of-file? Is that some inside joke I don't know about? I have no idea, but I smile anyway, acting like I get it.

"Honestly, I don't blame Eleanor. Reese is so…" Celeste's voice trails off, searching for the right word.

"Controlling?" Miranda supplies. "Obsessive? Toxic? Most-likely-to-commit-friend-icide on anyone who fails to go along with her every word?"

"Harsh," Celeste counters, shooting her friend a funny look. "I was going to say rigid. You know how she gets. She's been talking about MIT and Harvard since before we knew them. Eleanor never seemed to mind though."

"Well, she minds now." Miranda's eyebrows draw together. "You heard what she said."

Celeste nods, her shoulders vibrating with laughter. "The entire dining hall heard what she said. I can't believe she shouted that right in Reese's face."

"What?" I ask. "Shouted what?"

"I told you," Celeste answers me. "EOF!"

They both collapse into giggles. *OK, then. So much for girl talk.* I laugh along with them, forcing a fake chuckle, but I've given up on understanding the joke.

19

TOE THE LINE

MADDOX

Where is everyone?

I turn in my chair and peer through the glass wall of the study room. The other three spots around the conference table sit empty. No sign of my group. I half expected Reese and Eleanor to bail on our meeting after their epic death match in the dining hall this morning. But Nora? It's not like her to be late. Bright-eyed and bushy-tailed is more her style.

The thought makes me grin. I'll admit I was looking forward to this work session with Nora. Looking forward to it way more than I should…

I spin my chair in a circle, pushing off against the tabletop to pick up speed. The second floor of the library whizzes by in a whirl. Round and round and round. I'll be dizzy when I stop.

Too dizzy to stand up straight. Too dizzy to *think* straight. But I haven't been thinking straight for a while. Not since yesterday afternoon at The Overlook.

I stomp my feet on the ground to stop the chair, but the world keeps on spinning.

"Nora," I murmur, raking my fingers through my hair. What am I going to do about that girl?

I shouldn't have made a move on her. Reckless, that's what it was. I got swept up in the moment—all alone with her away from prying eyes—and the challenge of proving to her that I'm not some lying cheat.

I proved myself, all right. My ex-girlfriend's non-reaction has me baffled. I figured she'd tell her parents to yank my funding as soon as Reese showed her the interaction data. I've been holding my breath all day, waiting for the ax to fall.

Is it possible Reese didn't tell her about the kiss?

Maybe Reese didn't consider it worth mentioning. It wasn't a *real* kiss, after all. It could have been if I'd gone for it—and damn if it wasn't tempting—but I caught myself. There's a line between virtual and real, and I managed to pull back before I crossed it.

That's my plan with Nora. Toe the line, but don't step past. Not until I've figured out a way to proceed without Eleanor catching wind.

Behind me, the study room door creaks open. *Finally.* I sit up and straighten my shoulders as I turn to greet my group members. Reese alone lurks in the doorway, poking her head through the gap.

Her face looks different than usual. I can't remember the last time I saw her without the Day-Glo eye shadow and bubble-gum pink lipstick. I study her, struck by the overwhelming resemblance to her older brother. Aside from her hair, she and Emerson could be twins with their matching pale blue eyes and dimpled cheeks. Is that why she wears so much makeup? To set herself apart?

"Meeting's canceled," she tells me in a flat voice. She moves to close the door again.

I'm going to need more information. "Wait!" I prepare to chase after her, but she hesitates in the doorway and then enters the room.

"What's going on?" I ask her. "Are you and Eleanor—"

She gives her head a tiny shake to cut me off. Something in her eyes warns me not to mention that name again. I can't tell from Reese's expression if she's angry, hurt, or both. Maybe she doesn't know herself. She looks startled mostly—like she's been sucker punched. I can't say I blame her. Eleanor took us all by surprise with her announcement over breakfast.

Skipping senior year?

I guess it explains a few things about Eleanor's behavior lately. No wonder she wasn't too upset by my decision to break up with her. She must have been planning to dump me herself. Once this summer session ends, she's leaving Winthrop Academy for good. She's just miffed because I beat her to the punch.

I wonder...

Did the falling out between Eleanor and Reese have anything to do with me—and the recent uptick in rabbit-related activity on my InstaLove account? I'm dying to pump Reese for information, but I hold back. One look at her face warns me not to go there.

"Sit." I gesture toward the chair across from mine. "Talk to me. Are you OK?"

She looks down at the chair but doesn't take a seat. "I'm fine," she says softly. "It'll blow over. She's not really going. She wouldn't."

I'm not so sure, but I don't contradict Reese. She knows Eleanor better than anyone. Maybe she's right. This is all another game, designed by Eleanor to get a rise out of us. A week from now she'll laugh her tinkling laugh and announce she was only kidding. Stanford... Like hell she's going to Stanford. It's not even Ivy League!

Still, if Eleanor wanted to hurt Reese, she could hardly have picked a better way. *EOF...* Reese's favorite catchphrase, flung back in her face. Everyone in the dining hall fell silent when Eleanor shouted it. We all knew what it meant. That's one talent of Eleanor's I've always found incredible—that effortless way she's able to define a new piece of slang for everyone within earshot, purely from the context and the expression on her face.

EOF.

Not End of File.

End of *Friendship*.

No wonder Reese couldn't summon up an answer. She stood frozen, stunned silent, mouth quivering, and then she turned and fled from the room in front of everyone.

But she looks like she's recovered her composure, standing before me now. Reese tosses her hair and draws up her shoulders, rearranging her features into their usual businesslike expression. "Don't worry," she says to me. "We'll reschedule the meeting. It's a minor setback."

"I wasn't worried about the meeting, Reese."

She frowns. "What else?"

"Are you two OK? Are you still rooming together?"

"Of course." She blinks at me. "Everything's fine. Nothing's changed."

I can't help but raise my eyebrows. Reese scares me sometimes with her cold-bloodedness. Either the girl's in complete denial about the conversation that went down, or she's faking it.

Maybe that's the answer.

That makes sense, doesn't it? Maybe Reese and Eleanor came to their own "separation agreement"—their own set of terms and conditions, same as mine. Keep up appearances until the end of Maker Fair. Don't let anyone see the truth. Then go their separate ways with both their heads held high.

But that only leaves my head spinning with more questions. Like, who exactly is Eleanor trying to fool with all these agreements? And why?

NORA

I walk out of the girl's bathroom and nearly crash right into him.

"Whoa! Careful!"

Did Maddox track my location somehow? He was standing right outside the bathroom door. We collide and I nearly topple, but he grabs me by the shoulder to keep me upright.

I swear I'm not usually accident prone. Only when Maddox is nearby. Maybe I should make a hazard alert for *him*.

> **SYSTEM ALERT**
> Boy ahead! Locate nearest emergency exit. Brace for impact. Assume crash position. Stop, drop, and roll!

Better set the distance parameter for at least a hundred feet to be on the safe side. Although a hundred feet wouldn't be much help to me now. As I regain my footing, I calculate approximately half an inch of space between my face and the front of Maddox's shirt. Which means if I look up, his head will be right there. His eyes. His nose. His lips…

I take a hasty step backward.

"Come with me." His hand is still on my shoulder. It slides down the length of my arm to my wrist, raising goose bumps as it goes. He tugs me in the direction of the stairs.

I turn to follow him. For a moment, I think he might hold my hand, but he lets go as he turns toward the library's central staircase. "Change of venue," he says over his shoulder. "This way."

He waits for me to catch up at the bottom landing. His hand reaches for mine again. This time our palms meet. Our fingers interlock, and a thrill of electricity jolts through me. He turns his head, but not to look at me. His gaze tracks over my shoulder, scouring the area for anyone who might be watching us.

That only makes my heart beat faster and my hand grip his more firmly.

"Come on." He pulls me toward the stacks, leading me through a maze of floor-to-ceiling bookshelves. I break into a jog to keep up with his long strides.

"Where are we going?"

"Celestial navigation."

Um. Was that answer supposed to mean something? I mean, this library has a ton of skylights, but I'm pretty sure we can't see any stars in the middle of the day.

He pulls to an abrupt stop, and I crash into him again. This time it was no accident. He made me do it on purpose. His arm goes round my waist. I reach for the nearest shelf to steady myself and find myself face-to-face with rows of book spines.

By the Stars: A Workbook

Navigation for Beginners

Celestial Navigation in the GPS Era

Fundamentals of Celestial Navigation for Yachtsmen

"Are we going yachting?" I ask, pulling that last one off the shelf.

He shrugs and takes the book away from me. "Nah. I parked my yacht on the other side of campus."

"So why are we in this section?"

I can't imagine how anything in these books might be relevant to our project.

"Dead spot," he says by way of explanation. "No cameras in range of this shelf."

Wow. Should I be alarmed by the fact that he knows that?

"So…" He shifts uncomfortably. "We need to talk."

I nod. "I thought we were having a group meeting."

He ignores me, slouching against a bookshelf with his hands in the pockets of his perfectly creased khakis. "What were you laughing about with those girls in there?"

"Who?"

"Celeste and M. In the bathroom. I heard you talking."

My eyes fly open wide. "You were eavesdropping?"

He smiles at me and cocks his head. "If I were eavesdropping, then I wouldn't have to ask you what you were talking about, would I?"

I suppose that's true. But still. *A little creepy, Maddox…* "Maybe I should go back." I ease a half step away from him.

He reaches for my arm. "Wait. Hold up. I'm sorry. This is coming out wrong."

"I don't understand."

"I need to know if you told them about…" He points back and forth between our chests. "This. You and me."

"Is there a '*this*'?" I ask, mimicking his gesture.

His hand finds mine again. His thumb runs along my palm, sending off miniature fireworks in the pit of my stomach. "I would like there to be."

"OK, then—"

"But I need you not to tell anyone."

I pause a beat. Something tells me this is not how the typical conversation goes when a guy expresses romantic interest. "You mean so your *real* girlfriend doesn't find out?"

He blows out his breath. "She's not my real girlfriend. She's my ex. And she already knows. That's *why* you can't tell anyone."

I should let go of his hand. I can't stop looking at his thumb, tracing circles on my palm. "You understand how sketchy this all seems, right?"

"I know. I'm sorry. Eleanor's being…weird. Weirder than usual."

"So? You either care what she thinks, or you don't."

"It's more complicated than that."

"Is it?"

I retrieve my hand and tuck a strand of hair behind my ear. I don't like this. I shouldn't go along with it. Something about it feels icky. I may be surrounded by books for yachtspeople, but I have no idea how to navigate this ship. This isn't how this conversation is supposed to go. It shouldn't feel so scary. So confusing. I meet his eyes uncertainly, and Maddox takes my hand again. Every time he does that, I forget all the reasons why I should turn back.

He dips his head and looks into my face. "I like you, Nora."

I stare back with a million unspoken questions on the tip of my tongue.

"You like me back," he whispers. "I know you do."

True. I'm not enough of an actress to hide that fact from him. But if he really wants this ship to sail, I've got a few questions that he needs to answer. Like, for example, *why?* Why would someone like him be interested in someone like me? Why would someone with a girlfriend as incredible as Eleanor Winthrop want a girl as ordinary as Eleanor Weinberg?

A confident person wouldn't feel that way, but I can't help it. At least I'm not pathetic enough to utter the question out loud.

"Don't do that," he says, as if he can read the doubts written all over my face. "Don't compare yourself."

"It's kind of unavoidable, isn't it?"

"The two of you couldn't be more different."

"Gee, thanks."

He's so close now his forehead grazes mine. I'm staring at his lips. "I mean that as a compliment," he murmurs.

I close my eyes. I can't let that mouth of his distract me. It doesn't add up. She's smart. She's rich. She's popular. She's probably the prettiest girl here. "She's perfect," I whisper.

His hands rise to cup my face, and his thumbs play with the wisps of hair that escaped my ponytail. "I disagree."

"I have eyes, Maddox."

"I know. I like your eyes."

"That's not what I meant."

"What did you mean?"

"I mean I'm not clueless. I have a brain."

"I like your brain too." He smiles.

Why does his smile have to do that to me? I'm having a hard time making my brain operate at the moment. Is he going to kiss me? For real this time? I'm pretty sure he would if I closed my eyes and tipped back my head.

But should I? Do I dare?

He lets go of my face and turns his head away. "Shhh," he whispers. "Someone's coming."

He grabs a book and heads back toward the main staircase. My heart is in my throat as I stumble after him. We emerge from between the shelves and nearly run smack into Dr. Carlyle.

The program director looks back and forth between us. His eyes narrow as he peers down the bridge of his nose. "Everything OK, you two?"

"Great! Doing some research. Nora's idea." Maddox shoves the book he's holding into my hands, and I look down at the title.

Celestial Navigation in the GPS Era

Well, that's not incriminating at all.

"Navigation, huh?" Dr. Carlyle tips his head to one side. Is that laughter in his eyes? Something tells me he knows exactly what the Celestial Navigation section signifies…and the reason why the students of Winthrop Academy have such a keen interest in the topic.

"You can look at that upstairs, but leave it on a cart when you're finished. The stacks are off-limits for the summer."

"Oh. Right. OK!" I stammer. "Sorry. I didn't know."

"My bad," Maddox says. He guides me by the elbow toward the staircase. "Won't happen again, sir."

Dr. Carlyle's voice stops us before we reach the first step. "Have you two seen Miss Winthrop?"

I stumble, nearly tripping. Maddox's back goes straight. He turns around. "Eleanor?"

"Her mother's looking for her."

Maddox answers, and I detect a tremor in his voice. "I thought Mr. and Mrs. Winthrop weren't coming until Maker Fair."

"No," Dr. Carlyle replies. "On the phone. Tell Eleanor to give her mother a call if you see her, will you?"

"You got it, Dr. C." Maddox tosses a salute. "We'll let her know."

THE DROPBOX (ENTRY 5)

ELEANOR

https://bit.ly/dropboxL

Dropbox > Personal

File Name	Created on	Visible to
Entry 1.txt	7/1/2019	Deleted
Entry 2.txt	7/2/2019	Deleted
Entry 3.txt	7/9/2019	Deleted
Entry 4.txt	7/10/2019	Deleted
Entry 5.txt	7/17/2019	Only you

Another week down. I'm almost there. Only four days to go until Maker Fair. Too bad my partner is still only speaking to me through grunts and text messages. No real communication since I told Reese about Stanford, and it went about as badly as I thought. My dearest roommate is nothing if not predictable. When it comes to controlling my life, she's almost as bad as my mom and dad.

It's fine. I'll smooth it over with Reese. I know how to deal with her. It's my parents who worry me more. The news of my college acceptance took approximately three nanoseconds to spread beyond the hallowed walls of Winthrop Academy. I've been dodging my mom's calls for a week.

I bet she didn't think I had it in me. Didn't think I could get in anywhere without Mommy and Daddy pulling strings.

They can't be too upset though. I mean, it's Stanford. The Harvard of the West! It's only an hour flight from the cabin in Tahoe. I could do far worse. They'll be mad for a while because I didn't talk to them first, but they'll come around.

No, it's not the Stanford part that I worry about with my parents. It's my new choice of "roommate" that they might not like so much…

20

PREPARATIONS

MADDOX

The relentless heat has me moving in slow motion. I wipe my hand across my brow to clear away the sweat. We're approaching the end of July, and the recent heatwave shows no sign of breaking anytime soon. I wonder if I could talk Dr. C into turning on the air conditioning. They switched it on in the library, but not here in the large assembly hall where the Maker Fair will take place.

The stifling atmosphere must be keeping the other students away. Maker Fair is in four days, and Nora and I are the only ones working in the exhibition space. Everyone else found a cooler spot to complete their preparations, but there's no way around it for us. The structure we're building would be too large to transport.

"Ow!"

I look up from the plank of plywood I'm sanding. Nora drops her hammer and stuffs her thumb into her mouth.

I can't help but grin at her. I swear, I've never met anyone this accident-prone. All that brainpower, and yet she can't walk in a straight line without tripping? Somehow, it adds to her cuteness.

She takes her hand away from her mouth and shakes it out. "Stop laughing at me," she says. "That hurt!"

"Who's laughing?" I make my eyes all wide and innocent. "I didn't make a sound."

She glares at me. "You're laughing on the inside."

"I'm not laughing. I'm smiling. Is smiling allowed?"

"No." She picks up a towel and wipes her palms. "No smiling. You're distracting me."

"Then you're going to have to stop being so cute."

I drop my sandpaper and cross over to her, examining our progress as I go. The three-foot-high platform is taking shape. It'll be ready for our live demonstration in four days, once we finish sanding the edges and nailing down the steps.

I take Nora's hand. "Let me see." Her thumbnail looks red and angry, but at least she didn't draw blood. "You should put some ice on this," I tell her.

"Are you injured, Miss Weinberg?"

I jump at the voice. I didn't hear anyone creep up. Dr. C stands in the doorway of the assembly room behind me. He heads in our direction.

"No," Nora answers him, pulling her hand away. "Just clumsy. I'm fine."

I pick up the hammer she abandoned. "Maybe I should build the steps."

She scowls at me. "I know how to use a hammer."

"Go work on commenting our code. You understand it better than me anyway."

Dr. Carlyle interrupts, glancing toward the laptop Nora left on the work table behind us. "Will you show me, Nora? I'd like to see."

I shoot Nora a look, urging caution with my eyes. She can show him our program, but she better not give away all our secrets. We need to keep some surprises up our sleeves. There are two keys to scoring well at Maker Fair: interactivity and drama.

Our presentation should deliver on both fronts. It will consist of the video I recorded—Nora walking backward toward the edge of a two-hundred-foot cliff—projected onto the wall and replaying in a loop. Then, while the judges make their rounds, we'll draw a crowd to our booth with our live demonstration. That's where this platform comes in.

We'll invite volunteers to stand in the center and walk backward in any direction, stopping only when they see a warning alert. Nora's program will do the rest. The only issue is the distance parameter. I set it to a safe ten feet for real world applications, but we'll need it much smaller for platform-demo purposes. Two feet maybe? Three? It's easy enough to play around with it once we're ready to go live. It takes only one keystroke, thanks to the efficient way Nora designed the code.

I glance over to her, standing at her laptop with Dr. Carlyle. He leans in to read something on her screen. I can tell from the way his eyebrows arch that he's impressed.

He should be. It impressed the hell out of me too, the first time I laid eyes on Nora's handiwork—not to mention the effortless speed with which she spins out algorithms, like a spider weaving its web. I consider myself a strong coder, but I don't hold a candle to Nora when she gets in the zone.

Yeah. I scored big when I landed Nora for my partner. Not that I care so much about impressing Dr. Carlyle. It's Emerson Kemp whose head I'm hoping to turn. He's the one who took notice of Nora's admission application in the first place. He's coming to Maker Fair in four days to serve as a guest judge on the scoring committee, and he better like what he sees. This is about more than winning some first place prize and bragging rights for a year. I need to lock down that licensing deal…and hope it comes with a nice fat check.

My whole future depends on it.

NORA

My thumb throbs from where I hit it. I can already see a blood blister forming beneath the nail. Probably for the best that Maddox confiscated my hammer. I'm less likely to cause major bodily harm at a laptop keyboard.

It's not that I don't know my way around a set of tools. I've built plenty of stuff in my garage at home without incident. But I didn't have a partner working with me. A partner who gets all sweaty from manual labor in this stuffy room. A partner whose hair gets all dark and curly when it's damp. A partner whose shirt keeps sticking to his chest…

Thank goodness Dr. Carlyle turned up. I needed a distraction. There's no telling what kind of damage I might have inflicted if I attempted the use of power tools within a hundred-foot radius of the Maddox Danger Zone.

I can focus better with the program director peering over my shoulder. Dr. Carlyle's lips move silently as he reads through lines of code on my laptop screen. I haven't written up the comments yet to document what this section does. Should I explain it to him? It's obvious, right? Maybe not. Sometimes I have a hard time judging whether something intuitive to me will be equally self-explanatory to other people. Maddox has no problem following my logic. He's proven himself competent at editing and debugging, although any code he writes from scratch tends to be clunky. Not error-ridden or anything, but suboptimal. Full of redundancies and inefficient data structures.

At least Maddox doesn't mind when I show him a more elegant

solution. I discovered that about him in week two of the program. He tried to store user location specs using a HashMap when an ArrayList would take so much less memory. Some people would get all huffy about stuff like that, but not Maddox. He simply turned to me with a huge lopsided grin and said, "How are you this awesome?"

That's what I find most attractive about him. He may be easy on the eyes, but underneath all that, he's a true geek at heart. Like me.

Dr. Carlyle clears his throat. "Very impressive, Miss Weinberg." He points to my visor, sitting idle inside my open backpack. I normally have it on the cord around my neck, but it kept getting in the way when I was hammering. Dr. Carlyle gestures for me to pick it up. "I'd love to see a demonstration of the functionality."

"Sorry, it's not ready." I point toward the elevated platform, still under construction. "You have to stand up there for it to work," I explain. "We need to reinforce the center before it's sturdy enough to bear weight."

Dr. Carlyle frowns as he assesses the plywood structure. "How high is it off the ground?"

"Only three feet," I tell him quickly. Why does he sound so skeptical? If he thinks that's unsafe, wait till he sees the video Maddox plans to project on the wall.

The program director's face looks grim. He taps his foot against the hardwood floor, considering. *Oh no, is he going to veto our whole plan?* I look toward Maddox, trying desperately to make eye contact and summon him over. I've noticed over my almost three weeks in the program that Dr. Carlyle has a soft spot for that boy. Maddox must be his favorite student, the way the program director lets him get away with murder. If there's one area where my Maker Fair partner excels, it's talking himself out of trouble—and talking everyone around him into giving him his way.

I, on the other hand, have never successfully talked my way into anything. I can't even convince my parents to let me download an app used by ninety-nine percent of teenagers on the planet. Why, oh why didn't Maddox come over here to handle the program director? He really thought I should be the group spokesperson?

Dr. Carlyle scratches his chin.

Maddox is too busy swinging his hammer to look up. I'm on my own. What would a smooth talker say in this situation? What would Maddox do?

He would lie. That's what he would do. Lie through his teeth. I wave a hand vaguely toward the platform. "The extra padding is going all the way around the perimeter. Not that we need it, but as a safety precaution—"

"Padding?" Dr. Carlyle turns his attention back to me. "What sort of padding did you have planned?"

Yes, Nora. What sort of padding *did* you have planned?

See, this is the problem with lies. They have a way of multiplying. And right now my mind is a total blank.

"What are we talking about?" *Oh thank God.* Maddox to the rescue. He inserts himself in the space between Dr. Carlyle and me.

"The padding," I reply slowly, making heavy eye contact for emphasis. "You know, all the extra *safety* padding, to go around the edge of the platform?"

He doesn't miss a beat. I swear, he could win awards for his smooth-talking abilities. "Oh right. I meant to ask you, Dr. C. Is it cool if we borrow the gymnastics mats from the student fitness center?"

Dr. Carlyle frowns. "The fitness center is closed for the summer."

"Exactly! So nobody's using the mats."

Maddox turns on his most endearing grin, and Dr. Carlyle looks like he's wavering.

I bite my lip. "You can never be too careful," I add tentatively.

"Seriously." Maddox cocks his thumb at me. "Especially with this one around."

His face goes deeply somber, and I have to scrunch my mouth sideways to keep from cracking up. I could swear Dr. Carlyle might be on the brink of laughter himself, but he manages to maintain a stern look.

"All right, you two. Plenty of padding. Carry on."

As soon as the door swings closed behind him, Maddox's knees buckle and he collapses to the floor. He has his hand covering his eyes, but his mouth bubbles with laughter.

I kneel down on the floor beside him, and he sits up. "Padding, Nora? What the hell?"

"Sorry! He seemed concerned."

"Concerned about what? It's three feet off the ground!"

"But theoretically if someone fell off—"

"No one's falling off!" Maddox points to my laptop. "Didn't you show him the program?"

"Well, in case the program doesn't work for some reason…"

"It'll work." He smiles at me, the same impish grin he directed at Dr. Carlyle moments earlier. "I have total faith in your software development skills, Miss Weinberg."

Gosh, he's good. You'd think his player ways would have less effect on me since I know exactly what he's doing. But no. It doesn't seem to work that way.

He takes my hand and pulls us both to our feet. Then he turns my battered thumb to examine it. "Your hammering skills leave something to be desired, however."

I can hear the teasing laughter in his voice as he shifts closer. His head hovers over mine. A clumsy person might look up at him too quickly and clock him in the jaw with her forehead.

But I'm not that clumsy. Not quite.

I angle my head sideways before I lift my face. He smiles at me with that mischievous light still dancing in his eyes. I try my best to scowl, but I can't. I smile back in spite of my best efforts. I don't seem to have full control over my lips at the moment.

Or my lungs.

Or possibly my heart.

He's going to kiss me. Here. Now.

It's weird how clearly the thought comes to me, considering how my entire autonomic nervous system has ceased functioning. Somehow time has stopped, and I'm able to have a lengthy stream-of-consciousness conversation with myself in the instant before his lips lower themselves to mine.

This is what it must be like when you're dying, I suppose. There's a saying that your life flashes before your eyes, but I never understood that before. Like, how does anyone have *time* to review their entire life in those fleeting instants before the end comes? But I totally get it now. When you find yourself face-to-face with the thing you've always known would come for you someday, and yet you thought would never really get here. Somehow, in that instant, the speed of thought accelerates. You have time to think clearly. To know what will come next. To say to yourself, this is it.

This is it, Nora.

This is the thing.

This is how it happens.

My first kiss.

"Ummm. Are you OK?"

My eyes fly open. Maddox lingers a few inches from my face. My hand is still in his. But I can't help but note a distinct lack of lips on my lips. *What the heck?*

He strokes my injured thumb. "Did you pass out from internal blood loss?"

Now I really do scowl at him. I pull my hand away and stick

my tongue out, hoping he can't see my disappointment as I turn toward our construction area. "We should probably get back to it."

He grabs my elbow. "Wait. Hold up." There's a tenseness in his tone, and I don't know what to make of it. I've given up trying to read this boy. "Where's your visor?" he asks. He catches sight of my backpack, where I left it on the corner of our makeshift platform. "Go get it. Put it on."

Why? So we can do another avatar kiss? No. I'm done with that. "No more interaction prompts."

He raises an eyebrow.

"Mutual attraction detected," I say in a robotic computer voice. "Do you do something about it for real, Maddox? Or do you hide like a scared little rabbit behind your avatar?"

He groans, but he doesn't let me go. He pulls me closer. He stares at my lips, his breath tickling my cheek. But he still doesn't close the distance. He pulls back once again with an unreadable expression on his face. It doesn't look like rejection—more like longing tinged with regret.

He sighs and rests his forehead against mine. "I can't," he says in a strained voice. "It's complicated."

Everyone keeps saying that. Reese. Now Maddox. I swear, if one more person tells me it's complicated, I'll scream.

I push against his chest to shove him away, but he captures one of my hands and holds it to the spot just left of his breastbone. I can feel his heart thudding beneath my palm.

His eyes leave mine and travel over my shoulder toward the double doors of the assembly hall. "I'll explain," he tells me softly. "For real. I promise. But not here. Later. Somewhere private."

Something in his face warns me that he's serious. He's not playing games. Something has him scared. "Where? My room?"

He shakes his head. "No. Not the dorms. It's too close."

Too close to what? Is it Eleanor he's so afraid of? But *why?* "OK, then where?"

His Adam's apple bobs up and down. "I'll send you an InstaQuest. Later. Tonight. After curfew."

"I can't break curfew!"

"I'll take care of the cameras." His voice is so low it's barely audible. We stand close enough for his lips to brush against my ear. The sensation sends a shiver racing through me. "Wait in your room after dinner, and keep your eyes on your visor."

I open my mouth to protest again, but I don't have a chance. The doors of the assembly hall jolt open. Eleanor and Reese stand on the other side.

21

PLAYGROUND GAMES

MADDOX

I didn't intend to have it out with Eleanor today, but I don't have any choice. The time has come. She just caught me red-handed. I'm three inches from Nora with her palm pressed against my chest. Not exactly a businesslike position.

I let go of Nora's hand. My eyes skim past Eleanor and land on Reese. "Oh good. You're here. Lowercase needs you to look over something."

"I do?" Nora and I lock eyes. "Ohhh," she says slowly. "Right. I need to show Reese that…that thing." She spins away from me and grabs her laptop before heading toward the double doors.

Reese ignores her. She has her eyes cast sideways toward her roommate. Eleanor still hasn't moved a muscle since she stepped into the room. Her stillness feels more menacing than any movement she could make. At last, she tips back her head and casts her eyes upward toward the ceiling. "Go ahead," she says to Reese. "Moxie and I need to have a chat."

My thoughts exactly.

We stare each other down from opposite ends of the room. She has her hands on her hips. I draw myself up to my full height and mirror her position. The moment the doors swing closed behind Reese and Nora, she reaches into her shoulder bag for her visor.

"What are you doing?"

"I'm placing a call."

"Eleanor—"

"Call Mother," she says aloud, directing the visor. She drops her hands from her hips and saunters toward me. "It's ringing."

I move a few paces toward her. "Eleanor, can we please talk about this?"

She whips the visor off. Her eyes shoot daggers from behind the lenses. "You knew what would happen. We had an agreement, and you've obviously chosen to disregard it, so—"

"I didn't do anything!"

She stands by the far end of the platform and rests her hip against it. Nora's backpack sits beside her. She pushes it away, wrinkling her nose in distaste and replacing it with her own designer bag.

"That's not what it looked like from my angle," she says.

There's no point arguing. I'm done trying to smooth things

over. She wants to call her parents and tell them what a terrible person I am? Go ahead.

"Maybe I should call your parents for you." I reach for my own visor and slip it on. "I'm sure they'd be fascinated to hear how their precious offspring has taken up a new career in blackmail."

She lifts her chin and laughs her silvery laugh. I can't believe I ever found that sound attractive. Now, it only sets my teeth on edge.

"Blackmail?" she says sweetly. "That's a strong word."

She looks calm on the surface, but I know her hidden depths. There's a tension at the corners of her mouth that wasn't there a moment earlier. I called her bluff, threatening to go to her parents.

Her parents…

I pull in a breath and hold it deep inside. All this time, I assumed Eleanor's motives had to do with jealousy, but maybe there's more to it. She's *using* our fake relationship to cover something—something she doesn't want her parents to know about until after this program ends.

Eleanor's visor pokes out from her bag. I eye it thoughtfully. Was she really about to call her mother? If I grabbed that visor and looked behind the lenses, would I see any evidence of a phone call?

Or has all her talk about cutting off my funding been nothing more than a playground taunt?

Yeah. I see you, Eleanor Winthrop.

She always used to do that when we were little. Any time the game of freeze tag or red rover turned against her, she'd deal with it the same way: threaten to tattle to the nearest grown-up.

But she never followed through on those threats. Not if her opponents stood firm.

Maybe I'm on to something here. I press my advantage, choosing my words carefully. "Why are you doing this? This fake relationship thing. What are you trying to hide?"

Eleanor ignores my question with more forced laughter, but her eyes go hard. "I'll tell you what," she says, carrying on as if I hadn't spoken. "I'll give you one more chance. But you cannot so much as *look* at another girl for the rest of the program. Do you understand?" Her hands are on her hips again. "Especially during Maker Fair. You will stand next to *me*, not *her*. You will hold my hand. You will put your arm around me. And you damn well better make it look convincing—"

There. See? How could I have been so clueless? She basically confessed. Her parents will be in attendance at Maker Fair. She wants me to make it "look" convincing.

None of this is about our relationship. She's playing some twisted mind game with her parents. And me? I'm nothing more than a prop.

I can't believe I ever loved this girl. The lengths that she would go, the amount of damage she would cause…

"And if I refuse?" I ease my way toward her as I speak. "You're not seriously going to blow up my whole life. Over what?"

Her face remains perfectly calm. "You only have a life because my family handed it to you. And now I'm asking you"—she pokes me in the chest—"not blackmailing you, *asking* you, for one little favor in return. I really don't think that's so much to ask."

I stuff my hands in my pockets to keep them still. I could strangle her right now, with that fake angelic smile on her fake angelic face.

I'm done. If I had any lingering reservations about meeting Nora later, they're gone. I'll meet up with her. I'll kiss her dizzy. I'll do anything I like. Eleanor can go to hell for all I care. "Go ahead and call your parents. You tell them your side of the story, and I'll tell them mine."

Eleanor looks down sharply. She nudges Nora's backpack with her elbow. "Is she really worth it? You're going to lose your spot at Winthrop over *this*?"

I grab the backpack by one strap and move to toss it over my shoulder. Eleanor keeps hold of the other side.

"Let go," I say.

"No. You let go."

I give the backpack a tug, but I stop at the sound of ripping fabric. Somewhere on this bag, a seam has given way. I can't tell if it's the strap around my shoulder or the one clutched in Eleanor's fist.

She raises an eyebrow, daring me to tug my side again.

So this is what we've come to? This girl has been the center of my life since we were both two years old. I thought we'd matured since then, but no. After all that time, we're playing one last playground game. Tug-of-war.

"I'm heading back to Fenmore anyway," she says, twisting the canvas loop around her wrist. "I'll drop it off in her room."

"No."

She rolls her eyes. "Don't be so dramatic. I'm not going to light it on fire."

I see where that ripping sound came from. There's a thread unraveling by my shoulder, where the strap meets the fabric of the bag. Part of me wants to tug anyway, even if we leave the whole backpack in tatters, but I hold back. There are other ways to win at tug-of-war besides brute force. With a shrug, I let the strap slide off my shoulder and down my arm. "Fine. Have it your way, Eleanor. Have *everything* your way."

She smiles at me, but her eyes are frosty cold. "Good boy." Then she tosses Nora's backpack over one shoulder and turns away, heading for the door. "I knew you'd come around."

That's where she's wrong though. These games have gone on between us for too long already. It's time I put a stop to them, once and for all.

NORA

This can't be happening right now.

My backpack… How could I have been this careless? I was so

flustered in the assembly hall that I didn't stop to think. I grabbed my laptop but forgot to take my bag.

I know exactly where I left it, sitting open on the edge of the platform. I saw it there before I left the room with Reese. But when I returned to look for it, the backpack was nowhere to be found.

And neither was my visor.

My feet drag as I trudge down the winding path toward Fenmore Hall. I scuff the bottom of my shoe against the ground.

Maybe I should check with Maddox. Is it possible he took my bag back to his dorm, not realizing my visor was inside? I don't know, but I can't go running to Maddox like some needy little kid. Not after the way we left things. He made it clear he needed me to keep my distance until he summons me. He'll kill me if I show up uninvited at his room.

There's no way around it. I'll have to tell Reese my visor's missing. But I can't go to her room! No way. Not after the dirty look Eleanor shot at me back there, like she might vaporize me where I stood through pure, undiluted loathing.

Reese wasn't much friendlier after we left the assembly hall. We both knew we'd been dismissed to give Maddox and Eleanor space to talk. Neither of us bothered with the pretense once we left the room. "I warned you," was all she said as we made our way outside and took off in opposite directions.

Whatever college-related drama went on between Reese

and Eleanor, they seem to have patched up their differences. Reese is squarely on Team Eleanor. Otherwise known as: Team Erase-Nora-Weinberg-from-Existence.

I hang my head. Why can't I catch a break for once? I mean, Reese and Eleanor were never going to be my BFFs, but at least we'd come to a grudging truce for work-related matters. But now this. After the way they treated me when I dunked my visor in the pool, I can only imagine their abuse when they hear I lost it.

The main door to Fenmore Hall swings open before I can reach for the handle. Miranda emerges, her thicket of curly hair tied back into a ponytail. She looks different somehow— younger and more approachable—without the usual cap pulled down over her forehead. I guess it's too hot out for beanies, even for her.

"Hey!" Miranda calls to me, holding the door open. "What's the matter?"

I hesitate, and my eyes sweep over hers. Maybe I should confide in her. She's been nice to me lately—and by "nice" I mean acknowledging my presence instead of looking straight through me when we pass. If I told her about the visor, would she run interference on my behalf?

I'm desperate for an ally, but…*no*. Miranda and I are acquaintances, not friends. I have no friends in this place. Not really. Maybe I would have made some if I hadn't spent the past couple of weeks glued to Maddox's side, but it's too late to change that now.

Miranda might be friendly enough for small talk, but her allegiances are clear. If anything, she and Eleanor have been tighter than ever lately. I see them sitting together in the dining hall for practically every meal, even when Samirah isn't around.

I fan my face with my hand as I grab the door handle from her. "I'm fine," I lie. "Just overheated."

I don't stop for further chitchat. No doubt Miranda will find out the real reason for my misery at dinner tonight, when Eleanor fills her in. For now, I head to my own room with no visor. No backpack. No hope of retaining a shred of dignity. Only my laptop tucked beneath my arm.

I reach the top of the steps, and I draw up short.

Am I seeing things?

Oh, please tell me I'm not hallucinating...

I clap my hand against my chest as I stride quickly toward my door. There, hanging from the doorknob, is my backpack.

I set my laptop on the floor and hug the bag fiercely. Maddox must have spotted it in the assembly hall and brought it back here. I rush to pick it up and zip it open. My visor sits inside, filling the dark cavity with blue LED light.

I pluck it out of the bag and press my lips to the smooth black frame. Then I slip the lanyard around my neck where it belongs.

Crisis averted!

Well, no. I silently amend that last statement as I kick off my shoes and sink down at the edge of my bed. Minor predicament averted. The real crisis still looms over me like a thundercloud.

I cover my eyes with my hands and collapse backward onto my bed. Maddox...

I was so sure he was going to kiss me. I can picture the look on his face afterward. The look of a boy with mixed feelings. The look of a person being torn in two.

"*I can't,*" he said in that voice full of regret. "*It's complicated.*"

I suppose I should be happy. This is progress. The last time I confessed to liking a boy, he looked like he might vomit. On the scale of rejections, "*it's complicated*" scores a huge step up.

So why do I feel infinitely worse than I did when Trevor shot me down? Maddox didn't even reject me. He told me he'd explain. He promised to talk later. But now that the thrill has subsided, the disappointment chafes inside my chest, shredding my heart like a cheese grater.

Nothing with Maddox feels remotely like my crush on Trevor Chang. Not even close. The stakes are so much higher. This program ends in four days, and then we'll scatter to the winds. I'll head back to New Hampshire, Maddox to New York. I doubt we'll keep in touch. We'll never cross paths again...

The thought makes me feel like I might break.

Maddox and I will go our separate ways, whether he kisses me or not. So why does it matter so much? The answer stares back at me, impossible to ignore. There's only one explanation if I'm being honest with myself. What I feel for Maddox goes beyond a simple crush. He's been the object of my every waking thought since I got here. His face is the first image that pops into my head when I wake each morning and the last thing I think about before I drift to sleep. Is it possible that I might be in love with him?

Don't be ridiculous, Nora.

I can't help thinking of the first night of the program—the first time I played InstaLove on a visor—and that euphoric sensation of floating, my feet no longer connected to the ground.

Remember where that feeling left me that time? Didn't I vow to protect myself from making that mistake again?

I built an entire warning system to prevent any further missteps. But I didn't see the real hazard until it was too late. Too late to protect my heart. Too late to pull back from the precipice. I was too busy floating on air, and now I've stumbled over the edge.

I'm falling hard—and I have no idea where I'll land.

I sit back up. Reese was right. "*I warned you…*" I should've listened. This won't end well. Talk about hazardous terrain. I can only hope Maddox will reach out a hand and catch me before my heart ends up completely smashed.

"*I'll send you an InstaQuest,*" he told me. "*Later. Tonight. After curfew.*"

That's hours away. How am I supposed to survive the suspense until then? I slip on my visor, hoping by some miracle to see a new notification from his avatar. My most recent interaction fills the screen.

What the heck? My fingers tense, and my bedsheet bunches against my palms. *Did he change his avi? To that?*

"No," I moan out loud. "Whyyy?" Doesn't he know how often I log in and check my account, purely to see the expression on his avatar's face?

There's no expression now. No puppy-dog eyes to make me smile. No smirk to make me blush. His perfect features have been replaced by a fathomless gray square. And his username? He must have changed that too—shortened to his first initial.

M

THE DROPBOX
(ENTRY 6)

_____

ELEANOR

https://bit.ly/dropboxL

Dropbox > Personal

File Name	Created on	Visible to
Entry 1.txt	7/1/2019	Deleted
Entry 2.txt	7/2/2019	Deleted
Entry 3.txt	7/9/2019	Deleted
Entry 4.txt	7/10/2019	Deleted
Entry 5.txt	7/17/2019	Deleted
Entry 6.txt	7/17/2019	Only you

UGH UGH UGH! It's all screwed up! I can't believe
Moxie is giving me this much trouble. I expected
Reese to be the suspicious one, not Maddox!

Now Reese and I are chill. She totally caved after I shed a few tears and "confided" how much I need my best friend. Reese loves nothing more than to feel like she's the most important person in my life. She's so predictable.

But Mox? I think he just saw through me.

He realized that I need him more than he needs me. All this time, I had him distracted by my "jealous ex" routine, but somehow he saw behind the curtain. How????

It's that girl's fault. Lowercase. Maddox used to be so nice and easygoing before she got her hooks into him. He never questioned anything about our relationship. But now he's got a reason to think a little harder, to look a little closer at the fuzzy edges.

I can't believe I'm dealing with this now. I just need Maddox to keep his mouth shut a while longer!

OK. Breathe.

The plan can still work. Maker Fair is July 21. Eleven days before my birthday. Eleven days when I need to fall off the radar: Disappear-> Radio silence-> Lie lie lie-> Stall stall stall-> Make it until August 1-> Then happy birthday to moi!

And then it's a done deal.

The tricky part is Maker Fair. I wish my parents weren't coming. I already told them Moxie and I are going to Tahoe for two weeks afterward. I can't have him making eyes at another girl in front of their faces! They'll know something's not right. They'll go sniffing around, and then it's only a matter of time before they realize where I'm really going.

I can't let that happen. Maddox needs to stay on script. But I just lost all my leverage.

What now?

Think, L. Think!

If I can't control Maddox, then I'll need some distraction. Something to keep everyone otherwise occupied during the fair.

Distraction, the key to illusion. There's more than one way to make a rabbit disappear.

Right. I know what I have to do. Desperate times call for desperate measures. M vetoed that idea, but so what? I can do it on my own. I have little Lowercase's visor.

22

THE LESS YOU KNOW

NORA

Winthrop Student Mail Server

July 18, 2019

From: Office of Dr. Carlyle

To: Summer Students (All)

Subject: CAMPUS LOCKDOWN

Attention:

One of our students, Eleanor Winthrop, was reported missing this morning by her roommate. Miss Winthrop was last seen leaving the library yesterday evening, July 17, shortly before curfew. If you have any information that may assist in locating her, please reply to this message or speak to the residential adviser in your dormitory.

In the meantime, with the search ongoing, this campus is officially on lockdown. Remain in your assigned dormitory buildings at all times. Anyone returning to the off-campus location known as "The Overlook" will face severe disciplinary consequences.

I close my laptop and roll onto my back. My dorm room's white popcorn ceiling looms above. Strange how this position brings me back to my first night at Winthrop, full of misery and dread at the thought of staying here for three full weeks. As if falling in a swimming pool were the worst fate that could ever befall a person.

How little I knew.

Eleanor Winthrop has been missing for twenty-four hours, and the police aren't searching for her at the bottom of a swimming pool. They're searching at the bottom of the lake.

The whispered rumors were already flying when I woke this morning. I went to bed full of anxiety over Maddox—trying to interpret what he meant by graying out his avatar, and swallowing my disappointment over the InstaQuest he never sent—but I woke with Eleanor's name buzzing in my ears.

"She's missing…searching the lake…she told Reese she was heading to The Overlook…everyone's going up there to watch…" I spent

most of the day huddled with the others on that forbidden shelf of granite, watching the police divers work. They were still at it by the time we tramped back down to campus. I wonder if the divers will keep searching after dusk.

A knock sounds at my door. That reminds me of the first night here as well, lying in my bed in misbuttoned pajamas, with Maddox's nighttime visit to fetch his crumpled blazer off my floor.

Is that him now? Violating lockdown? I can tell it is from the cadence of his knuckles against the doorframe.

Knock, knock, knock-knock-knock.

"Come in," I whisper, sitting up.

The door cracks open wide enough for him to slip inside. He eases it closed behind him, and I wince at the loud click of the latch inside the doorjamb. For a moment, we both go still, listening for any sign of movement in the corridor. Long seconds tick by inside my head.

All quiet.

The tension eases in my shoulders. I slide off the bed and go to him. His face looks drawn, dark smudges beneath his eyes.

"Maddox, what are you doing? You shouldn't be here."

He reaches for my hand. Turns it over. Runs his thumb along my palm. "I know."

He should be in Grier. In his own bed. Staring at his own white popcorn ceiling. The last I saw him was on the clifftop along with all the others.

My gaze flicks over his shoulder toward the door he closed behind him, blocking the surveillance camera mounted on the other side. "Maddox, you can't doctor the video feeds anymore. Don't you see how bad that looks?"

He doesn't answer. He lets go of my hand and crosses the room, sinking heavily into my desk chair.

Something's happened. There's no way he would have risked coming here otherwise. He stares mutely at his legs, running his palms against his thighs to smooth the wrinkles in his khaki-colored pants. For once, he didn't iron them.

I wait for him to explain his presence, but the silence lengthens. I have no choice but to venture more whispered questions.

"What is it? Did you hear something? Did the searchers find her?"

My heart thrums, waiting for his answer. It felt the same earlier this afternoon, standing at The Overlook as we watched the police diver rise from the bottom of the lake.

"*Is it...*" someone had whispered. "*Is it her?*"

I'm not sure who spoke the question. The voices around me had intermingled, mixing and echoing, jumbled together with my thoughts. We could all see the answer in an instant. Whatever that diver was holding, it didn't look human. Way too small. I realized what it was when the diver reached the boat. He held the object out to a policewoman kneeling on the deck, and a fading ray of sunlight caught the smooth surface of the lenses.

An InSight Visor…

But still no sign of the girl who had been wearing it—not unless Maddox has some news.

"What?" I prompt him again. "Did they find something?"

He looks up and shakes his head. I release a breath from somewhere deep inside, waiting for him to say more. At last he whispers a few words. "It's all my fault."

I don't know what he means, but the sound of it sends my pulse racing. His eyes point at me, but they remain unfocused. Unseeing. Like I'm not really here—like I'm a ghost, or a piece of augmented reality painted in.

There's something creepy about it. My hand rises to my throat. "She might be fine. You know how she is. She's probably hiding somewhere, laughing her head off."

"Maybe."

I move toward him and kneel on the hardwood floor at his feet. "She's doing this to punish us, Maddox."

His hands resume their movement, sliding to his knees to pull the fabric taut, then lifting up to let the wrinkles reappear. He does it three times in a row before I grab his hand and fold it inside both of mine.

I don't know this Maddox. I don't know these mannerisms, or how to read the haunted look on his face. None of it reminds me of the boy I talked to yesterday, or the day before, or the day before…

He pulls me toward him, bringing me to rest in his lap. I've never been so close to a boy before. I should be thrilled, but I feel nothing. Not now. I wrap my arms around his shoulders, and he buries his face in my hair.

"It was supposed to be a game." His voice is muffled. His shoulders shake. Is he laughing? Crying? I hold him tighter and try to shush him, but he goes on. "She isn't hiding. She's gone."

"Why?" I whisper. "What are you not telling me?"

He's silent for a long time before he answers. "The less you know, the better."

I open my mouth to ask him what he means, but he presses a finger to his lips. My ears register the sound of footsteps in the corridor, followed by the buzz of students' voices. I strain to make out what they're saying, but I recognize only one word.

Eleanor.

"Wait here," I whisper to Maddox. "I'll go see what it is."

I step outside, careful not to swing the door open wide enough for anyone to see the contents of my room. Students fill the hallway from end to end. Ms. Cleary emerges from her suite, belting a terry cloth robe at her waist. Her hair hangs loose around her shoulders, partially concealing the look of bewilderment on her blotchy face. She opens her mouth as if to speak, but no words follow.

Whatever news there is, it didn't come from Ms. Cleary. My eyes search toward the other end of the hall. No sign of Eleanor. Reese stands outside their room, but a crowd of others block my path to her.

Two doors from mine, Samirah slips out into the hall. I head toward her.

"What happened?" I keep my voice hushed to blend in with the others, although I don't know why we're all speaking in muted tones. Like we're gathered at a hospital.

Or a funeral.

Samirah answers me so softly, I have to lean forward to understand her words. "They dredged the lake."

"Did they find something?"

"Eleanor," she whispers.

I thought I heard that name. I ask the natural next question, although I can already read the answer on the faces all around me. "Is she…is she OK?"

Samirah only shakes her head. I'm not sure if she's answering my question or telling me to shush.

I wrap my arms around myself to ward off the sudden chill. My eyes seek Reese again at the far end of the hallway. She stares straight back in my direction.

Her face is pale, with an eerie emptiness to her expression. Vacant. Hollow. *Lifeless.* Our eyes remain locked for a long moment, despite the length of corridor that separates us, but she shows no sign of recognition. She blinks and looks away.

Celeste stands at Reese's side. She loops her arm around Reese's shoulder, and Reese crumples against her. That reminds me of a funeral too.

The whispers swell around me.

"No way. Are they sure?"

"I can't believe…"

"What happens now?"

I'd like to know the answer, but something tells me not to ask. Not in front of all these people. I turn to reenter my room— Maddox needs to know what I just heard—but my door is already open before I reach for the doorknob. I look for the boy I left there moments earlier, but he's gone.

23

NEGATIVE

NORA

There's something wrong. Something just beyond my grasp, nagging at the fringes of my consciousness, but scurrying away every time I try to put my finger on it.

This feeling has been with me since I woke this morning. The contents of my fitful dreams faded the moment my eyes opened, leaving me with nothing but a tangle of damp sheets—and the unsettling sensation of a truth just out of reach.

I push away the feeling and head for the door. I need to stretch my legs. I don't intend to stray farther than the hallway bathroom, but the whispered fragments of a conversation lure me in the direction of Celeste and Miranda's room.

I pop my head in, and I'm confronted with a view of the same four girls I met on the first day of the program, in nearly identical formation. Miranda and Samirah sit on one bed, quietly holding hands. Chloe and Celeste, the girls I previously knew only as Pixie-Cut and Hair-Pouf, sit cross-legged on the bed opposite. There's only one notable absence from today's girl-talk session.

Where's Reese?

The last time I saw her, she had her head slumped against Celeste's shoulder. Celeste led her away somewhere, staggering beneath her weight. Reese had looked stricken at the time. Beyond devastated. *Destroyed.* I can only presume Celeste took her to the infirmary. I haven't seen Reese since, and the room she shared with Eleanor remains roped off with yellow crime scene tape.

"Come in," Celeste says, looking toward me.

I hover awkwardly in the threshold, half in and half out of the room. The desk chair is occupied by what appears to be part of a Maker Fair project, labeled with Miranda's name. It looks like some kind of souped-up potter's wheel with exposed circuit boards soldered to the floor pedals.

I'd love to take a seat, but I don't dare move the gadgetry. It doesn't look too sturdy.

"Yeah, come in," Samirah echoes. "Sit with us."

I stuff my hands in my pockets. "Thanks."

Chloe inches sideways to make room for me beside her, but I've already crossed to the desk. I perch on the edge, drawing my knees to my chest. Under any other circumstance, I'd be thrilled these girls acknowledged me. Are we all friends now? Maybe we're besties for life. Bonded by trauma. Maybe superficial social hierarchies don't hold up so well in the face of life and death.

Or maybe these girls are just restless. We're all confined to Fenmore for at least another day—not even allowed to leave for meals. I spied a breakfast cart inside Ms. Cleary's suite, laden with cereal and pastries. I suppose they'll wheel in another cart for lunch and dinner. We're waiting to be called into the program director's residence, where we'll be interviewed one at a time by a panel of adults: Dr. Carlyle, a grief counselor, and an investigator from the medical examiner's office, determining the circumstances surrounding the victim's death.

That last part seems to be the focus of the girls' conversation.

"I don't understand," Celeste says in a hushed tone. "Eleanor was the last person I would've expected to do it."

Samirah bows her head. "I guess you can't always tell if someone's depressed." She looks sideways at her girlfriend for confirmation, but Miranda avoids her eyes. She looks down, silent and sullen, studying the striped pattern in the bedsheets.

Depressed? Is that what Maddox meant last night in my room, when he said it was all his fault? But then why would he refuse to confide in me? "*The less you know, the better.*" As if he were shielding me from something that could hurt me more than him.

"I don't know," I say weakly. "I assume she fell by accident. There weren't any guardrails or anything."

Chloe sighs. "But why would she go up there in the first place?"

I've been asking myself the same question. Maddox brought me to that cliff on our InstaQuest. It can't be a coincidence. He'd obviously been there more than once. Does he use that same spot for all his rendezvous?

But why would he and Eleanor—

My thoughts are interrupted by a buzzing sound from the vicinity of my left hip. It startles me so much that I nearly topple off the desk.

That must be what had me feeling off-kilter before. There's a weight in my pocket that doesn't feel right. I've grown accustomed to its absence. It's been sheltering in the top drawer of my desk since this program began.

My phone.

I took it out this morning, replacing it in the desk drawer with my visor. No way am I ever using that cursed thing again. I don't care if I promised Reese not to use my phone for the duration of the program. As far as I'm concerned, this program is over. Maker Fair is canceled. As soon as my parents come to pick me up, this place and everyone in it will be nothing more than a memory.

The phone in my pocket buzzes again. An InstaLove notification flickers on the screen.

A private message?

The sight of the username makes my pulse rate jump.

PRIVATE MESSAGES WITH REESE

Reese: I know what you did.

There's something downright spooky about her timing. Can she tell that I'm using InstaLove on my phone?

Whatever, Reese. I'm done playing by her rules. She can't seriously expect me to use my visor now. My fingers shake as I text back.

Lowercase: I'm sorry, Reese. I had to switch. Don't be mad.

I hold my breath, hoping that's the end of the conversation, but she doesn't let me off that easily. She texts again.

Reese: You did it on purpose. Didn't you?

My forehead furrows, confused. I must have made some sound of surprise. The other four girls halt their conversation and look up.

"What is it?" Miranda asks. "Who are you texting?"

"No one," I lie as my fingers compose a new message.

Lowercase: What? What are you talking about?

Reese: I saw your code.

Lowercase: What code?

Reese: You wanted her out of the way? Well, you got your wish.

My heart is beating like a drum. Miranda rises, coming toward me, but I stand abruptly and head out of the room. Some instinct tells me not to let the other girls know what Reese said.

I'm in the corridor, halfway to my room, before I text back again.

> **Lowercase:** I don't know what you're talking about. What
>   code?
>
> **Reese:** The hazard alerts. Someone reset a parameter.
>
> **Lowercase:** What? Which parameter?
>
> **Reese:** I think you know.
>
> **Lowercase:** No, I really don't!
>
> **Reese:** The distance parameter. Does that ring any bells,
>   perhaps?

I know which one she means: the variable for how far from the hazard a user has to be before the alert goes off. But why is she texting me about it now?

> **Lowercase:** It's set to 10 feet.
>
> **Reese:** Someone changed it. Do you know what they reset
>   it to?

I reach my door and pull it closed behind me. Maddox must have changed the value in preparation for our demo. We'd talked about resetting it to 2 or 3. I'm about to say so, but Reese messages again before I can summon a reply. This time it isn't a text. She sends me a screenshot. A fragment of my code.

```
distance = -1 ;
```

"Negative?" I whisper, squinting at the screen. A negative number. But that would mean…that would mean…

The gorge rises in my throat. I suddenly understand what Reese is talking about—and why she's so upset.

Negative one.

I close my eyes, and in that instant, last night's dream comes back to me with terrifying clarity.

A girl.

A cliff.

A scream.

And a hazard alert she never saw.

Because the warning message didn't flare until she was one foot over the edge.

24

THE INTERVIEW

NORA

Negative one...

Someone reset a parameter.

Reese's accusation swims inside my head as I wait outside the door of Dr. Carlyle's office. It's quiet here in the waiting room. Three other chairs sit unoccupied, propped against the wall. Ms. Cleary escorted me from Fenmore for my interview, but she left me here in the program director's residence to wait alone.

Alone. Quiet. Too quiet. The only sound is the faint rumble of voices on the other side of the door. I can't tell if the person speaking is male or female, old or young, student or faculty. It may as well be silence. There's nothing to drown out the thoughts spinning in my head.

You did it on purpose. Didn't you?

You wanted her out of the way? Well, you got your wish.

distance = -1 ;

It should've been set to ten. Ten feet. I know it was, the last time I looked at the code. There's no way I could have overwritten it without realizing, is there? A typo? A misplaced elbow leaning on the keyboard of my laptop?

Maybe.

Or maybe someone else changed it.

Only one other person had edit privileges on that file. Not Reese. Not Eleanor. There's no way anyone hacked in. It was housed on a remote server, fully secure and encrypted. Only two people on this campus had access. Me...and my partner.

Maddox's face in my room last night—that haunted expression in his eyes—takes on a whole new meaning. "*It's all my fault,*" he said. Did he reset it? Did he sabotage it on purpose?

I don't want to believe that he did something to Eleanor, but I can't rule it out.

I hug my arms around my stomach and lean forward. My gaze returns to the closed door of Dr. Carlyle's office, then slides sideways over the wallpaper toward the open vestibule outside the waiting area. A camera hovers in the hallway, pointing in the direction of my chair. I can see partway down the corridor beyond. A red neon exit sign points the way outside.

Exit.

I'd love nothing more than to follow that suggestion. More

than anything, I long to go home. I want this nightmare to be over.

The office door swings open. For a moment, only shadows emerge. Then the two of them come out: Maddox, hands shoved in his pockets, looking down at the tassels on his shoes and Dr. Carlyle behind him, with a fatherly hand patting Maddox on the shoulder.

I can't read the expression on Maddox's face. He looks up and meets my eyes, but he doesn't speak. He only gives his head a tiny shake. *Not here.*

"Go straight back to your room," Dr. Carlyle instructs him. "We're still trying to get ahold of your grandmother."

Maddox nods, and Dr. Carlyle shifts his attention to me. "Miss Weinberg. Come in. We're ready for you." He slips back into his office, beckoning for me to follow.

I walk past Maddox. Neither of us speak, but we pass close enough to brush shoulders. For the briefest instant, his hand catches mine. Our fingers clasp. I feel his gentle squeeze. Reassuring me? Offering support? Or asking for my silence?

I can't tell.

Then he's gone, and I make my way into the director's office.

"Sit down, Miss Weinberg."

Dr. Carlyle sits behind a mahogany desk, flanked by two unfamiliar faces.

"This is Dr. Tanaka from the medical examiner's office," he explains, indicating the man on his left dressed in a blue oxford shirt and tie. "And Ms. Peterson here is a social worker trained in grief counseling."

I slip into the chair facing them. The social worker smiles at me warmly, but it doesn't do much to ease the tension in the room. "How are you coping with all of this, Eleanor?"

Eleanor.

That name fills the office like a gunshot. The social worker must see the surprise flash across my face because she glances sideways to Dr. Carlyle.

"Nora," he corrects, steepling his fingers on the desk. "I believe Miss Weinberg prefers to go by Nora."

I look down at my lap to cover my unease. "That's fine. I answer to whatever." My voice sounds funny. Distant and strained. "And I'm coping OK, I guess. I wasn't really friends with—with *her.*"

"You were group members though," Dr. Carlyle replies. "You were collaborating on a project."

I can't interpret the expression on his face. He looks blank, like a poker player concealing his hand. I'm outnumbered in this room, facing questions from three adults, and I can't tell if he's an ally or an adversary.

I stuff my fingers under my thighs to hide their trembling. "Yes—I mean, technically, we were—we were a four-person group. Reese, Eleanor, Maddox, and me. But not really. I mean—I didn't—She and I—" I'm stammering badly. I cut myself off mid-sentence, searching for words. "She and Reese were partners. I was working with Maddox on a separate part of the project."

Dr. Carlyle seems to accept this explanation. He turns in his chair toward the man beside him, offering him the floor.

"OK, Nora," Dr. Tanaka begins. "I'm here gathering information to help determine the decedent's cause and manner of death. I have a few questions that you might be able to help with."

Something about this interview doesn't sit right. I have the strongest feeling this is all a trap designed to trick me. This man is some kind of doctor, not a policeman, but that doesn't change the fact that he's questioning me like a suspect. I look for reassurance to the other two adults.

The social worker leans toward me. "You're not in any trouble, Nora. Dr. Tanaka here is talking to every student in the program."

"Shouldn't my parents be here?"

"That's why Dr. Carlyle and I are present." She has a folder on the desk in front of her, and she opens it to show me. My name sits at the top of a form, with my mother's signature at the bottom. "Your parents authorized Winthrop Academy to act *in loco parentis* for the duration of the program."

My eyes go to each one of them in turn. Dr. Carlyle looks grave, but Ms. Peterson casts me a maternal smile. "Go ahead, dear. It's all right."

I force a deep breath. I don't know why I'm so nervous. I

haven't done anything wrong. I had nothing whatsoever to do with Eleanor's disappearance. I never even had a conversation with the girl. From the moment I arrived on campus, she made a point never to direct a single word in my direction. Only sullen glares and high-handed disdain.

Dr. Tanaka picks up his pen. "When was the last time you saw the deceased?"

"Wednesday, in the main assembly hall." I glance toward the program director. "It was after you came to look over our progress. Eleanor and Reese showed up together."

The medical examiner's pen glints in the lamplight as he jots notes on a yellow legal pad. "How would you describe Miss Winthrop's mood?"

I blow out my cheeks, picturing Eleanor's face as she stood glaring at us from the hall's double doors. Her mood? Not happy. "I guess she seemed…annoyed."

"Did she say what she was annoyed about?"

"Maddox could tell you better. Or Reese. I honestly didn't know her very well."

"Yes." Dr. Tanaka doesn't look up from his page. "We've already spoken with Mr. Drake and Miss Kemp at some length."

I don't know why those words make my fingers clench beneath my thighs. Maddox wouldn't say anything bad about me, I don't think, but Reese is a different story. Did she tell them about the parameter? How much did she say?

You did it on purpose. Didn't you?

You wanted her out of the way? Well, you got your wish.

I didn't know how to defend myself against those texted accusations, but I realize now I have an answer. *Of course!* I sit up straighter, forcing my fingers to unfurl. My hazard alert program had to be downloaded and installed on a user's visor before it would do anything. Maddox and I were planning to push an update to everyone in the program before the Maker Fair demo, but so far it had been installed on only one visor. Not Eleanor's. *Mine.*

The medical examiner stops writing notes. He reaches to retrieve something from the briefcase that sits on the floor at his feet. A clear plastic envelope thunks down on the desk. My stomach twists at the sight of it.

"Do you recognize this item?" he asks.

I nod in confirmation. He has his legal pad propped up so I can't see his notes, but it occurs to me that my relief may have been premature. Something in his tone makes my mouth go dry.

"It's an InSight Visor," I say softly.

"This was found by police divers near the location of the victim's body. Do you have any idea how it got there?"

The victim's body…

The sound of those words makes me flinch. Somehow, until this moment, a part of me had held out hope that it was all a mistake. A trick. A carefully constructed illusion, planned by Eleanor herself.

"Nora?" Dr. Carlyle prompts.

"Are you sure…" I whisper. "Are you sure it was her?"

They all stare back at me. "Yes, dear," the grief counselor says gently. "I'm so sorry, I thought you'd heard. Eleanor Winthrop's remains were identified this morning. She appeared to have fallen from…"

Oh my God.

Dr. Tanaka clears his throat. "Nora, I need you to answer the question. Do you have any idea how this InSight Visor ended up in the water?"

I don't know what to say. My thoughts fly in a million different directions. "N-no," I stammer. "I guess she must have been wearing it when she—when she—" I stop, unable to complete my sentence. My eyes dart to the visor once again.

Someone has applied a neon-orange sticker to the inside of the frames beside the serial number. Dr. Tanaka points to it with the capped end of his pen. "Yes, Miss Kemp turned over the user data she'd collected. This serial number was not originally assigned to Eleanor Winthrop. Do you know anything about that?"

I shake my head, unable to speak.

"It turns out that this visor was assigned to you, Eleanor *Weinberg*, on July 1. My colleagues were also able to lift some latent fingerprints that I imagine belong to you."

Dr. Carlyle's face finally registers a discernible emotion. His mouth drops open, and his eyebrows arch upward behind the wire frames of his glasses.

My hand rises to my throat. I tug at my shirt collar. Why is this room so hot? Stiflingly hot. The three questioners await my explanation, and their gazes feel like heat lamps searing into me.

I look down at my knees. I'm too tangled up in this business. Way too close for comfort.

"Go ahead, Nora," Ms. Peterson prompts me. "Do you have any explanation?"

What does she expect me to say?

Warning messages are going off like fireworks in the back of my mind. I don't need a visor to help me picture them.

> **SYSTEM ALERT**
> Warning! You are approaching an unseen hazard. Stop moving and proceed with extreme caution.

I should stop. End this interview. There's a reason all three of them are on the opposite side of the desk. They're all lined up against me. Every word I say brings me closer to the brink of danger. Who knows what awful things Reese already told them.

They haven't asked about the negative parameter yet, but I have a feeling the questions are coming. *Who changed it? Did you do it on purpose? Who else could have sabotaged that code but you?*

Only one other person had edit privileges on the subfolder where my code resides. Maddox.

"It was supposed to be a game…" That's what he said to me last night. *"The less you know, the better…"*

Why? The better to protect me? Or the easier to throw me under the bus? The fact that my visor was retrieved from the bottom of the lake—that's not going to help me look any less suspicious.

"Miss Weinberg." Dr. Tanaka taps his pen against his pad. "Do you have any idea how Eleanor Winthrop came to be wearing your visor on the night she fell to her death?"

My brain whirs uselessly, searching my memory for anything else I could tell them. Anything concrete. Any shred of evidence to back up the fact that I'm telling the truth.

"The backpack!"

I say the words too loudly. All three of their heads snap up at once, struck by my vehemence. I lean forward, resting my fingertips on the edge of Dr. Carlyle's desk, as my words tumble out in a rush.

"I lost my backpack Wednesday afternoon. My visor was inside. I left it in the assembly hall, and someone returned it to my room later. They must have switched my visor for a different one. You'll see it—I'm sure you will—if you go back and look!"

Dr. Carlyle raises a hand to slow me down. "Hold on, Nora. I'm not sure I understand. If we go back and look at what?"

I'm breathless now. I stop and force myself to inhale. "The security camera footage. Go look at Wednesday afternoon. You keep the recordings archived somewhere, right? You must!"

Dr. Carlyle nods. "For seventy-two hours."

"All that footage has been turned over to our office," the medical examiner adds. "We have our analysts reviewing it."

I close my eyes, and my heart resumes a halfway normal rhythm. They have the footage. That means they have the truth. It's not my word against Reese's—or against Maddox's.

There's only one small doubt that remains in the back of my mind. Should I tell them? Or will it only make things worse?

"The thing is," I say softly as I smooth my dampened palms against my thighs. "There's a chance—"

"Can you speak up, Nora?" Dr. Carlyle interrupts. "I didn't catch that."

"There's a hack."

He watches me intently, waiting for me to say more.

"The security camera system," I explain. "It's not exactly... secure."

Dr. Carlyle's jaw drops open yet again. "Nora, are you saying that you've hacked—"

"No, no!" I protest. "Not me. The others. Maddox, Reese, and Eleanor. They've been gaming the camera feeds for years."

25

PICK YOUR BATTLES

_____

MADDOX

I pace my room like it's a jail cell. It might as well be. I'll trade it for a jail cell soon enough.

To think I was so concerned about Eleanor and her money. As if some unpaid medical bills were the worst thing I had to fear. What a joke.

The walls of this room are closing in. It's only a matter of time before it all comes crashing down. The unaltered security footage is archived for seventy-two hours. It's all been turned over to the investigators. They have analysts combing through it. They'll find what they're looking for soon—if they haven't found it already.

I still don't understand exactly what went down the night Eleanor disappeared. I only know how it looks for me.

Bad.

I haven't slept for a couple of days. My eyes feel hot and gritty, but I can't make my brain shut off. I keep reliving that afternoon and evening in my head, going over it again and again, as if I can somehow turn back time and make the whole mess go away.

But I can't. I know that. Just like I can't change the archived footage. The present can be gamed, but the past is unalterable.

And yet here I go again, rehashing it…

I spent most of the day in the assembly hall with Nora until Eleanor walked in on us. That was the last time I saw Eleanor alive, and I'll never forget the final words I said to her: *"Have it your way. Have everything your way."*

Then I let her walk away, with Nora's backpack slung over her shoulder.

Pick your battles, I told myself at the time. Looks like I picked wrong.

I failed to consider that Nora's visor might be in that bag. How I could have overlooked that detail, I'll never know.

I sent an InstaQuest to Nora that night, and I hacked all the camera feeds on the path from the dorms to the edge of campus so no one would see us breaking curfew. But it wasn't Nora who accepted the invitation and followed the trail of little rabbits meant for her eyes only. It wasn't Nora who climbed the locked gate at the western edge of campus.

It was Eleanor.

She must have found Nora's visor and used it. That's the only way she could have intercepted the InstaQuest I sent.

She had to have gotten up there before me. I found the clifftop empty, and I waited for hours at The Overlook for Nora to arrive. I thought she blew me off. It wasn't until the following morning that I realized what must have happened. Eleanor was missing—and when I went to check the archived footage, there she was in black and white, headed to The Overlook ten minutes ahead of me.

I press my palms against my temples and wipe them down the length of my face.

There's no way anyone will believe I had nothing to do with Eleanor's fall. I've known it since the morning she vanished, and I spent that whole day praying I was wrong. She'd faked it somehow, I told myself. She'd pop up any second, laughing that maddening laugh. She was merely playing a prank—a sick joke to get me kicked out of school.

The inserted GIFs still remain in the source code where I left them. I didn't dare hack in to take them down and revert to the unaltered feeds. Not with Eleanor missing, and campus security on high alert.

Maybe I should delete them now. My eyes shift sideways toward my laptop, but I'm distracted before I can type a keystroke. A knock sounds at my door.

I jump to my feet. It must be Dr. Carlyle—or maybe that investigator from the medical examiner's office, back to question me in a far less friendly tone. I can only hope it's not the police here to arrest me.

My eyes fly around my room. There's another way out, a fire escape beyond my window. I could make a run for it.

But how far could I possibly get?

No. No point delaying the inevitable. Time to face the firing squad. I take a deep breath and square my shoulders. Then I swing open the door.

NORA

I sink down on the stone bench and close my eyes. I held myself together for the duration of the interview in Dr. Carlyle's office, but my nerves caught up with me as soon as I stepped outside. My knees have turned to rubber, too weak to support my weight.

I need to talk to Maddox.

I can't stop thinking about the evidence Dr. Tanaka showed me before he sent me on my way. Bits and pieces of data—fragments of disjointed conversations—that the forensic analysts were able to retrieve from the memory card of the waterlogged InSight Visor. Most of it had come from me before the visors were switched. There was only one thing at the end I didn't recognize.

Congratulations, Lowercase!

Your crush Maddox has invited you on a True Love InstaQuest!

[CONTINUE] [DECLINE]

At first I thought I was looking at the remnants of our clifftop beta test. But the time stamp made no sense. Three days ago? A few minutes after curfew? I was about to tell the interviewer that it must be a mistake, but then he pulled out one more screenshot from his file—and the sight of it turned my blood to ice.

> **Maddox:** No more scared little rabbits, Nora. I'll explain everything. Come to The Overlook. Tonight. I'll be waiting.

Try as I might, I can't avoid the inevitable conclusion.

Maddox sabotaged the alert system. He was the only one who could have changed that parameter. He set it to -1 and then he sent me the invitation, knowing it would be after sundown by the time I made the hike uphill. Too dark to see clearly. So easy to make a misstep without a hazard warning to alert me to the danger.

Only the wrong Eleanor showed up. The other Eleanor had my visor. She intercepted that message and went to the cliff to confront Maddox in my place.

I don't want to believe that Maddox would intentionally hurt me. The boy I like. The one I thought I might *love*...

But what were those feelings based on? A few weeks of app-facilitated flirtation. I can't escape the cold, hard facts. I barely know him. The boy I thought I loved doesn't exist. He's an illusion. A piece of augmented reality. A more palatable version of the real Maddox beneath—a Maddox I've never really known.

My stomach won't stop clenching and unclenching. I keep reviewing every interaction I've ever had with him, searching for some clue to what's been real and what's been fake.

The boy with the easy smile who rescued me from a swimming pool…who made me laugh and blush and shiver when he grazed my shoulders with his fingertips…who reached out to me when I had no friends…who saved me from weeks of partnerless loserdom…the boy who invited me on an InstaQuest to tell me how he really feels…

"I'll explain. For real. I promise. But not here. Later. Somewhere private."

Or the boy I spied in Eleanor Winthrop's dorm room the first week of the program…doctoring the campus security system…scheming with his so-called ex…showing me a totally different side to his character if I'd had enough sense to pay attention.

"Because she'll do all the work and let me coast."

It's like he's two different people, two different versions. The real Maddox and the avatar. I don't know which is which.

A muffled sound escapes my lips. There's something else, some tiny bubble of anxiety floating around my brain. I close my eyes and concentrate to bring it to the surface.

The visors…

My spine goes ramrod straight. Whoever took mine from my

backpack didn't just steal it—they switched it for another pair. Was that Eleanor's visor in my bag?

That would explain some things, like why Maddox's account had that weird creepy avatar and username.

M

Maddox didn't change that. Eleanor must have done it from her end. She deleted his name and grayed out his image. But why?

There's only one reason I can think of: because she couldn't bear to look at him any longer. She couldn't stand the sight of his deceitful, conniving face.

Honestly, I can't say I blame her.

26

A KNOCK AT THE DOOR

MADDOX

The hinges groan as I swing my door open. I brace, preparing for the worst, and don't resume breathing until I see the man on the other side.

Not Dr. Carlyle.

Not the police.

Instead, I'm face-to-face with a blond, blue-eyed golden boy in a Metallica T-shirt and ripped jeans. He looks different from the last time I saw him, with his formerly shoulder-length hair cut to a short, spiky crop. I could recognize him purely from his outfit though. His signature style hasn't changed since his Summer Program glory days. No one else would dare dress so casually on this campus—no one but the Maker Program's most famous alum.

Emerson Kemp was the last person I expected to darken my doorway, but I can't complain about the temporary reprieve.

"Hey," I greet him crisply. "What are you doing here?"

He peers past me over my shoulder, his eyes scanning around my room. "Hey man, have you seen my sister?"

"No. Why would Reese be—"

He cuts me off, shaking his head. "Some girl named… I forget. Something with an M…"

"Miranda?" I supply. "Was she wearing a gray wool cap?"

"Yeah. Sure." He makes a noise in the back of his throat to signal his lack of interest. "Miranda. Whatever. Some girl lurking around outside. She told me Reese might have been headed over here."

I can't help but look at him askance. *Outside?* That can't be right. Why would either of those girls be anywhere besides their own dorms? Aren't we all supposed to be on lockdown?

Emerson cranes to see past me. I step back and sweep my arm to indicate the emptiness of my room. "I haven't seen her. Why would Reese come here?"

"Looking for that new girl. Lowercase." Emerson's eyes shift back and forth. He slouches against my doorframe and swipes his hand across his forehead, mopping away the sweat that beads at his hairline. "I take it you haven't seen Lowercase either."

"Earlier," I tell him. "At Dr. C's office for her interview. Why? What's going on?"

Emerson gestures for me to come close. He drops his voice.

"I'm here to pick up Reese. The school demanded someone from the family come take her off their hands."

I wince, sucking in the air between my teeth. That doesn't sound good. I haven't talked to Reese since we all heard the news, but she can't be taking it well. She loved Eleanor like a sister. The two of them were inseparable since the day they met in second grade. "Are they worried Reese might try to hurt herself?"

"No, not really." Emerson looks sideways down the hall to make sure there's no one else within earshot. "More like she might try to hurt someone *else*."

Who? *Me?*

I fold my arms across my chest. Not that I'm alarmed, really. What could Reese possibly do to me? The girl has a wicked temper, but I'm pretty sure I could take her in a fight.

Still, not a great sign that Reese has her ire pointed in my direction. How much of the truth has she figured out? She has access to all that InstaLove data—everything except for private messages. She must know about the quest I sent. Does she think I did something to Eleanor on purpose?

I take a step backward into my room. There's something else... Something Emerson said...

Miranda told him Reese came here, but not looking for me. Looking for *Lowercase.*

"Nora?" My attention jolts back to Emerson's face. "Does Reese blame Nora? She had nothing to do with it!"

"Apparently, my sister disagrees."

I sit down heavily on the edge of my bed. This whole damned mess has my head spinning. I need to talk to Reese. I should have done it days ago, as soon as Eleanor went missing. I should have told Reese about the InstaQuest that night. I should have told *someone*.

Instead I chose the coward's way. Silence and denial. Hoping if I kept my mouth shut, I might magically get out of this mess unscathed.

And Nora could be the one to pay the price.

I rake my fingers through my hair. "Reese wouldn't—she wouldn't do anything violent, would she?"

NORA

I can't sit still. I rise from the bench and walk briskly in the direction of Fenmore Hall.

I should have headed back there directly from my interview, instead of stopping here to look at my phone. I left my visor in my room, tucked out of sight inside my desk. Unattended. *Unprotected.* I didn't even bother to lock the drawer!

How was I so oblivious? I should have taken it with me to the interview. I never should have let it out of my sight. I can only pray it will still be there when I return.

I need that visor. It might be my only hope.

There's only one thing I know for sure. Maddox reset the

distance parameter, and he'll let me take the blame if I don't defend myself. He must have had some reason to change it—some motive to want me dead. He never gave me any reason to feel unsafe, but maybe he said something to Eleanor…

And if I have her visor, that means I have access to their Interaction History.

I reach the staircase inside Fenmore, gripping the bannister as I take the steps two at a time. The door of my dorm room stands open a crack. Did I leave it that way in my haste to get to Dr. Carlyle's office? For the life of me, I can't remember.

I hurry inside and shut the door behind me, breathing hard from my run across campus. I lunge for the desk drawer and yank it open. There it is, right where I left it. My visor illuminates the drawer with the light from its blue LED.

"Oh, thank God," I breathe, as I press the lenses to my eyes.

Welcome back, L!

I flick away the welcome notification and navigate to the history option, scanning through the columns of avatars for that faceless gray box I saw before.

M

My palms feel hot and sticky. I wipe them against my thighs.

Something tells me that it's wrong to eavesdrop on a dead girl. I should stop now. Take off this visor. Proceed directly to Dr. Carlyle's office, and let the adults sort everything out. But will they listen to me?

I doubt it. Not after Maddox filled their heads with lies. I need to go to them with more than my own suspicions. I need proof.

I double-blink at the gray avatar to pull up their messages. Their last exchange populates on my screen.

PRIVATE MESSAGES WITH M

M: I can't stop thinking about you.

L: I know.

M: Do you really?

L: I tend to have that effect on people 😉

M: Haha this is true.

L: I can't stop thinking about you either.

M: No one knows, right?

L: How many times are you going to ask me that?

M: Eleanor...

L: No one knows! I'm being super careful.

M: What about Reese?

L: No. She has no clue.

M: Good.

L: But I want to be alone with you again.

M: Soon.

L: Before Maker Fair, right? We'll sneak off somewhere for
a little bit?

M: Not while we're on campus. No.

L: Whaaa? Why not?

M: We've been over this!

L: Since when were you such a nervous wreck?

M: We can't risk it. All those cameras everywhere.

L: That never stopped you before.

M: Just stick to the plan, OK? Promise me.

I can't breathe.

This is not the text exchange of two exes who recently split up.

"I can't stop thinking about you…"

"I can't stop thinking about you either…"

Well, that answers *that*.

Maddox never broke up with Eleanor. Of course not. I should have known. But I still don't understand what they were up to. Why would they bother sneaking around when everyone knew they were together?

None of this makes sense. I frown as my eyes track downward, scrolling to read more of the exchange.

And that's when I see it.

The words I was seeking.

All the proof I need.

That says what I think it does, right? I'm not taking it out of context? I go to reread it again, but my view is blocked by another notification.

> There are one or more InstaLove user(s) nearby. Interact to
> raise your score!

A knock sounds on my door, firm and insistent. I freeze, whipping off the visor. That better not be Maddox. I pray it's someone else. I'm not ready to confront him. Not yet.

Not until I've figured out the truth.

27

IN THE DARK

MADDOX

My fault.

My fault.

Everything's my fault.

The words echo in my head like the *drip, drip, drip* of a leaky faucet. Impossible to ignore. Impossible to turn off.

Why am I such a weakling? I've handled everything wrong. *Everything.* And now Nora might be in danger—all because I lacked the intestinal fortitude to own up to my mistakes.

For some reason, I can hear Eleanor's tinkly laughter in my head, calling me the nickname she bestowed on me from our childhood sandbox days. Moxie. I finally get the joke. If there's anything in this world that I have less of, it's moxie.

I should have told Dr. C the truth—and I should have told Reese

too. It was my fault Eleanor fell. I finally stood up to her, refused to
play her games, and she came to The Overlook to confront me.

But I didn't say any of that when I sat in the program director's office. I played dumb. I lied my ass off, too scared of the
consequences if I told the truth. Now Reese blames Nora, and
she isn't playing games. If the look on her brother's face was any
indication, Reese is out for blood, and Nora has no idea of the
approaching danger.

Another girl I've led to the brink of disaster, completely in the
dark.

```
if moxie-level <= 0 :
    maddox ('covers his ass')
    eleanor ('takes the fall')
```

No.

No, no, no.

I can't let it end the same way twice. I have to find Nora—or
Reese—before they find each other.

"I'll help you search," I offered Emerson just now, bounding
in his wake when he turned to leave. I'm not supposed to wander
from my room, but that's the least of my transgressions at this
point. Emerson accepted with a curt nod, and we set off down
Winthrop's network of pathways in opposite directions, scouring
campus for any trace of the girls.

So far, nothing.

I pick up my pace and don my visor as I go, hoping it might alert me to the presence of their avatars.

> There are one or more InstaLove user(s) nearby. Interact to raise your score!

That sounds promising. I turn the corner, with a burst of hope quickening my steps. "Please be Nora," I murmur under my breath. But that would be too easy. Of course it isn't her.

> Samirah

An interaction prompt pops up, but I ignore it. I whip off my visor and rub my eyes.

"Hey!" Samirah says. "Have you seen Miranda?"

"She isn't in her room?"

"No, she never came back after her interview."

I frown, my impatience growing with every second that slips by. There are only two avatars I'm interested in locating at the moment. Miranda isn't on the list.

Samirah chews at her thumbnail. "I'm just worried. She seemed upset earlier."

"She's out here somewhere," I reply. "Emerson bumped into her before."

"Emerson Kemp? He's here?"

I nod vaguely and move to step past her, but I pull up short before I've gone three paces. I stop and turn around. "Actually… Do you want to help? As long as we're all out here searching for people…"

Samirah's eyes narrow. "Why? Who are you searching for?"

"Reese," I say. "Or Nora. Before they find each other—"

"Oh! I saw Reese."

Something catches in my throat. "You did? Where?"

"Fenmore! I just passed her. She was heading up the stairs."

NORA

The knock sounds again as my eyes dart around my room. I don't feel safe confronting Maddox. Here. Alone. No witnesses. Not when he knows how to hack the surveillance cameras.

There's not enough furniture in here to hide. Should I try the closet? Or maybe take the fire escape?

I shove aside the window shade and yank at the sash, but the window is jammed. The white paint chips away beneath my fingernails as I tug in vain.

"Going somewhere?"

A voice speaks behind me from the open doorway. I whirl around, clapping my hand to my chest to calm my labored breathing.

Not Maddox. Thank God.

"Reese!" I lean against my desk, removing my visor gently so as not to clear the message exchange I was viewing. "You should see this. I figured out—"

I break off mids-entence. Something in Reese's face makes goose bumps rise on my arms. She removes her visor as well, and there's a look in her eyes that sends my pulse racing—a look that says she's not interested in hearing anything I have to say.

She comes toward me and I back away, but there's nowhere to go. She has me cornered.

"Wait!" I hold both hands in front of me, palms out, to stop her progress. "Listen to me. I know who reset the distance parameter! I have the proof right here."

The visor dangles from its cord around my neck. I pull it off and hold it out, but she doesn't take it from me. Her face darkens as she sweeps her hair out of her eyes.

I hold my breath, unsure whether my words can get through to her. She's already come to her own conclusions. I doubt anything I say can change her mind, but I have no choice. I have to make her listen. "Reese," I try again, taking a tentative step toward her. I hold out the visor before me like a shield. "Please. Look at this. You'll see."

Something seems to shift inside her head. Her eyes meet mine.

"It's Eleanor's visor," I tell her quickly, seeing her hesitate. "She switched with me!"

Reese shakes her head, blue hair scattering about her shoulders.

The pin-straight strands she normally keeps so sleek now look messy and uncombed. She glares at me down the bridge of her nose. "That's not true. She would've told me."

No, Reese. She didn't tell you everything. I lower my eyes to the floor and address my words to her feet. "She didn't tell you about Stanford."

There's a long silence. My eyes dart to Reese again. She hunches forward as if someone punched her in the stomach. I reach to touch her arm, but she jerks away. "You have no idea what you're talking about."

That much is true. I'm an outsider here at Winthrop. I barely understand half the things the other students say to one another— but none of that matters now. All I know is I need Reese to stop flinging false accusations in my direction.

"Look at this," I insist, holding the visor out to her again. "Capital L. That was Eleanor's username, right?"

Reese scowls at me, but she takes the visor from my hands and slips it on.

I hear her gasp, and I know what she's reading: the part of the message exchange I was looking at before she knocked on my door.

PRIVATE MESSAGES WITH M

L: It's no big deal. A reset parameter. Everyone will think it's a typo!

M: Uhhh that's a terrible idea.

> **L:** It's the only way! Will you please listen to me?
>
> **M:** You want it set to 0?
>
> **L:** Yes...no even better! Set it to -1!
>
> **M:** Babe, you can't be serious. Don't you know how dangerous that is?
>
> **L:** It's only a 3-foot drop! We just want the demo to fail so everyone's distracted.

"Do you see?" I ask Reese breathlessly. "The distance parameter! Did you see that part?"

Reese takes off the visor, but she doesn't look at me. Her eyes shift over my shoulder toward the door. I'm not sure she realizes I'm still standing here.

"M," she murmurs. "It was M."

Her body quivers like a tightly wound spring. There's a violence in her eyes that makes me take a half step backward.

"Reese, we should show this to Dr. Carlyle. He'll know what to do." I reach for the visor, but she snatches it away. Before I can say another word, she steps around me and takes off, heading for the stairs.

"Wait!" I clatter after her. "Where are you going?"

Reese answers me over her shoulder, but she shows no sign of slowing down. "I'll take it from here." She sprints ahead of me, heading outside, and she turns right at the first fork in the gravel paths.

"Stop!" I call out, following in her wake. "The director's

residence is the other way!" But it's clear Reese has a different destination in mind as she dashes past Grier and heads toward the western edge of campus.

I know what lies that way.

A locked gate. A rough-hewn staircase made of rock. A trail-head. A cliff.

Every instinct inside of me screams not to go up there again. But I have no choice. She has the visor—the only proof of my own innocence. I don't dare let it out of my sight.

28

A GATHERING STORM

NORA

Reese has nearly reached the tree line by the time she stops. She draws to a halt so abruptly that I have to sidestep to avoid crashing into her. Eleanor's visor covers her eyes, and her hands grope before her as if she's blindfolded.

I circle in front of her. I'm close enough to see her nostrils flare with each indrawn breath, but she doesn't acknowledge my presence. Is she ignoring me? Or perhaps I really am invisible this time.

"Reese?" My voice falters, but I force myself to speak up. "What are you doing? Is the visor malfunctioning?"

She doesn't respond. Instead, she takes a long stride forward. I have to step off the edge of the path to make room.

"Reese!" I say more loudly. "Reese, can you hear me?"

"Shhh," she whispers harshly. One hand swats at me like I'm

some annoying gnat circling around her head. "Go away. You're not needed."

What's happening right now?

Maybe I should go back. Forget the visor. I should report directly to Dr. Carlyle's office and tell him about the messages I read. The director's residence lies all the way on the other side of campus. I turn my head in that direction, weighing my options.

A line of storm clouds gathers at the horizon beyond the campus buildings. I can sense the change in the air that comes with an approaching storm.

I can't go back. Without the visor, it's my word against Maddox's—my awkward lack of poise against Winthrop Academy's most accomplished smooth talker. I can see Dr. Carlyle now, clapping a hand on Maddox's shoulder, striving to keep a straight face, but all the while living vicariously through the antics of his favorite student.

No. If it's my word against Maddox, I don't stand a chance…

And it's not like I could retrieve those messages from anywhere else. I'm sure Maddox deleted any trace of that exchange from his own visor. It might be stored by InstaLove on a remote server somewhere, but even Reese didn't have access to that data. "*I'll be monitoring your InstaLove usage,*" I remember her saying when she first handed me my visor. "*Everything except for private messages.*"

I swallow hard, watching Reese. She holds out both hands in front of her, and all ten of her fingers wiggle up and down.

Suddenly it hits me, what she's doing. I could almost smack myself in the forehead for being so dense.

Typing!

She didn't head in this direction because of The Overlook. She must have spotted a communication kiosk over here. Now she's inside, typing out a message at some augmented-reality keyboard that only she can see.

"Are you sending an InstaQuest?" I ask. "Now?"

Her fingers continue typing as she growls out an answer from between her teeth. "Obviously."

"Who? Maddox?"

She gives a snort, but the corners of her mouth lift upward. "I'm inviting our friend M for a little *tête à tête*."

MADDOX

I race to Fenmore with Samirah at my heels, praying we're not too late. We need to get to Nora's room before Reese finds her. I pass the front stoop in a flying leap and shoulder my way through the heavy doors, but my path is blocked as I step into the dormitory's entrance hall. Emerson hustles down the stairs, followed by Dr. Carlyle.

"Maddox? Samirah?" The program director peers down at us from behind the wire rims of his glasses. "What are you doing out here? I told you to wait in your rooms!"

"It's my fault," Emerson explains. "I asked Maddox to help me look for Reese."

"She's in there!" My voice sounds ragged as I point toward the second floor. "Upstairs! We have to—"

I don't have time to explain. I move to push past both of them, but Emerson stops me.

"No, she's not."

"But Samirah said…"

"I saw Reese going up there," Samirah contributes, looking decidedly uneasy beneath Dr. Carlyle's scrutiny. "I came out here because Miranda—"

"Miranda's missing too." I speak tersely. Every instinct in me screams to get a move on. My body vibrates up and down on the balls of my feet. *Forget Miranda. Find Nora. Find Reese!* If the girls aren't upstairs in their rooms, then we need to search. "We should all split up. Or maybe—" I break off and snap my finger as a better idea hits me. "The feeds! The surveillance feeds! If we log into the security server, we should be able to spot them. Unless…"

"Unless what, Maddox?" Dr. Carlyle has his hands on his hips, with a look on his face I hardly recognize. There's something missing in his expression. An undercurrent of bemused affection. A look that says he knows I'm getting up to no good, and he might not condone my methods, but he approves of my enterprising spirit. That's how he's always looked at me.

But now there's a tightness to his voice that I haven't heard before. Not angry, exactly. I've seen Dr. Carlyle lose his temper once or twice, but this is different…and far more unnerving.

There's a hint of desperation behind those wire rims—like a man who thought he stood on solid ground, only to feel the earth give way beneath his feet—a man whose carefully crafted illusion of control has begun to flicker around the edges.

"Yes, Maddox?" he prompts. "Did you have something else to tell me?"

He phrases it as a question, but I can tell it's not. The surveillance feeds… The hack… All the blood in my body turns to ice as I realize the truth.

He knows.

Dr. Carlyle watches me, eyes flashing with silent accusation, but Emerson intercedes before the program director can get a word out. He clutches a smartphone in his hand and taps at it quickly with his thumbs.

"Maddox is right. The surveillance feeds… I can't believe I forgot about those!"

Dr. C freezes, catching sight of Emerson's screen. "Is that—"

"We're in," Emerson mutters without looking up. "Here are the live feeds from Fenmore second floor, but I don't see any sign—"

"Emerson!" Dr. Carlyle thunders, finding his voice at last. "What the hell do you think you're doing?"

Emerson turns toward him, matching thunder with a steely gaze. "I'm looking for my sister," he says. "Whom you would not have lost in the first place, if this institution had the slightest sense for cybersecurity."

Whoa.

The two of them stand toe to toe. Chests puffed out. And now I'm the one at a loss for words. I have to hand it to Emerson. The guy has balls of steel. Three years ago, he was a student here, and not a particularly well-regarded one. Emerson nearly faced expulsion for the sheer variety of ways he broke school rules. Only Eleanor, pleading with her parents for leniency, saved his ass. But now, with his ripped jeans and heavy metal T-shirt, Emerson stares down Dr. Carlyle like he owns this place.

Dr. Carlyle blinks first. He takes a step backward, conceding the point. He removes a handkerchief from the pocket of his blazer and mops his brow.

Emerson returns his attention to his phone. "What about the western edge of campus? Isn't anyone monitoring the feeds over there?"

"No." I say the word, but my voice is too hoarse for anyone to hear. Campus security might be watching the video feeds, but they won't see Reese or Nora…or even Miranda. All those feeds have been altered since the night I sent the InstaQuest—the night Eleanor disappeared.

I need to tell them, but my throat is too tight to speak. I clear it to get their attention and choke out a few short words. "You won't find them."

Dr. Carlyle glances toward me.

"Not on the live feeds." I address my words to the program director's pointed oxford shoes. "Only in the archives."

I feel sick to my stomach, like I've been standing in the sun too long, even though the sky above has gone a dreary gray. I lean against the stone balustrade beside me and bury my head in my hands.

Emerson will catch my meaning. He knows about the hack. Hell, he invented it. He looks toward me, eyebrows raised, but Samirah interrupts before he can utter a question.

"Look!" She peers over Emerson's shoulder at his phone, pointing to the screen. "There! There she is!"

I look up, and my pulse quickens with hope. *Nora?*

But no. I see my mistake from the expression that transforms Samirah's face. Not Nora. Not Reese. She just caught sight of Miranda.

29

THE OVERLOOK

NORA

You'd think the universe had sent me enough warning messages to last a lifetime. But no. Here I am again, huffing and puffing from the steep climb upward to The Overlook, with my sandals chafing at my feet and sweat pouring down my temples.

The view of the lake below does nothing to soothe my jangled nerves. The storm clouds overhead reflect against the choppy surface, turning the water from blue to an ominous shade of dark gray.

The wind has grown insistent. It whips at my hair, and a raindrop lands on my shoulder. I hold out my hand, palm up.

Drop. Drop, plop.

Those aren't the misty raindrops of a passing summer sprinkle. They're the fat kind that serve as a warning of an oncoming downpour.

Great. An exposed cliff in a thunderstorm? Probably not the wisest place to be. But I can't go back. Not without Reese. Not without the visor.

I glance at the girl before me. Reese stands at the center of the clifftop with Eleanor's visor concealing her eyes. She has her back to me, facing toward the yellow police tape and the ledge beyond.

I wipe my wet hand against my shorts and retreat closer to the trailhead under the branches of the nearest tree. "We shouldn't be up here," I call to Reese. "There's a storm coming!"

She merely shrugs. "So leave if you're afraid. Run along."

If only I had my cell phone. I reached for it as Reese flung herself over the locked metal gate at the bottom of the trail, but I found my pocket empty. I must have left it in my room. Now I'm caught up here empty-handed. No visor. No phone. No way to call for help beyond the sound of my own voice, and the hasty message I traced in the dirt with the edge of my shoe before I clambered after Reese. I can only hope that some responsible adult—Dr. Carlyle, security, the police—will notice it and come after us.

Reese lifts the visor from her face and turns to confront me. "You should go back, Lowercase. This doesn't concern you."

Lowercase.

Something in the way she says that nickname makes me tremble. How can she still call me that, after everything that's happened? I always assumed Eleanor was the one who refused to let me go by my real name, but I don't know that for a fact. I never heard Eleanor say so to my face. It was Reese who changed the username on my InstaLove account. Reese invented that nickname in the first place. Didn't she?

I think back, visualizing the scene on the first day of the program, surrounded by five laughing girls in Reese's room. No, it wasn't Reese. It was one of the others who first suggested "Lowercase." Maybe Mirand—

Wait a sec.

Miranda...

Of course it was Miranda! How could I have overlooked that? How many times have I heard Maddox refer to her by the shortened form of her name?

M!

My eyes fly back to Reese. She lifts the visor to her face again. Her lips press together, and her jaw works from the way she grinds her teeth. Whoever lies on the receiving end of that InstaQuest, they haven't responded yet. I assumed it was Maddox, but perhaps the letter M stands for a different name entirely.

There's something else—some other detail I'm missing. I look down and force myself to focus.

M.

The single letter, M.

I've heard Maddox speak that nickname aloud, but I've *seen* it somewhere too. Weeks ago, at the beginning of the program, I saw it on a screen, not a visor. My laptop?

A hazy memory resurfaces. I was sitting with my laptop on

that hidden bench behind the hedges, looking through the Maker Project ideas on TeenHack.

And there it was, that single-letter username: M.

What project had M posted? I recall feeling creeped out by it, but I can't remember the details. Definitely not the modified potter's wheel I saw in Miranda's room…

I can feel my brain turning—trying and failing to retrieve a memory—like the spinning rainbow wheel on my laptop whenever my CPU usage spikes. I blink to clear the sensation.

It doesn't matter anyway. Judging from Reese's body language, I'll find out M's identity soon enough. She pulls her hands from her pockets, and her fingers ball at her sides in two closed fists.

"Come on, M," she mutters. "Get your lying ass up here."

MADDOX

My chest deflates as I look to the video feeds displayed on Emerson's phone. A figure emerges from behind a closed office door, with a middle-aged woman behind her. The two of them hug briefly. Then the girl tugs her beanie lower over her forehead.

Miranda.

"That's my office," Dr. Carlyle says under his breath. "She's with Ms. Peterson. She must have gone back for more grief counseling."

Samirah looks to him. "Can I…"

He nods before she gets the words out, and Samirah takes off in the direction of the program director's residence. To meet her girlfriend. To offer support and love. Because that's what two people in a healthy relationship do.

But I wouldn't know much about that, would I?

I swipe the back of my hand across my mouth and sink down on the marble steps. "What about Nora? What about Reese?"

"I'm looking," Emerson replies.

"Try the gate. The one that leads to The Overlook. It's serial number 19X9852."

Dr. Carlyle lifts an eyebrow. "You know that off the top of your head, Maddox?"

I avoid his gaze—and the accusation in his voice. Yes, I know the serial number. I looked it up last night. That camera holds the evidence of my involvement in Eleanor's fall. I probably signed my own death certificate by bringing it up in front of Dr. C.

But I can't think about that now. Nora's in danger. That's the only thing that matters.

I keep my eyes trained on Emerson as he examines the image on his phone. "Nothing there on the live feed," he says.

Of course not. The live video still bears the altered image I didn't have the courage to remove. "What about the archived footage?"

From where I sit, my eyes are level with the cell phone in Emerson's hands. I can't see the screen, only the edge of his black rubber cell phone case cradled between his palms. I have no idea what he's looking at when he sucks in a harsh breath.

"Emerson?" Dr. Carlyle prompts.

I lower my head, bracing for the blow about to fall. Emerson must have rewound too far back. Did he see me scaling the chicken wire fence?

"What the…" Emerson murmurs. His voice drops so low that .next word comes out no louder than an exhalation of breath. "…hell?"

I rise and attempt a peek at the image on his screen, but he jerks the phone away. He shields it with his shoulder. I can only make out the black text box I've come to know so well.

InstaLove…

An InstaQuest…

"Who?" I ask him. "Who sent you that? Is it Reese?"

He answers in a strangled voice. "I think it's—it's from—"

But he never finishes his sentence. With no further explanation, he turns and bolts through the heavy wooden doors.

THE DROPBOX
(FINAL ENTRY)

ELEANOR

https://bit.ly/dropboxL

Dropbox > Personal

File Name	Created on	Visible to
Entry 1.txt	7/1/2019	Deleted
Entry 2.txt	7/2/2019	Deleted
Entry 3.txt	7/9/2019	Deleted
Entry 4.txt	7/10/2019	Deleted
Entry 5.txt	7/17/2019	Deleted
Entry 6.txt	7/17/2019	Deleted
Entry 7.txt	7/17/2019	Deleted

Breathe, L. Just breathe!

UGH. Third journal entry today. I've completely lost
my chill.

I can't remember if I logged out before I switched
the visors. It's been messing with my head all
afternoon. I did, right? I must have. I remember
selecting "Sign Out" from the menu and seeing the
prompt to confirm.

And then I chose YES, right? And I blinked? I don't
know why I have the weirdest feeling that I didn't.
I've been making too many mistakes. It isn't like
me. I forgot to clear the browser history from this
terminal before I logged out and went to dinner.
Anyone could have found it. Anyone! I should delete
this whole dropbox. Stop writing things down. If
someone hacked in and found it…

M would kill me. He's convinced I'm going to slip
up, and someone's going to find out about us. It's
getting kind of insulting tbh. Would it really be
so catastrophic if people knew we were together? I
know, I know, I'm not 18, and he has his CEO image->
500 employees depending on him-> Investors wouldn't
like it-> Blah blah blah blah blah.

Whatever, Emerson. Sometimes I think he loves his
stupid company more than me. I'm blowing up my
whole life to move out West. To be with him. My

parents are going to freak when they find out. They've always disapproved of M. And Reese... Reese will never speak to me again. Like, how is that conversation going to go?

Hi, Reese. Yes, you are my best friend that I tell everything, except for this one secret I've been keeping…that I've been in love with your brother right under your nose…and my "relationship" with Maddox? The boy I told you broke my heart?

That was never real.

Fake fake fake. Nothing like a little augmented reality to cover up the truth. Your brother taught me that, Reese. Fake it till you make it. That's his motto. Mine too, now.

It will all be so much easier after my birthday. Once I'm of age in California, we can apply for the marriage license that day. My parents will come around once it's legal, once they know how serious we are.

If only Emerson would listen to me! All he has to do is change one parameter. So easy! Then Maddox's Maker Fair demo will crash and burn, and nobody will question why Maddox is comforting poor Lowercase with her bumped head.

But no. M won't do it, will he? God forbid he get

his hands dirty. And I couldn't access the server
to change it myself. Not even with the visor.
Unlike me, clueless little Lowercase actually has
the presence of mind to LOG OUT of file servers
before she closes them.

Whyyy???

So now, there's only one move left. Desperate times
call for desperate measures. I need to come clean.
Tell Maddox the truth. He'll cover for me in front
of my parents if I'm honest with him. I know he
will.

I should have gone that route from the beginning.
Maddox wouldn't have minded. Not after we broke up.
I bet he would've helped me out of the goodness of
his heart. Because he's actually a good person.
He's not faking anything. Not like M. Not like me.
It's not too late to fix it. Go. Now. Talk to
Maddox. Make it right.

OK, that's the plan. You got this, L.

Just breathe.

30

M

NORA

The first few warning raindrops have given way to a steady downpour. Tree limbs groan overhead in a sudden gust of wind. Those scattered branches won't do much to protect me from getting soaked to the skin.

Reese, fully exposed to the elements out there on the shelf of rock, doesn't seem to care. Water drips down her forehead, but she's oblivious to the reality surrounding her. She keeps her full attention devoted to the visor—and whatever game she's using it to play.

Something about her expression scares me more than the dark storm clouds. *I need to get out of here. Now.*

I turn to go, but pull up short. A new sound greets my ears. Footsteps, growing stronger by the second. Whoever M may be,

I'll find out soon enough. There's someone running up the trail in our direction.

Maddox or Miranda? I'm not sure I care to encounter either of them on the narrow, rocky steps back down to campus. I shift my weight from side to side, hesitating.

The footsteps grow more urgent. They splash through puddled water as they make their way closer. Reese must hear it too. She turns toward the trailhead and squares her shoulders.

The owner of those footsteps climbs the final rise. At last, a head comes into view.

Not Maddox, thankfully.

Not Miranda either.

I'm rooted to the spot as recognition dawns. I've never seen that face in the flesh before, but I know it from pictures. I must have read a hundred articles with his headshot at the top. Reese's voice confirms his identity.

"Emerson."

I squeeze my eyes shut, sending up a silent word of thanks. *Emerson Kemp.* An adult. Here to take charge and put an end to his sister's erratic behavior. He must have followed us up here.

He stops a few feet from where I stand, breathing hard from the climb. His hands go to his hips as he struggles for air, and his head turns back and forth between Reese and myself. "What are you two doing up here?"

"I—I—"

Reese cuts off my stammers, her voice rising to be heard over the rumble of distant thunder. "I don't know, Emerson. I might ask you the same question."

She takes off her visor, and there's a menace in her eyes I don't understand. Instinctively, I take a step away, retreating closer to the man in shredded jeans and a sopping wet T-shirt.

"I got an InstaQuest." Emerson pants, his eyes traveling all around him. "El... She's still up here somewhere! Did you get one too?"

He holds up an oversize smartphone, cupping it with his hand to shield the screen from water. I squint to read the text through the intensifying sheets of rain.

> **L:** M, I'm here. Come find me. Don't tell anyone, OK? I'll explain when you get here. Come alone.

An InstaQuest.

From L.

To M.

My eyes fly open wide as the full truth hits me. The nicknames... *Of course.* I realize what they stand for—what Reese must have known the moment she saw the letters on the screen.

Eleanor and Emerson.

L and M.

Emerson tucks the phone away in his pocket. He looks frantic, water running down his face in rivulets. His spiky blond hair has darkened to the color of straw. "Help me find her!" He takes a few steps onto the rain-slick slab of rock where Reese stands. "Help me look! She's still alive!"

A flash of lightning fills the sky. I count the beats inside my head until its followed by the roar of thunder.

One one-thousand...two one-thousand...three one-thousand...

Crash.

The sound makes me jump. Emerson retreats. Reese takes off her visor, lowers her forehead, and glares.

"What is with you?" Emerson yells at her. "Don't just stand there! Help!"

She holds up the visor and waves it at him. "Eleanor's gone, jackass. The InstaQuest was from me."

The two of them look like they both want to kill each other. I edge back toward the trailhead as the claps of thunder grow closer. A torrent of rushing water tumbles down the rocky staircase, stopping me in my tracks. I don't dare attempt the treacherous descent. "Oh no," I whisper, but my voice is barely loud enough to reach my own ears.

I turn back to Reese and Emerson, but the sight of them does nothing to ease my rising panic. They stand face-to-face on the clifftop, a few short feet from the edge.

This is not going to end well. "You guys!" I call out to them. "Maybe we should talk about this somewhere else?"

Reese ignores me, keeping her full fury trained on her

brother. "It was you? That's why she was graduating early? To be with you?"

My jaw goes slack. Eleanor's sudden change of college plans… No wonder she picked Stanford, a stone's throw from Emerson's corporate headquarters in Silicon Valley.

He doesn't bother to deny it. "Don't be a baby, Reese."

"I'm a *baby*? I'm not allowed to be upset that you were stealing my best friend?"

He shakes his head. "She knew you'd react this way. That's why we couldn't tell you."

"She was *my* friend. Not yours!"

"Actually, she was getting really tired of how possessive you were."

Reese wraps her arms around herself, quivering with the force of each word she utters. "You killed her!"

He reaches for her elbow. "Calm down. You know that isn't true." Reese jerks her arm out of his grasp as he continues. "I loved Eleanor. It was serious between us. You don't even know…"

"Are you stupid?" Reese's voice rises sharply, echoing off the rocks. "You killed her! Don't you realize what you did?"

Emerson looks dumbfounded, but I know what she means.

The distance parameter.

My code was stored on the InstaLove corporate servers. Eleanor didn't have access to edit that parameter herself, but if anyone would have admin privileges on that file server, it was the company's CEO.

"You sabotaged the code!" Reese shouts in his face. "Negative one, remember? She didn't get a hazard alert. She fell because of you!"

Emerson swipes a hand across his face to clear away the rainwater. "That? No—that—that was a prank. She said it was a three-foot drop. I wasn't going to at first, but it seemed harmless enough…"

"She fell from here!" Reese's mouth twists as she delivers the devastating truth. "She came up here at night! She didn't get a warning message! Because of you!" She rushes at Emerson and pummels at his chest. He sidesteps, dangerously close to the precipice, to avoid her raging fists.

"Watch out!" I call. My heart beats a mile a minute. Reese is out of control. Someone's going to get hurt. I hesitate, unsure if I should stay here in the shelter of the trees, help Emerson subdue his sister, or attempt the flooded trail.

I look toward the trailhead, chewing my lip. Another flash of lightning blazes, close enough that I can smell the ozone in the air. *Nope.* I'm not going anywhere. Not right now. The storm's right over us. I don't need to count the beats before the thunderclap rings out.

The ear-splitting roar is punctuated by an even louder noise behind me—the sound of Reese's scream.

31

SOS

MADDOX

I can't believe Emerson.

He left us standing here without one word of explanation. The moment he saw that InstaQuest he took off at a run, unfazed by the howling wind and rain.

I should have gone with him. I tried, but Dr. Carlyle stopped me. No way was he letting another student barrel off into a thunderstorm. I stood by helplessly as Emerson turned the corner around Grier Hall and disappeared. I have a sick feeling in my stomach that I know where he's heading.

Maybe Dr. Carlyle has a point. The Overlook is treacherous enough without the added danger of flash floods and lightning strikes. Nora wouldn't be reckless enough to head that way in a storm...

Not unless she didn't have a choice.

Dr. Carlyle blocks my path outside. I turn and race upstairs toward the second floor instead. "This way!" I call over my shoulder. "We need a laptop. Now!"

I shove my way through the first open door. Nora's room. Empty. Her laptop sits abandoned on her desk. I flip it open as Dr. Carlyle enters. My fingers fly through the keystrokes, pulling up the command prompt.

```
Winthrop Secure Server [10.0.10.240]
<c> 2015 Intellisoft Solutions. All
    rights reserved.


C:\ Augmented-Reality.exe_
```

I can't believe I typed that filename in front of him. If my fate weren't sealed already, this would do it. But I don't have time to worry about saving my own neck. I beckon Dr. Carlyle to watch over my shoulder as the system logs in. An array of video feeds populate the screen, and I maximize one of them. "Look! Look at this!"

The grainy image shows a locked gate, a rusted No Trespassing sign dappled by golden sunshine, and the gently swaying shadows of leafy branches.

"There's no one there," Dr. Carlyle says. He reaches for the laptop, but I knock his hand away.

"Watch!" I pull up the source code editor and scroll to the

lines of code I left in place for the past three days. I delete the OVERLAY statement. Hit return. On the other half of the screen, the live feed updates. Back to real time. The weather changes in an instant, from hazy sunshine to pouring rain.

"Dear lord," Dr. C mutters, but I ignore him. There's something else different about the scene. Those markings on the ground weren't there yesterday when I hiked to The Overlook to watch the search. I zoom in close to get a better look.

Three letters come into focus, scrawled in the mud at the base of the locked gate.

S O S

"It's them! We have to get up there!"

The image goes blank for a split second, replaced by pure white light. Then a peal of thunder roars outside, loud enough to make the window of Nora's dorm room rattle. Dr. Carlyle claps a hand on my shoulder to keep me in place.

"No, Maddox." He shakes his head grimly. "It's too unsafe. No one's going anywhere until this storm passes."

NORA

I whirl around at the sound of Reese's cry. Emerson kneels on the ground with his sister motionless before him. There's an odor I can't quite place, coming from their direction—a faint electrical smell, like burning wire.

What happened? I stumble a few paces toward them. *Was she hit by lightning?* Something dark oozes from Reese's left temple, staining the clifftop at Emerson's knees.

I lift my eyes to him, and only then do I notice the object he's holding. He shields it from the rain with his chest, juggling it back and forth between his hands like a hot potato. Sizzling hot.

My mouth drops open, and another piece of the puzzle clicks into place. *Of course.* That Maker Project from TeenHack… I remember thinking it sounded detailed enough to work in real life.

M

Turn any cell phone battery into an electroshock security device (stun gun). Detailed step-by-step instructions...

"What did you do?" My eyes fly to his face. "Did you *tase* her?"

Emerson turns toward me. "I—I didn't mean—She was trying to—" He cuts himself off, swallowing the words. He looks almost as shocked as I feel.

"What's the voltage on that thing?"

"It shouldn't be enough to knock her out!" A trickle of blood seeps from Reese's forehead. Emerson stuffs the phone in his pocket and mops her face with the hem of his T-shirt. "She must've hit her head when she went down."

I rush to his side. "Is she breathing?"

He nods, looking past me toward the trailhead. He grabs Reese beneath the armpits and drags her away from the edge of the cliff. "Help me. Take her feet."

I obey. We won't be able to carry her down the flooded steps, but maybe we can find a place to shelter until the storm passes. We make it only a few feet before Emerson lets go of her armpits and sinks down onto his haunches. He drops his head into his hands.

I glance at the waterlogged trail. The rushing water looks more turbulent than it did a moment ago. But how deep is it? Maybe I can make it down without being washed away. Maybe if I scoot on my butt from step to step… *Maybe.* "You stay here with her," I say to Emerson, approaching the top of the staircase. "I'll go for help."

"No. Stay." Emerson stands and catches me by the arm. His eyes meet mine and narrow slightly, as if he's seeing me here for the first time. "Wait," he mutters. "Who are you? Are you Lowercase?"

I nod and lower my gaze, suddenly self-conscious. My eyes land on the rectangular outline in his pocket. I could almost smack myself in the forehead for not thinking of it sooner. That thing is more than a stun gun. It's his phone! "Do you have cell service?" I ask, gesturing impatiently. "Call 911!"

Emerson remains still. He studies me, his forehead furrowed as if struggling to make sense of my words. Finally, he removes the phone and flicks it on. "Good," he says slowly. "This is good. This is what we'll do…"

I wait for him to place a call, but he doesn't. Instead, he points the phone's camera lens at my face. He squints at his screen for a moment, then drops his arm to his side. "Come here." He takes a step toward me. "I need your help." He grabs my wrist and tugs, pulling me away from Reese, back in the direction of the clifftop.

I wrench my arm, resisting. "Stop! What are you doing?"

"Relax." He releases his grip. "We need to shoot a video."

"What video?"

He holds up the camera lens again. "Listen to me. You won't get in any trouble. You changed the code by accident."

What?

"The hazard alert code," he continues. "You wrote it, right? So... maybe you made a typo. You changed the parameter yourself."

I shake my head slowly back and forth. "No. I didn't. You know that—"

But I realize he isn't asking me a question. He's telling me the lie he wants me to repeat.

I press my palm across my mouth. *What's wrong with him? His sister has a head injury, and he's worried about some computer program?*

He edges a step closer, and I backpedal. I can hear the police tape behind me, fluttering in the wind and pounding rain. He holds his phone in one hand, but he no longer wields it like a camera. More like a weapon—a stun gun. *Would a shock from that thing be enough to make me stumble backward?*

"This is important," he says. "This isn't a joke. Have you heard of corporate liability?"

"Your sister is bleeding!"

"I know, and I will help her in a sec. But this is business. I have a *fiduciary* responsibility to my investors. Do you know what that word means?" He pronounces it slowly like he's talking to a little kid, but he doesn't stop to explain. He comes closer still— uncomfortably close. "Of course you don't," he murmurs. "You're just some teenager at camp. No one will blame you. You made an innocent mistake."

I stay frozen where I stand, too afraid to back up any farther.

Emerson stops his relentless approach. He frames me in his camera sights again. "OK? Got it? I'm starting the video. Say you changed the code, and that you're sorry. You're so, *so* sorry. And then we'll call 911, and no one will get in trouble. Do you understand?"

No. I don't understand. I only know that I feel trapped. I don't know this man, and I definitely don't trust him. I clamp my lips shut tight. I'm not doing it. He can't make me speak words that I don't want to say.

But the problem is I'm cornered—trapped on this exposed slab of rock, rapidly filling with puddles. He blocks my path back to the safety of the trees.

I don't dare try to push past him.

I don't dare do what he says.

32

TASED AND CONFUSED

NORA

Emerson inches closer, brandishing the stun gun end of his phone.
I raise my palms before me as he approaches.

He stops a few feet away and stoops down, reaching for an
object at his feet. The visor. *Eleanor's* visor. Reese must have
dropped it when she hit her head.

Emerson slips his phone in his pocket and picks up the visor
with both hands. He contemplates it in silence, cradling it gently
between his fingers. Then, with a burst of sudden violence, he
cracks the frame against his thigh. The plastic snaps, exposing the
wiring within. He yanks at a few metallic strands and then heaves
the destroyed device off to his left.

My whole body trembles as I watch it fly over the edge of the cliff. It careens downward, bouncing off the rocks, before it disappears from view into the fog-cloaked lake.

"Why?" I start to say, but the question dies in my throat. I know exactly why he did that. The visor's outer casing may be waterproof, but the inner circuitry will corrode once it's exposed to the elements. Any data it contained—any proof of my innocence and Emerson's guilt…

Gone. Wiped away.

He controls the corporate server where any records would be stored. That visor was my only hope. And now it's lost forever.

I sway on my feet as Emerson lifts his remorseless eyes to me again. Why do I get the sense that those glasses aren't the only evidence he intends to toss over the edge? Once I make that video confession, there's no telling what he might do—what lengths he might travel to make sure I'm not around to contradict my recorded statement.

I have to get out of here. *Now.* While his Taser-phone is still lodged in his pocket. This might be my only chance. If I can dodge past him to the safety of the trees…

I lunge forward, but I'm too slow. Emerson lurches sideways to block my path. He grabs me by the wrist and wrenches my arm behind my back.

I let out a yelp as his grip on my arm tightens. I try to turn my head, but something stops me—the hard rubber case of Emerson's cell phone, no longer tucked away. He presses it firmly against my temple.

"Don't be stupid," his voice growls in my ear. "Do what I say, and we can put this whole unpleasant experience behind us."

No. I don't believe you.

I think the words, but I don't say them out loud. "OK," I whisper instead. "I'll do it. I'll make the video. Just let me go!"

I can't tell if he heard me. The stun gun maintains its steady pressure against my head as he turns me around and marches me in front of him, closer and closer to the precipice.

"Stop!" The police tape slaps against my shins, and I squeeze my eyes closed. I know what I'll see if I look down. Angry water, crashing against sharp rocks. "Please!" I rear back, unable to take another step without tripping. "Please stop. Please!"

He releases my arm. "Turn around and face me. We'll take the video here."

I do as he says. He aims the camera lens at my face, ready to record my statement. "What do you want me to say again?" I hug my arms around my body to stop from shaking, but I don't listen to his answer. I don't intend to say a word. I'm only playing for time.

His eyes go to his cell phone screen. "Hold on. You're out of focus."

The rain is letting up. The storm has moved out over the lake, but it left the surface of the clifftop soaking wet. I glance down and a sour taste fills the back of my throat. A mere six inches of slick rock separate my heels from the ledge.

How do I get out of this? How?

I can't risk another attempt to push past Emerson. There's no telling where I might skid if we collide.

He raises his eyes, meeting mine. "Go ahead," he orders. "We're recording. Tell the camera what you told me."

"W-what?"

"Tell us who reset the parameter. Don't be scared. Was it you?"

I still don't have a plan, and I'm running out of time. I stare into Emerson's camera lens and open my mouth to speak, but I close it again before uttering a word. A flash of movement catches my peripheral vision from the trees behind Emerson's back.

This isn't over. Not yet.

MADDOX

"No one's going anywhere until this storm passes."

Dr. Carlyle presses his lips into a stern line. I rise from Nora's desk and face him. Doesn't he see the SOS signal on the surveillance feed?

"We can't just sit here," I argue. "We have to do something—"

I break off, following his movements. Dr. Carlyle draws a cell phone from his pocket.

"Good," I say, although he hardly seems to register my words. "Call someone. Call 911!"

He nods once, then holds the phone to his ear and turns away.

I strain to hear Dr. Carlyle's side of the conversation. He

has his hand cupped over his mouth as he murmurs information into the phone. Other sounds drown out his voice. The dorm room window clatters in its frame as the full fury of the thunderstorm passes overhead. Outside, trees sway violently, with a few loose branches flying free in the gusting wind. The thought of anyone at The Overlook in this weather makes my stomach churn.

"They can't be up there," I whisper to myself. They must have taken cover as the storm blew in.

Nora has enough sense of self-preservation not to stand on an exposed clifftop in a thunderstorm. But Reese…

A ribbon of lightning crackles through the sky, followed by a thunderclap loud enough to make me flinch.

Nora's laptop still sits open on her desk. Dr. Carlyle has his eyes glued to it as he talks. I watch the live feeds over his shoulder. "There!" I cry, pointing toward a flash of movement in one corner of the screen.

Dr. Carlyle clicks to maximize the window, but my heart sinks again as the image expands. Three figures climb the stone steps of the library and take shelter inside the large glass doors. Their faces come into view as they turn toward the camera.

Miranda, Samirah, and Ms. Peterson.

Dr. Carlyle removes his glasses and wipes away the gathering steam on the lapel of his jacket. He minimizes the window once again. "False alarm. Not them." His muffled voice drones into his phone. "…still two students unaccounted for…Nora Weinberg…Reese Kemp… Yes, that's right. And one adult who may be with them…"

One adult.

Emerson.

The tightness in my chest relaxes its grip. That InstaQuest I saw on his phone before he left—a distress signal, like the SOS scrawled in mud. It must have come from Reese. I can only hope he reached the girls before the storm kicked up.

But why did Emerson take off without a word? It would only have taken him a second to show Dr. Carlyle the message he received. I close my eyes, struggling to remember the fleeting instants before he ditched us. His jaw fell open as his eyes flashed to his phone. And then he muttered softly. "*What the…*"

He paused before the next word. All the blood seemed to drain from his face, and I had to strain to make out what he said.

What the…hell?

That's what I thought I heard, but maybe I was wrong. For a moment, I go completely still.

Not *hell.*

L. The letter *L…*

No wonder he went deathly pale—like someone who just saw a ghost. That InstaQuest didn't come from Reese. It must have come from Eleanor's account.

But how?

And why? Why him? Of all people to receive that prompt and take off like a shot. Why Emerson?

A hand grips me on the shoulder, pulling me out of my thoughts. "Maddox? Are you all right?"

I look up, startled. My eyes go to Dr. Carlyle's face and then to the laptop screen. "What? Did you find them? Are they—"

"No." He releases my arm. "I'm going out with the search team. They have another way to access the location from the main road."

"Let's go!"

"Maddox, no. *I'm* going. You need to wait here."

I give my head a violent shake. My chest heaves up and down. I know what he's going to tell me. *It isn't safe. I'm just a kid. I've done enough to make this mess already…*

Instead, he removes his glasses. He slowly meets my eyes, and my words of protest die on my lips. Something in his look silences me. I feel exposed, unmasked, like he can see straight through me.

What does he see? The real me? And who is that exactly? The kid he always viewed with bemused indulgence? Or the boy who was weak, who lied to cover up other people's secrets. The boy who broke his trust.

I hold my breath, waiting for him to speak—waiting for his final verdict to come down.

"Please," I whisper. "Please let me help."

The moment seems to last forever. Then, at last, he nods.

"OK, son." He pats me on the shoulder, and his glasses resume their usual perch on the bridge of his nose. "Come on, then. Let's go."

33

OVER MY DEAD BODY

NORA

Emerson's camera lens bores into me, with the cliff's edge at my back. He waits for me to make my forced confession. I seal my lips together, stalling for precious seconds.

I didn't imagine that flash of movement from the trees behind his back. With a huge force of will, I resist the urge to look that way. I keep my eyes glued to Emerson's phone. He hasn't noticed, and I don't want to alert him. He can't hear anything over the rumbling thunder, and he can't see the hazard that staggered to her feet behind his back.

Reese. She's awake, watching us, wiping the blood out of her eyes.

At last, her voice rings out. "What are you doing?"

Emerson's shoulders jump, but the camera remains fixed on my face. "Are you OK?" he calls to her, with a quick swivel of his head. "Why don't you sit down? Lowercase here was about to make a video."

Reese looks to me, and I freeze. *Help me,* I scream inside my head, but I don't dare say those words out loud. I can only hope she's clearheaded enough to understand. I speak slowly, dragging out the syllables, but my eyes are locked on Reese. "I...I did it. I reset the distance parameter. It was me."

She blinks at me, her expression cloudy. Somewhere in that concussed brain of hers, she knows I'm not speaking the truth. She knows who changed that parameter as well as I do. *Come on, Reese. You know I'm lying. Say it!*

"No," she calls out from her position by the trees. "That isn't true!"

I close my eyes, breathing easier. Emerson lowers the phone. "Dammit, Reese! Not now. I'm recording! We'll have to start again."

"What's going on?" Reese demands.

Emerson ignores her, directing his words to me. "Go ahead. Start talking."

My eyes lock with his, then move to Reese. Two sets of ice-blue eyes peer back at me, nearly identical. Which one do I trust? There's only one move left. I can only hope it's the right decision. I look past Emerson to Reese, and I raise my voice to be heard as the words tumble forth in a rush. "Go get help. Now. He's forcing me to say this. You're my witness, Reese. Go!"

One set of blue eyes narrow dangerously. The other eyes widen at my words.

"Now, Reese! Hurry!"

But Reese is moving in slow motion. She teeters on her feet. The gash on her forehead continues to drip, blood mixing with rainwater. She ponders the diluted red tint that stains her hand like watercolor paint. Then, finally, she looks up. Her face changes, and the fogginess leaves her eyes.

"Please," I whisper. "Please."

Emerson darts another glance over his shoulder. He lets out an exasperated huff. "Stay there, Reese. I'm handling this."

She answers slowly. A roll of distant thunder drowns out her words, but I can read her lips. "Over my dead body."

Emerson raises the phone. "Talk," he commands me. "Hurry up."

My mouth flaps open, but I can't make more than a squeak come out. My eyes flash back and forth between Emerson and Reese behind him. "OK," I manage at last. "I...I did it. I reset—"

Reese interrupts before I can finish my sentence, her voice rising to be heard over mine. "No. You're the one who changed it, Em! You!"

"Oh my God!" Emerson drops the phone again. He stuffs it in the back pocket of his jeans and turns to face her. "You're such a child. Shut up!"

Reese's shoulders heave. Her breath goes in and out, flaring her nostrils with each harsh rasp, like an angry bull preparing to charge.

Emerson holds up his palms in his sister's direction. "Calm down, OK? Listen to me. I have to protect InstaLove. You know the PR nightmare we'll be in if it comes out that—"

But Reese refuses to be soothed. She cuts him off, her voice growing more wild. "Eleanor is *dead*! And you—you—you're worried about your precious app?"

A gust of wind buffets against me, billowing my hair and clothes. I lean forward to keep my balance as stray leaves and branches skitter past my heels into the yawning void beyond.

Emerson's tone changes, breathless as he pleads his case before his sister. "It was an accident! I had no idea Eleanor would come up here that night. She must've been looking for Maddox. Don't you see?"

No. I don't see, but I latch on to the name that Emerson spoke. *Maddox.* If anyone might realize I'm trapped up here—if anyone will see the SOS message I left at the gate below—it's him.

Please, Maddox, I pray silently. *Please. Please check the feeds. Please find us.*

Emerson still blocks my path to safety, but he has his back to me, his attention locked on his sister. He lifts his arms toward her. "Listen! I know you're grieving. I'm grieving too. More than you! I *loved* her."

"You think I didn't?" Reese shrieks the words at him. "She was my best friend in the world! You think that isn't love?"

I barely register their conversation. I look down, and all I can see is the upper left corner of Emerson's cell phone case, poking out of his back pocket.

Forget Maddox. I can't wait around for someone to rescue me. Now, while Emerson's distracted… It's my only chance to get out of this alive.

Everything happens all at once. I reach for the phone in Emerson's pocket. Triumph clicks in my chest as I pull it free. I sidestep, nimble on my feet for once in my life, attempting to move past him before he can react.

But Emerson isn't thinking about his phone. His eyes are on his sister. He stumbles backward into me as a flash of electric blue sweeps across the clifftop in our direction. "Reese!" he screams out. "No!"

But it's too late. She bowls into him headfirst, butting him in the stomach. They both go skidding backward. I lunge sideways to get out of their way.

I almost make it.

Almost.

But Emerson reaches for my arm. His hand catches my elbow. I flail, struggling to keep my balance as my shoes slide across the rocks, and the yellow caution tape snaps against my ankles.

34

LOSING GRIP

MADDOX

I don't recognize this stretch of road. In all my years at Winthrop, I've never traveled this direction. I've hardly left the safe perimeter of the wrought iron gates surrounding campus. When I have, it was only to make my way to the Greyhound bus stop that lies the other way.

But today we turned right instead of left, heading uphill along this winding road—the kind of road that makes your heart clutch with each hairpin turn as tires screech and scramble on rain-soaked pavement. Two narrow lanes, barely wide enough for a pair of cars to pass, writhe their way upward. A sheer wall of granite rises on one side, and on the other, nothing but a guardrail and a wide expanse of mist.

I stare into that blankness out the backseat window. Every

so often, a break in the milky white allows a glimpse of the lake below.

The car whips around another switchback, and I grip the edges of the leather seat with all my strength. *Too fast. Out of control.* The police officer at the wheel must know what he's doing. He must have driven this route before. But like this? In the wind and rain, with his siren blaring?

I thrust my fingers into my hair, annoyed by its shaggy presence on my forehead. It keeps falling in my eyes, blocking my view as I strain to make out any sign of human movement—any reason for hope.

There's only silence and tension in this car. Dr. Carlyle sits up front in the passenger seat. My gaze travels to his face, reflected in the rearview mirror. He has his head bowed, hands clasped, lips moving in a wordless murmur.

Praying? I never knew he was religious.

Maybe he's not.

Maybe I should be praying too, instead of staring uselessly into the inscrutable fog.

I look to the driver instead. The policeman has his eyes trained forward, concentrating on the road. I long to ask him if we're almost there, but I hold back.

Something tells me that my voice in the backseat won't be welcome. I shouldn't be here. I could tell they both were thinking that a few moments ago, as the terse phrases of the dispatcher buzzed across the squad car's two-way radio.

...incident in progress...

...10–39...

...all units...

...major injuries...

Major? How major? Can't this car go any faster?

I squeeze my hands into fists and press hard against my thighs. The tendons in my wrists bunch and gather. At last my eyes fall on something other than granite, fog, and trees. A line of vehicles gather in the shoulder of the road up ahead with flashers blinking. I force myself to breathe in rhythm with the lights. The car glides slower, toward a break in the guardrail. A steep trail leads downward through the gap.

We're still rolling slightly, but I don't wait. I whip off my seatbelt and thrust the door open. Dr. Carlyle's voice shouts after me, but I can't hear what he says. My feet skid across the pavement as I hurtle into the mist.

NORA

The caution tape breaks as my legs pass through. It barely slows me down.

It all happens so fast I hardly register the fear, or the pain of the sharp rocks that scrape against my shins. I hear only the sickening sound of screams.

Three anguished voices blend together.

One of those voices is mine.

Some instinct makes me clench my arms. I grapple with my hands to stop my fall. My fingers find a crevice in the rocky surface of the clifftop, and my arms wrench in their sockets as my feet and torso slide over the edge.

In a terrifying flash, Reese and Emerson tumble past my dangling legs. Their cries fade in my ears as they both fall.

Gone.

Both gone.

There's no one left to go for help. No one coming to rescue me. I'm all alone, clinging to this jagged shelf of granite, with death ten fingertips away.

My pulse thunders in my ears. My hands are soaked. I can feel my hold slipping. I keep my eyes focused on my forearms and grip with all my strength.

I have no idea how long I dangle there—a few fleeting seconds at most. But somehow, in that instant, the speed of thought accelerates.

This isn't happening. I press my eyes closed and will the words inside my head to be true. None of this is happening. None of this is *real.*

But I know I'm lying to myself.

This is it, Nora.

A sob forms in my throat, but I swallow it back down. I can't let go. I *can't.*

I won't die here like this when I've barely even lived. When I've never gone to college…or built an app…or founded my first company… When I've never even kissed a boy, much less been in love. Not for real. Not without the aid of a silly game.

There's no game to rescue me now. No avatar to hide behind. Just me. Nora Weinberg. Am I strong enough to live, or do I die?

My eyes fix on my arms, focusing every ounce of energy I possess on a single thought: *Pull.*

Pull yourself up, Nora.

You can do it.

You have to.

You have too much left to do.

My elbows bend, slow and shaky, muscles popping with the strain. *I have muscles in my forearms.* I don't know why that fact strikes me as noteworthy, but it repeats like a drumbeat in my head. *Muscles in my forearms… How is this real life?*

There's a feeling in my belly I haven't felt before—a power I didn't know I have. It rises upward, past my lungs and past my heart, until it bursts forth from my lips in a primal scream. My shoulders rise along with it. Up over the edge now. I kick my legs upward as my cry breaks free. With one final burst of effort, my left knee catches on the corner of the rocky ledge, and I lever myself back over the top.

Safe.

Alive.

Still breathing.

I crawl a few feet from the edge and then collapse. Now that I'm not dying, my body has turned to rubber. I can't summon the strength to move.

My ears still work though. I hear a sound, wailing in the distance, faint at first but growing stronger.

Sirens.

The police?

Footsteps, then. Pounding through the brush from somewhere overhead. Shouts. My name.

"Nora! Nora!"

There are feet all around me, filling the clifftop. Then arms. Firm and strong. Pulling me close. Pulling me upright. Clenching around my shoulders.

I know those arms. I've stared at them often enough to recognize them. I turn and cling to his chest with all the strength I have remaining.

"Nora. Nora, what happened?"

He sits awkwardly on the wet rock, with his legs splayed out on either side of me, rocking me back and forth. His khaki trousers, more than wrinkled now. Ripped at the knee. Stained with mud.

"Nora," Maddox says into my hair, his voice no more than a harsh sob. "Say something. Are you OK?"

"No," I whisper back.

I'm not OK. But I'm alive.

35

LOST AND FOUND

NORA

TEENHACK

OBITUARY

Emerson Kemp, InstaLove Founder and CEO, Has Died at Age 21

Berkshire, MA—

After an extensive search and rescue effort, authorities from the Berkshire County Sheriff's Office have now confirmed that Emerson Kemp and his sister Reese passed away last week in a tragic accident. An InstaLove spokesperson released the following statement: "It is with heavy hearts that we confirm the passing of our CEO, Emerson Kemp, who died a hero attempting to rescue his sister and another

student after they became trapped by flash flooding... MORE

I click the website closed, feeling queasy. I set my phone facedown on the wooden table that's served as my nightstand for as long as I've lived in this house. I shouldn't have gone online. I should have known better, but my curiosity got the best of me.

He died a hero…

Not exactly, TeenHack. I'm the only person alive who knows what really went down on that clifftop, and Emerson Kemp died trying to cover his ass. But I suppose there could be no more fitting obituary. He was all about augmented reality to the bitter end.

My cell phone buzzes, and I pick it up. *Finally.* I've been expecting this call all evening. My heart squeezes as the incoming request fills my screen:

> **Maddox Drake**
>
> would like FaceTime...

It's weird seeing Maddox's face pictured there. His actual face. No more avatars for either of us. And no more InstaLove for anyone. The app has been down all week, pending investigation into the accidents. But there's no escaping the fact that the InstaQuest functionality led three users to the place where they met their end. I don't see how the company can come back from that—especially without its CEO.

No, that obituary in TeenHack wasn't just for Emerson. His beloved company died with him.

I hit "Accept" on my phone, and Maddox greets me with a wave.

"Hey, Nor—"

His face pixelates, and I miss the end of his sentence as the video feed freezes. My Wi-Fi signal isn't strong enough here in my bedroom. I creep into the hallway and down the stairs, careful not to make much noise. It's after midnight, and my parents are already in bed.

Maddox's image springs back to life as I take a seat at the kitchen table. "Hello? Nora?"

"Hi," I whisper as loudly as I dare with sleeping parents overhead. "I'm here. Can you hear me?"

"Loud and clear." Maddox flashes a thumbs-up. His voice comes through, diminished slightly by the street noise in the background. He always calls me from the fire escape outside his window so he won't disturb his grandmother. His face is half-illuminated by a streetlight, partially lost in shadow.

"How are you holding up?" he asks.

Good question. It's been only a week since I hugged Maddox goodbye and headed home in the backseat of my parents' car, but it feels like the longest week of my life. One minute I'm fine—normal Nora, same as ever—and the next minute I feel like I've aged ten years.

At least this week has shown me one thing: Maddox isn't playing games. He actually cares about me, and he's proven it by calling every night.

I release a long sigh. "I'm OK. Did you hear from the sheriff's office again?"

He nods, and his face goes grave. Something about his expression makes my mouth dry. For both of us, our past few days have been punctuated by phone calls with the investigators and sessions with the trauma counselor that Winthrop Academy insisted on providing. It's become routine in a way, but something in Maddox's face warns me that today was anything but business-as-usual.

"What?" I ask him softly. "Did you find out something new?"

He lowers his voice, and I have to turn up my phone volume to hear him. "There was a journal. Eleanor—" He breaks off, and his Adam's apple bobs. "They found it in a Dropbox. She'd deleted all the entries, but the forensics people were able to restore most of it."

My pajama top feels tight around my neck. I loosen the top button. "And the investigators told you about it?"

"They had me read it. They needed help interpreting. It wasn't exactly clear who's who with all the nicknames and abbreviations she used."

No kidding. Good to know I'm not the only one who found Eleanor Winthrop's communication style somewhat baffling. Maddox pauses, and I can see from his face he's desperate to tell me whatever the journal revealed.

Do I want to hear this? Maddox has a trauma counselor too, and I could tell him to talk to her. That would probably be the healthiest thing for me. But I can't resist. More than anything, I want to know the truth. I want to understand what happened— what *really* happened—and why.

"Go on," I prompt him. "What did it say?"

He brings the phone close so that his face takes up most of the screen. "It all makes more sense now... Why she kept messing with me, what she was trying to hide." He stops and wets his lips. I hold my breath, waiting for him to continue. "Get this," he says at last. "She and Emerson were planning to elope."

I squint, wondering if I heard him wrong. "Like get *married?*" He nods, but my confusion only grows. "Wasn't she way too young?"

"I know! You have to be eighteen without your parents' permission, and her birthday was coming up. But still—"

"Wait," I interrupt him. "Slow down. I thought she was going to college in the fall."

"Yeah, that's why she applied to Stanford. So she could be with Emerson on the west coast while she went to school." His voice rises as he continues. "Don't you get it? She was using me to cover up their relationship. So her parents wouldn't realize she was with *him* until after she turned eighteen—after it was a done deal."

His eyes are wide and shining. The look on his face brings me back to a time before—a time that feels like ancient history: that afternoon in the Winthrop library, day two of the program, when Maddox commandeered my laptop to outline the idea for our project. "*Don't you get it?*" he kept saying, talking a mile a minute as I struggled to catch up. He was two steps ahead of me that day, and this conversation leaves me with the same sensation. My mind swims with more questions than I can formulate into words.

I'll stick with the main one. "Why?"

"Because!" The picture shakes and pixelates as he clambers to his feet, and I can hear nothing but the rattle of the metal fire escape beneath him. His face is lost in shadow. I can barely make out the outlines of his features. "Because," he says more slowly. "Her parents never liked Emerson. Not since we were kids. He was always in trouble, breaking rules. They thought he was a bad influence."

A bad influence? Talk about the understatement of the year...

Every time I close my eyes, I can't help but picture that stone-cold look on Emerson's face the last time I saw him alive. Not *bad* so much as *ruthless*—a person who would stop at nothing to get exactly what he wanted. I shiver, hugging my arm against my body to keep the phone from shaking.

On his end, Maddox shifts again, squatting down so that the streetlamp lights his features. His face grows solemn, and he swipes the back of his hand across his eyes. He's a different Maddox now. Not the boy from the library that day, brimming with enthusiasm. More like the boy who came to my room the night after Eleanor went missing—sad and scared and haunted by secrets he doesn't know how to tell.

It's funny. I spent so much time trying to reconcile the Maddox in my room that night with the boy I knew in the weeks before. But I get it now. I understand him so much better. There isn't a real Maddox and a fake one. He's both. All energy and charisma one moment, brooding darkness the next.

Right now, he looks exhausted, his eyes shot through with pink.

"Maddox," I say softly. "Are you getting enough sleep?"

"Sure." He clears his throat, but his voice sounds choked with more than fatigue. I can't forget the fact that Eleanor was once his girlfriend, and Reese was one of his closest friends. I can't imagine how it must feel to lose both of them at once. My experience at The Overlook shook me to the core, but I was an outsider to that Winthrop inner circle. I'm not dealing with the kind of grief Maddox must be feeling—or the way his entire world has ceased to exist.

I'm back home with my parents, back on solid ground, but Maddox's whole future is up in the air. His plans for senior year have fallen out from under him. Winthrop Academy announced yesterday that it would shutter its gates for the first time since its founding, pending a total overhaul of campus security. The entire student body was left scrambling. Maddox has no idea where he'll land.

Somewhere above me, a door creaks open. My mom's footsteps patter on the stairs. She must be coming down to check on me.

The clock on the microwave announces that it's nearly one o'clock in the morning.

"My mom's up," I whisper. "I should go."

A look flashes across his face, impossible to miss—an emotion I know well, but never expected to see reflected back on Maddox's features. Pure loneliness. I feel a pang at the sight of it, even as he covers it up with a tight smile. "OK," he says. "Good night."

"Maddox," I whisper before he can hang up. "Wait."

My mom comes into the kitchen, yawning and blinking against the change in light. "Nora? Sweetie, what are you doing up after bedtime?"

I meet her eyes and point to the phone. "Talking to Maddox." My voice is calm, and my next words follow before I have a chance to stop and think. "Mom, I'm inviting him to come visit. I think it's for the best."

"Oh?" she answers vaguely, glancing at the face on my phone. Maddox looks surprised, but he doesn't say a word, waiting for my mom's reaction. "We should talk about this in the morning with your father."

"No." I turn in my chair to face her. She doesn't get it yet. She hasn't grown accustomed to this new Nora—Nora 2.0, who doesn't have a bedtime. Who has a boy she FaceTimes every night. A boy she cares about. A boy she might someday even kiss…

"Maddox needs me," I tell her firmly. "He's coming here, or else I'm going to him. One way or another, we need to be together."

My mom pauses, studying my face like I'm a stranger she's seeing for the first time in her life. Maybe she is. Maybe I've always been invisible to everyone around me—invisible even to myself.

For the longest time, I thought I needed an app to cover up my weaknesses. But that's all behind me now. I see who I am. I meet my own eyes on my cell phone, and I can't help but smile. I'm that girl right there, pictured in the little FaceTime window in the corner of the screen. Nora Weinberg, unfiltered and unaugmented. A girl who came within an inch of not existing anymore—a girl who turned out to be stronger in real life than she ever could have dreamed.

ACKNOWLEDGMENTS

First and foremost, I would like to thank all my faithful readers. Your continued support—buying my books, borrowing them from libraries, and recommending them to friends—makes it possible for me to continue putting new stories into the world. This book only exists because of you.

There are several readers I must acknowledge in particular. Thank you to my critique partner Amy Giles, who provided invaluable feedback on this work. I'm also deeply indebted to the small army of Wattpad followers who served as my beta readers on the first draft of this book: Ermina Tajik, Reneilwe Masha, Maria Richmond, Kyle Chokas, Maya Jalukar, Tylinn Bronkhorst, Annie Bentley, Tora Ghosh, Sania Merchant, Sabaat Najeeb, Mariam Eqbal, Saba Gul, Siri Varshini, Anna Zhao, Nathaniel Luscombe, Amruta Gokhale, Angéline Lafleur, Spencer Hastings,

Asmita Jakhmola, Tracy Duplantis, Ashley Childs, Llewellyn Jehu, Kaitlyn Miller, Anjali Patel, Kaylie Montgomery, Hannah Lipow, Anna Irwin, Rawan Tamer, Ana Carla Tovar Flores, Emily Rafferty, and Melissa Gong. A huge thank-you goes out to each and every one of you for your comments, your criticism, and your endless encouragement.

To my agent, Myrsini Stephanides, thank you for being by my side every step of the way. Your wise counsel has never steered me wrong. I'm also incredibly grateful to my editor, Kate Prosswimmer, for her insight and enthusiasm, and for everything she does to shepherd my words into the world. Thank you, Kate!

The entire Sourcebooks team deserves my deepest gratitude. Beth Oleniczak and the whole marketing and publicity group have done so much to make sure my books find their way into the hands of readers. My heartfelt thanks also goes out to Lauren Dombrowski and the production team who bring my stories to the printed page. Thank you all, and a word of thanks in particular to Vanessa Han, who designed the gorgeous cover.

Finally, I must take a moment to acknowledge my family: Helene, Alex, Ted, Debbie, Gail, Allan, Jeanne, and my children. I'm so grateful for your love and support. Above all, a resounding thank-you goes out to my husband, David, for his patience and his partnership in each new project I undertake. I couldn't do it without you.

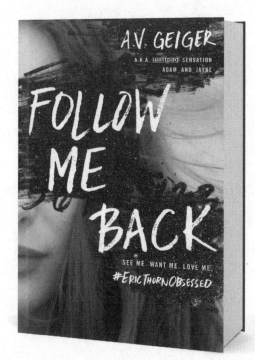

THE INTERROGATION (FRAGMENT 1)

December 31, 2016, 8:42 p.m.

Case #: 124.678.21–001

OFFICIAL TRANSCRIPTION

OF POLICE INTERVIEW

—START PAGE 1—

INVESTIGATOR: Sorry to keep you waiting, Mr. Thorn. We'd like to ask you a few questions.

THORN: Where's Tessa?

INVESTIGATOR: I'm Lieutenant Charles Foster. This is Detective Terence Newman. For the record, today is December 31 at 8:42 p.m. This interview is being recorded.

THORN: Is she here? Is she in the building?

INVESTIGATOR: Mr. Thorn, please sit down. This is an ongoing criminal investigation.

THORN: Tell me where she is!

INVESTIGATOR: We can't discuss that until we've taken your statement.

THORN: She's safe though, right? Will you tell me that much?

INVESTIGATOR: Son, the sooner you cooperate, the sooner we'll get this whole thing sorted out.

THORN: OK. OK. What do you want to know?

INVESTIGATOR: Thank you. Please state your full name, date of birth, and occupation for the record.

THORN: Eric Taylor Thorn. Date of birth, March 18, 1998. What was the third thing?

INVESTIGATOR: Occupation.

THORN: I don't...I don't even know anymore. Take your pick. Singer. Songwriter. Actor. Underwear model. Professional media whore? Does that qualify as an occupation?

INVESTIGATOR: That's fine, Mr. Thorn. Take it easy. This should only take a few minutes.

THORN: Should I have a lawyer?

INVESTIGATOR: You have the right to call an attorney at any time.

THORN: Am I under arrest?

INVESTIGATOR: We just have some questions. As I said, the sooner we have your statement, the sooner—

THORN: OK. Forget it. Tell me what you want to know.

INVESTIGATOR: Let's start at the beginning.

THORN: The beginning. What's the beginning? The day I got my record deal? The day I first picked up a guitar? I was about four years old.

INVESTIGATOR: We're talking about Tessa Hart. Tell us how you and Ms. Hart first became involved.

THORN: Over Twitter. Last summer. I think it was sometime in August. It started before that though. Before I even set up the account... [pause]

INVESTIGATOR: Please continue.

THORN: I guess... [pause] I guess if you have to start the story somewhere, I'd say the whole thing actually started in June with Dorian Cromwell. You know, from the boy band.

INVESTIGATOR: Are you saying this case is connected to what happened to Dorian Cromwell?

THORN: No, not really. Sorry, I'm not making any sense. I just meant the story was all over the news. And then the trial with that messed-up girl. All because he followed her back.

INVESTIGATOR: I'm afraid I'm still not following. How does the Dorian Cromwell case relate to your relationship with Tessa Hart?

THORN: It's funny. I knew it the moment I heard the story. I knew in my gut what must have happened to him. People say they'll always remember where they were when Kennedy was shot. Or where they were on 9/11. That's kind of how it was for me. I was driving down the Santa Monica Freeway with the top down, listening to the Top 40 on the radio. And the announcer broke in, right in the middle of number twelve. I wasn't even paying attention, but that was weird. You knew it was something big because they stopped in the middle of the song. They didn't know exactly what had happened yet. It took a few days to get to the bottom of it. About that girl, that fan. They didn't even know for sure it was a murder at that point. They only knew that it was Dorian Cromwell. That's what they said. Those were the exact words: Dorian Cromwell, lead singer of Fourth Dimension, was found dead this morning in London, floating facedown in the Thames.

1
PROJECTING

August 12, 2016

"You're not obsessed. You're projecting."

"Projecting?" Tessa looked up from the thick coil of long, brown hair that she'd been braiding and unbraiding for the past half hour. She met eyes uncertainly with her psychotherapist, Dr. Regan, sitting on the other side of the bedroom.

"It's a common defense mechanism," Dr. Regan said. Her tone remained emotionless as usual—the human equivalent of a white noise machine—but she shifted uncomfortably as she spoke. She sat perched in a low-slung, pink beanbag chair with her legs crossed at the ankles, striving to maintain a professional demeanor. Normally, she only met with clients in her office, but she made an exception for Tessa.

Tessa's gaze dropped to the older woman's panty hose, bunching at the knees, and she couldn't help but feel a grudging admiration. It took serious mental fortitude to brave the heat of the West Texas summer dressed in nylons. Tessa herself wore nothing but a tank top and cotton sleep shorts that barely skimmed the tops of her slender thighs.

"Projection," Dr. Regan said. "We use that term when an individual takes her own thoughts and feelings and attributes them to another person—in your case, to a celebrity."

"But I've never met Eric Thorn. I've never even been to one of his concerts."

Dr. Regan picked up Tessa's thought journal and flipped to the beginning. She made no comment on the drawings scribbled across the cover: a hodgepodge of hearts, woodland creatures, and eyeless human faces. *Forget projection*, Tessa thought, wrinkling her nose. They should probably discuss the fact that she couldn't even stand her own doodle-people looking at her.

Dr. Regan indicated one of Tessa's early entries. "Tell me about this. What piqued your interest enough to write something down about him?"

"About Eric?" Tessa reached for the spiral-bound journal, and her eyes swept over the page. "I was watching TMZ, I guess. They'd caught him walking around New York City with some actress from *Pretty Little Liars*. So naturally they assumed he was dating her."

"But that's not what you wrote down."

"Of course not. Have you seen TMZ? It's like fan fiction but less believable."

One of Dr. Regan's brows quirked upward, the closest she ever came to a real facial expression. She pushed her horn-rimmed glasses up her nose. "Tell me what you wrote instead."

Tessa pulled her knees against her chest. She felt a vague unease as she remembered how the grainy paparazzi footage had held her transfixed. Eric and that girl… He hadn't looked like he was on a date. Not even close. The video showed him walking briskly, with a furtive glance over his shoulder as he picked up the pace. Then the camera zoomed in close. Those piercing blue eyes of his had looked straight out of the screen. And the look on his face…

"He didn't look like some happy guy with a new girlfriend," Tessa told her therapist. "Not to me."

"What did he look like to you?"

Tessa closed her eyes. "Like he was scared out of his mind."

ABOUT THE AUTHOR

A. V. Geiger is the author of young adult thrillers *Follow Me Back* and *Tell Me No Lies*. An epidemiologist by training, she first learned to code during a high school summer program for students pursuing STEM careers, and she has always enjoyed a professional life that combines both creativity and logic. Nowadays, when she's not crafting thriller plots, she puts her tech skills to the best possible use by programming silly video games with her children. Their latest creation, "Bunny Hunter," involves a rabbit chasing a python. Learn more about A. V. Geiger and her books at avgeiger.com.